Praise for *The Cabin at the End of the World*

"A tremendous book—thought-provoking and terrifying, with tension that winds up like a chain. *The Cabin at the End of the World* is Tremblay's personal best. It's that good."

—Stephen King

"*The Cabin at the End of the World* is a thriller that grapples with the timely and the timeless. I tore through it in record time. I just couldn't wait to see where Tremblay was going to take me next." —Victor LaValle, author of *The Changeling*

"The apocalypse begins with a home invasion in this tripwire-taut horror thriller. . . . [Tremblay's] profoundly unsettling novel invites readers to ask themselves whether, when faced with the unbelievable, they would do the unthinkable to prevent it." —*Publishers Weekly* (starred review)

"*The Cabin at the End of the World* is a clinic in suspense, a story that opens with high-wire tension and never lets up from there. The blend of human horror and human heart is superb. Paul Tremblay is rapidly becoming one of my favorite suspense writers." —Michael Koryta, *New York Times* bestselling author of *How It Happened*

"A blinding tale of survival and sacrifice that matches the power of belief with man's potential for unbridled violence."

—*Kirkus Reviews*

"Paul Tremblay loads emotion and tension into every paragraph on every page of *The Cabin at the End of the World*. It is a dream come true, a heartfelt, emotionally charged journey into our worst nightmares. The last few pages are especially moving, a feat for the author, a feast for the reader. A horrifying, scary-as-hell tearjerker, so unusual, so special."

—Caroline Kepnes, author of *You* and *Providence*

"Tremblay once again demonstrates his talent for terrifying readers. Offering a terrible situation with no good outcome, this is the author at his best. Highly recommended for Tremblay's fans and those who relish end-of-the-world scenarios."

—*Library Journal* (starred review)

"Tremblay captures the intense emotional struggle . . . of Wen, Andrew, and Eric, while dread and terror permeate every sentence. This is a novel with the heart and tone of *The Road*, by Cormac McCarthy, but will also appeal to fans of Ruth Ware, Josh Malerman, and Joe Hill."   —*Booklist* (starred review)

"Think *The Desperate Hours* meets *10 Cloverfield Lane*, but way, way stranger. With *The Cabin at the End of the World*, Paul Tremblay gives us a gloriously claustrophobic and gory tale of faith and paranoia. Signs and wonders and homemade battle-axes, oh my!"   —Stewart O'Nan, author of *The Speed Queen* and *A Prayer for the Dying*

THE CABIN AT THE END OF THE WORLD

PAUL TREMBLAY

THE CABIN AT THE END OF THE WORLD

A NOVEL

 WILLIAM MORROW *AN IMPRINT OF* HARPERCOLLINS*PUBLISHERS*

Grateful acknowledgment is made to Clutch for permission to reprint an excerpt from "Animal Farm," words and music by Clutch © 1995; to Nadia Bulkin for permission to reprint an excerpt from "Seven Minutes in Heaven," *She Said Destroy* © 2017; and to Future of the Left for permission to reprint an excerpt from "The Hope That House Built," words and music by Future of the Left © 2009.

A hardcover edition of this book was published in 2018 by William Morrow, an imprint of HarperCollins Publishers.

FIRST WILLIAM MORROW PAPERBACK EDITION PUBLISHED 2019.

Designed by Fritz Metsch
Title and part title photograph by Ekaterina Kondratova/Shutterstock

―――

The Library of Congress has catalogued a previous edition as follows:

Names: Tremblay, Paul, author.
Title: The cabin at the end of the world : a novel / Paul Tremblay.
Description: First edition. | New York, NY : William Morrow, [2018] | Identifiers: LCCN 2017048369 (print) | LCCN 2017052235 (ebook) | ISBN 9780062679123 (E-Book) | ISBN 9780062679109 (hardback) | ISBN 9780062679116 (paperback)
Subjects: LCSH: Psychological fiction. | BISAC: FICTION / Horror. | GSAFD: Suspense fiction.
Classification: LCC PS3620.R445 (ebook) | LCC PS3620.R445 C33 2018 (print) |
    DDC 813/.6—dc23
LC record available at https://lccn.loc.gov/2017048369

―――

ISBN 978-0-06-267911-6 (pbk.)

23 24 25 26 27 LBC 19 18 17 16 15

for Lisa, Cole, Emma, and for us

Then back in the ground / We look at our hands / And wonder aloud / Could anyone choose to die / In the end everybody wins / In the end everybody wins

—Future of the Left, "The Hope That House Built"

Meanwhile, planes drop from the sky / People disappear and bullets fly . . . Wouldn't be surprised if they have their way / (Tastes just like chicken they say.)

—Clutch, "Animal Farm"

. . . because when the blanket of death came for us we kicked it off and were left naked and shivering in the world.

—Nadia Bulkin, "Seven Minutes in Heaven," *She Said Destroy*

COME AND SEE

ONE

Wen

The girl with the dark hair walks down the wooden front stairs and lowers herself into the yellowing lagoon of ankle-high grass. A warm breeze ripples through the blades, leaves, and crab-like petals of clover flowers. She studies the front yard, watching for the twitchy, mechanical motion and frantic jumps of grass-hoppers. The glass jar cradled against her chest smells faintly of grape jelly and is sticky on the inside. She unscrews the aerated lid.

Wen promised Daddy Andrew she would release the grass-hoppers before they got cooked inside the homemade terrar-ium. The grasshoppers will be okay because she'll make sure to keep the jar out of direct sunlight. She worries, though, that they could hurt themselves by jumping into the sharp edges of the lid's punched-in holes. She'll catch smaller grasshoppers, ones that don't jump as high or as powerfully, and because of their compact size there will be more leg-stretching room inside the jar. She will talk to the grasshoppers in a low, soothing voice, and hopefully they will be less likely to panic and mash themselves against the dangerous metal stalactites. Satisfied with her up-dated plan, she pulls up a fistful of grass, roots and all, leaving a pockmark in the front yard's sea of green and yellow. She care-fully deposits and arranges the grass in the jar, then wipes her hands on her gray Wonder Woman T-shirt.

Wen's eighth birthday is in six days. Her dads not so secretly wonder (she has overheard them discussing this) if the day is her actual date of birth or one assigned to her by the orphanage in China's Hubei Province. For her age she is in the fifty-sixth percentile for height and forty-second for weight, or at least she was when she went to the pediatrician six months ago. She made Dr. Meyer explain the context of those numbers in detail. As pleased as she was to be above the fifty-line for height, she was angry to be below it for weight. Wen is as direct and determined as she is athletic and wiry, often besting her dads in battles of wills and in scripted wrestling matches on their bed. Her eyes are a deep, dark brown, with thin caterpillar eyebrows that wiggle on their own. Along the right edge of her philtrum is the hint of a scar that is only visible in a certain light and if you know to look for it (so she is told). The thin white slash is the remaining evidence of a cleft lip repaired with multiple surgeries between the ages of two and four. She remembers the first and final trips to the hospital, but not the ones in between. That those middle visits and procedures have been somehow lost bothers her. Wen is friendly, outgoing, and as goofy as any other child her age, but isn't easy with her reconstructed smiles. Her smiles have to be earned.

It's a cloudless summer day in northern New Hampshire, only a handful of miles from the Canadian border. Sunlight shimmers on the leaves of the trees magnanimously lording over the small cabin, the lonely red dot on the southern shore of Gaudet Lake. Wen sets the jar down in a shady patch adjacent to the front stairs. She wades out into the grass, her arms outstretched, as though treading water. She swishes her right foot back and forth through the tops of the grass like Daddy Andrew showed her. He grew up on a farm in Vermont, so he's the grasshopper-finding expert. He said her foot is to act like a scythe, but without actually cutting down the grass. She didn't know what he meant and he launched into an explanation of what the tool was and how it was used. He took out his smartphone to search images of scythes before they both remembered there was no cell phone service at the cabin. Daddy Andrew drew a scythe on a napkin instead; a crescent-shaped knife at the end of a long stick, something a warrior or an orc from *The Lord of the Rings* movies would carry. It looked really dangerous and she didn't understand why people needed something so large and extreme to cut grass, but Wen loved the idea of pretending her leg was the handle and her foot was the long curved blade.

A brown grasshopper, big enough to span the distance across her hand, with loud, rasping wings flies up from underneath her foot and bounces off her chest. Wen stumbles backward at impact, almost falling down.

She giggles and says, "Okay, you're too big."

She resumes her exploratory swipes with her scythe-foot. A much smaller grasshopper jumps so high she loses sight of it somewhere in its skyward, elliptical arc, but she tracks it as it lands a few feet to her left. It's the same fluorescent green as a tennis ball and the perfect size, not much bigger than the clumps of seeds at the ends of the longer grass stalks. If only she can catch it. Its movements are quick and difficult to anticipate, and it leaps away the moment before the quivering trap of her hands is in place. She laughs and follows a manic zigzag around the yard. She tells it that she means no harm, she will let it go eventually, and she just wants to learn about it so she can help all the other grasshoppers be healthy and happy.

Wen eventually catches the miniacrobat at the edge of the lawn and the gravel driveway. Cupped in the cave of her hands, this is the first grasshopper she's ever caught. She whisper-shouts, "Yes!" The grasshopper is so slight she can only feel it when it tries to jump through her closed fingers. The urge to open her hands a crack for a little peek is almost a compulsion, but she wisely resists. She sprints across the yard and deposits the grasshopper into the jar and quickly screws on the lid. The grasshopper bounces like an electron, pinging against the glass and tin, and then stops abruptly, perches on the greenery, and rests.

Wen says, "Okay. You are number one." She pulls a palm-sized notebook out of her back pocket, the front page already gridded into wavy rows and columns with headings, and she writes down the number one, an estimate of its size (she writes, inaccurately, "2 inches"), color ("green"), boy or girl ("girl Caroline"), energy level ("hi"). She returns the jar to its shaded spot and wanders back into the front yard. She quickly catches four more grasshoppers of similar size: two brown, one green, and one a color somewhere in the spectrum between. She names them after schoolmates: Liv, Orvin, Sara, and Gita.

As she searches for a sixth grasshopper, she hears someone walking or jogging on the forever-long dirt road that winds by the cabin and traces the lake's shoreline before snaking off into the surrounding woods. When they arrived two days ago, it took them twenty-one minutes and forty-nine seconds to drive the length of the dirt road. Wen timed it. Granted, Daddy Eric was driving way too slowly, like always.

The sounds of feet mashing and grinding into the dirt and stone are louder, closer. Something big is trudging its way down the road. Really big. Maybe it's a bear. Daddy Eric made her promise she would yell for them and run inside if she saw any animal bigger than a squirrel. Should she be excited or scared? She doesn't see anything through the crowd of trees. Wen stands in the middle of the lawn, ready to run if necessary. Is she fast enough to get inside the cabin if it is a dangerous animal? She hopes it's a bear. She wants to see one. She can play dead if she has to. The maybe-bear is at the tree-obscured mouth of the driveway. Her curiosity shifts gears into becoming annoyed to have to be dealing with whatever/whoever is there because she's in the middle of an important project.

A man rounds the bend and walks briskly down the driveway like he's coming home. Wen is not a good judge of height as all adults exist in that cloud-filled space above her, but he is easily taller than her dads. He might be taller than anyone she has ever met, and he's as wide as a couple of tree trunks pushed together.

The man waves with a hand that might as well be a bear's paw, and he smiles at Wen. Given her many lip reconstruction procedures, Wen has always focused on and studied smiles. Too many people have smiles that don't mean what a smile is supposed to mean. Their smiles are often cruel and mocking, like how a bully's grin is the same as a fist. Worse are the confused and sad smiles from adults. Wen remembers presurgeries and postsurgeries not needing a mirror to know her face wasn't like everyone else's yet because of the crumbly, you-poor-poor-thing smiles on faces in waiting rooms and lobbies and parking garages.

This man's smile is warm and wide. His face opens its curtains naturally. Wen can't fully describe the difference between a real smile and a fake one, but she knows it when she sees it. He is not faking. His is the real thing, so real as to be contagious, and Wen gives him a tight-lipped smile she covers with the back of her hand.

The man is dressed inappropriately for jogging or hiking in the woods. His clunky black shoes with thick rubber soles piled beneath his feet stand him up even taller; they are not sneakers and they are not the nice dress-up shoes Daddy Eric wears. They are more like the Doc Martens Daddy Andrew wears. Wen remembers the brand because she likes that his shoes are named after a person. The man wears dusty blue jeans and a white dress shirt, tucked in and buttoned all the way to the top, squeezing the collar around his fire-hydrant neck.

He says, "Hi there." His voice is not as big as he is, not even close. He sounds like a teenager, like one of the student counselors in her after-school program.

"Hi."

"My name is Leonard."

Wen doesn't give her name and before she can say *let me go get my dads,* Leonard asks her a question.

"Is it okay if we talk a little before I talk to your parents? I definitely want to talk to them, too, but let's you and I chat first. Is that okay?"

"I don't know. I'm not supposed to talk to strangers."

"You're right and you're very smart. I promise that I'm here to be your friend and I'm not going to be a stranger for long." He smiles again. It's almost as big as a laugh.

She returns it and doesn't cover this one up with her hand.

"Can I ask you what your name is?"

Wen knows she should say nothing more, turn around, and go inside, and go inside quickly. She's had the stranger-danger talk with her dads countless times, and living in the city, it makes sense for her to be vigilant because there are so many people there. An unimaginable number of people walk on the sidewalks and fill the subways and live and work and shop inside the tall buildings and there're people in cars and buses that jam the streets at all hours, and she understands how there could be one bad person mixed in with the good people and how that bad person could be in an alley or a van or a doorway or the playground or the corner market. But up here, in the woods and on the lake, standing in the grass, under the sun and the sleepy trees and blue sky, she feels safe, and she believes this Leonard looks okay. She says so inside her head: *He looks okay.*

Leonard stands at the border of the driveway and grass, only a few steps away from Wen. His hair is wheat colored and moppy, swirling in layers, swoops of icing on a cake. His eyes are round and brown like a teddy bear's eyes. He is younger than her dads. His face is pale and smooth and he doesn't have a hint of the beard-stubble shadow Daddy Andrew gets by the end of each day. Maybe Leonard is in college. Should she ask him what college he goes to? She could then tell him that Daddy Andrew teaches at Boston University.

She says, "My name is Wenling. But my dads and my friends and everyone at school calls me Wen."

"Well, it is very nice to meet you, Wen. So tell me what you're up to. Why aren't you swimming in the lake on such a beautiful afternoon?"

That's something an adult would say. Maybe he isn't a college student. She says, "The lake is very cold. So I'm catching grass-hoppers."

"You are? Oh, I love to catch grasshoppers. Used to do it all the time when I was a kid. So much fun."

"It is. But this is more serious." She juts out her lower jaw, a purposeful imitation of Daddy Eric when she asks him a question with an answer that isn't yes right away, but will be yes eventually if she waits long enough.

"It is?"

"I'm catching them and naming them and studying them so I can find out if they are healthy. People do that when they study animals and I want to help animals when I grow up." Wen is a little light-headed from talking so fast. Teachers at school tell her to slow down because they can't understand her when she gets going like this. Substitute teacher Ms. Iglesias told her once that it was like the words leaked out of her mouth, and Wen didn't like Ms. Iglesias at all after that.

"I'm very impressed. Do you need any help? I'd love to help. I know I'm much bigger now than when I was a kid." He holds out his hands and shrugs like he can't believe what he's become. "But I'm still very gentle."

Wen says, "Okay. I'll hold the jar so the other ones don't jump out, and maybe you can catch a couple more for me. No big ones, please. They can't be big. No room. Just the small ones. I'll show you." She walks to the stairs to retrieve her jar. She goes up on her tiptoes and peers through the cabin's open windows that flank the front door. She looks for her dads, to see if they are watching or listening. They are not in the kitchen or the living room. They must be out on the back deck, reclined in the lounge chairs, sunning themselves (Daddy Eric will most certainly get sunburned and then insist his lobster-red skin doesn't hurt or need aloe), and reading a book or listening to music or boring podcasts. She briefly considers going out back to tell them about catching grasshoppers with Leonard. Instead she picks up the jar. The grasshoppers react like heated popcorn, pattering against the lid. Wen shushes her charges and goes to Leonard, who is in the middle of the lawn, already hunched over and scanning the grass.

Wen sidles up next to him. She holds out the jar and says, "See? No big ones, please."

"Got it."

"Do you want me to catch them and you can watch?"

"I'd really like to catch one at least. It's been a long time. I'm not fast like you anymore, so I'll just move real slow to not scare them. Oh, hey, there's one." He bends and stretches out his arms on either side of the grasshopper that is hanging upside down from the tip of a dried-out stalk. The grasshopper doesn't move, hypnotized by the giant eclipsing the sun. Leonard's hands slowly come together and swallow it up.

"Wow. You're good."

"Thanks. Now how do we want to do this? Maybe you should put the jar on the ground, let the ones inside calm down a little, and then we can open the lid and put this one in, too."

Wen does as he suggests. Leonard goes down to one knee and stares at the jar. Wen mimics his movements. She wants to ask if the grasshopper is jumping around in the darkness of his hands, if he feels it crawling on his skin.

They wait in silence until he says, "Okay. Let's try it." Wen unscrews the lid. Leonard slides one hand over the other until he is holding the grasshopper in one mighty fist and then delicately tilts the lid open with the newly freed hand. He drops the grasshopper inside the jar, replaces the lid, and turns it once clockwise. They look at each other and laugh.

He says, "We did it. You want one more?"

"Yeah." Wen has her notebook out and writes in the appropriate columns: "2 inches, green, boy Lenard, medeum." She giggles to herself that she named the grasshopper after him.

Leonard makes quick work of catching another grasshopper and deposits it inside the jar without incident or inmate escape.

Wen writes: "1 inch, brown, girl Izzy, low."

He asks, "How many do you have now?"

"Seven."

"That's a powerful, magic number."

"Don't you mean lucky?"

"No, it's only sometimes lucky."

His response is annoying as everyone knows seven is a lucky number. "I think it's lucky, and I think it's lucky for grasshoppers."

"You are probably right."

"Okay. That's enough then."

"What do we do now?"

"You can help me watch them." She puts the jar down on the ground and the two of them sit cross-legged and across from each other with the jar in the middle. Wen has her notebook and pencil out. A gust of wind rattles the paper held beneath her palms.

Leonard asks, "Did you punch the holes in the lid yourself?"

"Daddy Eric did it. We found an old hammer and screwdriver in the basement." The basement was a scary place with shadows and spiderwebs in all the corners and angles and it smelled like the deep dark bottom of a lake. The cement slab floor was cold and gritty on her bare feet. She was supposed to put shoes on to go down there, but she had been too excited and forgot. Ropes, rusted gardening tools, and old life jackets hung from exposed wooden beams, the battered bones of the cabin. Wen wished their condo in Cambridge had a basement like this one. Of course, once they were back upstairs, Daddy Eric declared the basement was off-limits. Wen protested but he said there was too much sharp and rusty stuff down there, stuff that wasn't theirs to be touching or using in the first place. In the face of the *no basement allowed* proclamation, Daddy Andrew groaned from the love seat in the living area and said, "Daddy Fun is so strict." *Daddy Fun* was the mostly playful nickname for the family worrier and the one quickest to say no. Daddy Eric, ever calm, said, "I'm serious. You should see it down there. It's a deathtrap." Daddy Andrew said, "I'm sure it's terrible. Speaking of a trap!" and he pulled Wen into a sneak-attack hug, spun her around, and gave her what he called his "face kiss": lips planted on the space between her cheek and nose and he playfully smooshed the rest of his big face into hers. His beard stubble tickled and scratched and she giggled, screamed, and squirmed out of it. She ran to the front door with her jar and Daddy Andrew called after her, "But we have to listen to Daddy Fun because he loves us, right?" Wen shouted, "No," back and her dads reacted with mock outrage as she closed the front door behind her.

Wen looks up from the jar and Leonard is staring at her. He's bigger than a boulder, and his head is tilted and his eyes are either squinting in the bright sun or are narrowed like he's trying to figure her out.

"What? What are you looking at?"

"I'm sorry, that's rude of me. I thought it was, I don't know, cute—"

"Cute?" Wen folds her arms across her chest.

"I mean cool. Cool! Cool that you use your dad's first name like that. Daddy Eric, right?"

Wen sighs. "I have two dads." Wen keeps her arms folded. "I use their first names so they know who I'm talking to." Her friend from school, Rodney, has two dads, too, but he's moving to Brookline later this summer. Sasha has two moms, but Wen doesn't like her very much; she's way too bossy. Some of the other kids in the neighborhood and at school only have one mom or one dad, and some have what is called a stepparent, or someone they call mom's or dad's partner or someone else without any sort of special name at all. Most of the kids she knows have one mom and one dad, though. All the kids on her favorite shows on the Disney Channel have one mom and one dad, too. There are days when Wen goes around at recess or the playground (but never at Chinese school) tapping kids on the shoulders and telling them she has two dads to see their reaction. Most of the kids aren't fazed by it; there have been some kids who are mad at one of their own parents and tell her they wished they had two dads or two moms. There are other days when she thinks every whisper or conversation across the room is about her and she wishes her teachers or after-school counselors would stop asking her questions about her dads and telling her that *it's so great*.

Leonard says, "Ah, of course. That makes sense."

"I think everyone should use first names. It's more friendly. I don't get why I have to call people Mr. and Miss and Mrs. just because they're older. After you meet Daddy Eric, he is going to tell me to call you Mr. Something."

"That's not my last name."

"What?"

"Something."

"Huh?"

"Never mind. You have my official permission to call me Leonard."

"Okay. Leonard, do you think having two dads is weird?"

"No. No way. Do other people tell you that having two dads is weird?"

She shrugs. "Maybe. Sometimes." There was one boy, Scott, who told her that God didn't like her dads and they were fags, and he got suspended and moved into a different class. She and her dads had a family meeting and had what they called *a big, serious talk*. Her dads warned her that some people won't understand their family and might say *ignorant* (their word) and hurtful things to her and it might not be their fault because of what they've been taught by other ignorant people with too much hate in their hearts, and, yes, it was very sad. Wen assumed they were talking about the same bad or stranger-danger people that hide in the city and want to take her away, but the more they talked to her about what Scott had said and why others might say things like that, too, the more it seemed like they were talking about everyday kind of people. Weren't the three of them everyday kind of people? She pretended to understand for her dads' sake, but she didn't and still doesn't. Why do she and her family need to be understood or explained to anyone else? She is happy and proud her dads trusted her enough to have the *big, serious talk*, but she also doesn't like to think about it.

Leonard says, "I don't think it's weird. I think you and your dads make a beautiful family."

"I do, too."

Leonard adjusts his sitting position, twists around so he's looking behind him at their black SUV pulled up close to the cabin in the small gravel lot, and then he eyes the length of the empty driveway and looks toward the obscured road. He turns back around, exhales, rubs his chin, and says, "They don't do much, do they?"

Wen thinks he's talking about her dads and she is ready to yell at him, tell him that they do a lot and that they are important people with important jobs.

Leonard must sense the building Vesuvius eruption and he points at the jar and says, "I mean the grasshoppers. They don't do much. They're just kind of sitting there, chilling. Like us."

"Oh no. Do you think they are sick?" Wen bends to the jar, her face only inches from the glass.

He says, "No, I think they are fine. Grasshoppers only hop when they need to. It takes a lot of energy to jump like that. They're probably tired from our chasing them down. I'd be more concerned if they were bouncing off the walls like mad."

"I guess so. But I'm worried." Wen sits up and writes "tired, sick, unhappy, hungry, scared?" in her notebook.

"Hey, can I ask how old you are, Wen?"

"I'll be eight in six days."

Leonard's smile falters a little bit, like her answer to the question is a sad thing. "Really. Well, happy almost-birthday."

"I am having two parties." Wen takes a deep breath and then says, rapid-fire, "One up here at the cabin with just us and we're going to eat buffalo meat burgers not buffalo style like the chicken, and then corn on the cob and ice cream cake and at night we're going to light fireworks and I get to stay up until midnight and watch for shooting stars. And then . . ." Wen stops and giggles because she can't keep up with how fast she wants to talk. Leonard laughs, too. Wen regroups and adds, "And when I get back home me and my two best friends, Usman and Kelsey, and maybe Gita, are going to the Museum of Science and the electricity exhibit and the butterfly room and maybe the planetarium and then ride on the duck boats, I think, and then more cake and ice cream."

"Wow. I see this has all been carefully planned and negotiated."

"I can't wait to be eight." A loose strand of hair falls out of her ponytail and in front of her face. She quickly stashes it behind her ear.

"You know what? I think I have something for you. Nothing too great, but let's call it an early birthday present."

Wen knits her brow and folds her arms again. Her dads told her in no uncertain terms to not trust strangers especially if they offer you a gift. She really hasn't been out here by herself for too long with Leonard, but it's starting to feel a little long. "What is it? Why do you want to give it to me?"

"I know, it seems weird, and it's funny, but I thought I might meet you or someone like you today and I was walking down the road out here and I saw this"—he starts fiddling with the breast pocket of his shirt—"and for some reason I thought I should pick it up, even though I never do that kind of thing normally. So I picked it. And now I want you to have it."

Leonard pulls out a small, droopy flower with a halo of thin white petals.

As uncomfortable as she was a moment ago at the thought of a gift from a stranger, Wen is disappointed and doesn't try to hide it. She says, "A flower?"

"If you don't want to keep it, we can put it in the jar with the grasshoppers."

Wen suddenly feels bad, like she is being mean even though she isn't trying to be mean. She tries a joke: "They're called grass-hoppers not flower-hoppers." But she feels worse because that sounds mean for real.

Leonard laughs and says, "True. We probably shouldn't tam-per with their habitat too much."

Wen almost mock-faints into the grass she's so relieved. Leon-ard extends the flower over the grasshopper jar, across the ex-panse of lawn between them. Wen takes it, careful not to brush his hand accidentally.

He says, "It's a little squished from being in my pocket, but still mostly in one piece."

Wen sits up straight and reshapes the curled stem that's about as long as her pointer finger. The stem feels loose and will prob-ably fall off soon. The middle part of the flower is a little yellow ball. The seven petals are long, skinny, and white. Does he expect her to stick it in her hair or behind her ear or run inside to put it in a glass of water? She has a better idea. She says, "It already looks kinda dead. Can we pull it apart and make a game of it?"

"You can do whatever you want with it."

"We'll take turns pulling off a petal and when we do we ask a question the other person has to answer. I'll go first." Wen plucks a petal. "How old are you?"

"I am twenty-four and a half years old. The half is still important to me."

Wen passes the flower back to Leonard and says, "Make sure you only pluck one at a time."

"I will do my very best with these big mitts." He follows Wen's instructions and carefully plucks a petal. He pinches his fingertips tightly together to ensure he only pulls out one. "There. Phew." He passes back the flower.

"What's my question?"

"Right. Sorry. Um . . ."

"The questions should be fast and the answers fast, too."

"Yes, sorry. Um, what's your favorite movie?"

"Big Hero Six."

"I like that one, too." He says it matter-of-factly, and for the first time since they've met, she wonders if he is lying to her.

Leonard passes the flower back. Wen plucks a petal; her hand is quick. She says, "Everyone usually asks what is your favorite food. I want to know what your least favorite food is."

"That's easy. Broccoli. I hate it." Leonard takes the flower and pulls a petal. He quickly looks behind him and back down the driveway again and asks, "What is your first memory?"

Wen isn't expecting that question. She almost says the question isn't fair and is too hard, but she doesn't want to be accused of making up the rules as she goes, which she's been accused of before by her friends. She's sensitive about being fair when playing games. "My first memory is being in a big room." She spreads her arms wide and her notebook slips off her lap and into the grass. "I was very small, maybe even a baby, and there were doctors and nurses looking at me." She doesn't tell Leonard all of it, that there were other beds and cribs in the room with her, and the walls were green tiled (she remembers that ugly green vividly), and there were kids crying in the room, and the doctors and nurses were leaning in close to her and had heads as big as moons and they were Chinese like her.

Wen reaches over the jar, almost knocking it over, in a hurry to get the flower back from Leonard before he breaks the rules and asks a follow-up question. Another petal is plucked away and she rolls it up into a ball between her fingers. "What monster scares you?"

Leonard doesn't hesitate. "The giant ones like Godzilla. Or the dinosaurs in the *Jurassic Park* movies. Those movies scared the heck out of me. I used to have nightmares all the time about being eaten or squashed by T. rex."

Wen has never been afraid of giant monsters but hearing Leonard talk about them and then looking at the trees stretching beyond where she'll ever reach, and how they bend and wave easy in the breeze, she can understand being afraid of big things.

Leonard's turn with the flower. He plucks and asks, "How did you get that tiny white scar on your lip?"

"You can see it?"

"Barely. Only a little, when you turn a certain way."

Wen looks down and pushes out her lips in attempt to see it. Of course it's there. She sees it whenever she looks in the mirror, and sometimes she wants it to go away, to never be seen again, and sometimes she hopes it'll be there forever and she traces the slash with a finger like she's darkening a line with a pencil.

"I'm sorry, I don't mean to make you uncomfortable. I shouldn't have asked that. I'm sorry."

Wen shifts and adjusts her legs, and says, "I'm okay."

The fissure in her cleft lip went all the way up to her right nostril so the two sets of empty, dark spaces overlapped and became one. Last fall, Wen begged her dads to let her see baby photos, the youngest ones of her that they had, the ones from before the surgeries and before they adopted her. It took some convincing, but her dads eventually acquiesced. They had a set of five pictures of her lying on her back on a white blanket, awake and her balled-up fists hovering next to her unrecognizable face. Wen was unexpectedly shaken by the photos and convinced she was, for the first time, looking at her real self and this real her was gone, forgotten, banished, or worse, that imperfect unwanted child was hidden, locked away inside of her somewhere. Wen was so upset her hands shook and the tremors spread throughout her body. After her dads consoled her, she calmed down and gave them an oddly formal thank you for letting her look at the photos. She requested they be put away because she would never look at them again. But she did look at them again, and often. Her dads kept the wooden box of photos under their bed and Wen would sneak into their room to look at them whenever she could. There were more photos in the box, including pictures of her dads in China; Daddy Eric looked weird with thin, wispy hair clinging to his head—which he has since shaved bald for as long as she can remember—and Daddy Andrew looked exactly the same with his dark, long hair. There were pictures of the three of them in the orphanage, too, with one picture of her dads holding her up between them. She was the size of a loaf of bread and wrapped up tightly in a blanket, only the top of her head and her eyes peeking out at the camera. She would look at the pictures with her dads in them first, and then the photos of just her. The scary the-real-her-was-in-the-baby-photos feeling went away the more she looked.

Yes, that was her little baby head with a shock of unruly black hair perched above the unmolded clay of her face. Wen traced the boundaries of skin and space of her cleft lip in the photos and then manipulated and moved her own lip around, trying to recapture what it must've felt like having the disconnect, owning all that empty space. Each time she slid the box back under the bed, she wondered if her biological parents gave her up to the orphanage because of how she looked. Eric and Andrew have always been open about Wen having been born in China and adopted. They have bought her many books, encourage her to learn as much about Chinese culture as she can, and this past January, they enrolled Wen in a Chinese school (in addition to her regular, everyday school) with classes on Saturday mornings to help her learn to read and write Chinese. She rarely asks her dads about her biological parents. Almost nothing is known about them; her dads were told that Wen was left anonymously at the orphanage. Daddy Andrew once speculated that her parents might've been too poor to properly care for her and only hoped she could have a better life elsewhere.

She says, "I had what they call a cleft lip when I was a baby. And they fixed it. It took a lot of doctors a long time to fix it."

"They did an amazing job and your face is beautiful."

She wishes he wouldn't say that and so she ignores it. Maybe it's time to get one or both of her dads. She's not afraid or worried about Leonard, not exactly, but something is starting to feel off. She brings up one of her dads as though mentioning him is the same as calling him to come out here. "Daddy Andrew has a big scar that starts behind his ear and goes down to his neck. He keeps his hair long so you can't see it unless he shows it to you."

"How did he get it?"

"He got hit in the head by accident when he was a kid. Someone was swinging a baseball bat and didn't see him standing there."

Leonard says, "Ouch."

Wen thinks about telling him that Daddy Eric shaves his head and sometimes he asks Wen to check his head for nicks and scars. There are never any scars like hers or Daddy Andrew's and if she finds a little red cut, it's always healed up and gone by the next time she looks.

She says, "It's not fair, you know."

"What isn't fair?"

"You can see my scar and I can't see anything wrong with you."

"Just because you have a scar doesn't mean you have something wrong with you, Wen. That's very important. I—"

Wen sighs and interrupts. "I know. I know. That's not what I mean."

Leonard twists around again and stays twisted around, as though he sees something, but there's nothing behind him other than the SUV, the driveway, and the trees. Then there're faint sounds coming from somewhere in the woods beyond, or coming from the road. They both sit quietly and listen, and the sounds grow louder.

Leonard turns back to Wen and says, "I don't have any scars like you or your dad, but if you could see my heart, you'd see that it's broken." He doesn't have a smile on his face anymore. His face looks sad, like the real kind of sad and he even might start crying.

"Why is it broken?"

The sounds can now be heard plainly and without them having to be quiet. Familiar sounds, feet tramping and stomping their way down the dirt road, like earlier when Leonard showed up. Where did Leonard come from anyway? She should've asked. She knows she should've. He had to have come from far away. This time it sounds like a whole bunch of Leonards (or bears? Maybe this time it's actually bears) are walking down the road.

Wen asks, "Are there more people coming? Are they your friends? Are they nice?"

Leonard says, "Yes, there are more people coming. You are my friend now, Wen. I wouldn't lie to you about that. Just like I won't lie to you about them. I don't know if I'd call them my friends, exactly. I don't know them very well, but we have an important job to do. The most important job in the history of the world. I hope you can understand that."

Wen stands up. "I have to go now." The sounds are closer. They are at the end of the driveway but not quite around the bend and the trees yet. She doesn't want to see these other people. Maybe if she doesn't see them, refuses to see them, they'll go away. They are so loud. Maybe instead of bears it'll be Leonard's giant monsters and dinosaurs coming to get them both.

Leonard says, "Before you go inside to get your dads, you have to listen to me. This is important." Leonard crawls out of his sitting position and onto one knee, and his eyes brim with tears. "Are you listening?"

Wen nods her head and takes a step back. Three people turn the corner onto the driveway: two women and one man. They are dressed in blue jeans and button-down shirts of different colors; black, red, and white. The taller of the two women has white skin and brown hair, and her white shirt is a different kind of white than Leonard's. His shirt glows like the moon, whereas hers is dull, washed, almost gray. Wen catalogs the apparent coordination in how Leonard and the three strangers dress as something important to tell her dads. She will tell them everything and they will know why the four of them are all wearing jeans and button-down shirts, and maybe her dads can explain why the three new strangers are carrying strange long-handled tools.

Leonard says, "You are a beautiful person, inside and out. One of the most beautiful people I've ever met, Wen. Your family is perfect and beautiful, too. Please know that. This isn't about you. It's about everyone."

None of the tools are scythes but they look like menacing, nightmarish versions of them, with rough scribbles at the ends of the poles instead of smooth crescent blades. All three of the wooden handles are long and thick, perhaps once owning shovel blades or rake heads. The stocky man wearing a red shirt has a flower of rusty hand shovel and/or trowel blades, nailed and screwed to the end of the handle. On the other end of his handle, pointed down by his feet, is a thick, blunt, red block of dented and chipped metal, the head of a well-used sledgehammer. Now that he's closer, his handle looks bigger, thicker, like he's holding a boat's oar with the paddle sawed off. Even as Wen walks backward, toward the cabin, she sees the tops of screws and nail heads haphazardly ringing both ends of his wooden handle like fly hairs. The shorter woman wears a black shirt, and at the end of her wooden handle is a pinwheel of raking claws, crooked metal fingers jammed together into a large ragged ball so her tool looks like the most dangerous lollipop in the world. The other woman wears the off-white shirt and at the end of her tool is a single blade head, bent and curled over itself at one end, like a scroll, and then tapering into a right triangle with a sharp point at the other.

Wen's choppy, unsure backward steps become deep, equally unsure, lunges. She says, "I'm going inside now." She has to say it to ensure she will enter the cabin and not stand and stare.

Leonard is on his knees with his great and terrible arms out-stretched. His face is big and sad in the way all honest faces are sad. He says, "None of what's going to happen is your fault. You haven't done anything wrong, but the three of you will have to make some tough decisions. Terrible decisions, I'm afraid. I wish with all of my broken heart you didn't have to."

Wen fumbles up the stairs, still going backward, with eyes only for the confusing amalgams of wood and metal the strangers are carrying.

Leonard yells, but he doesn't sound angry or distressed. He's yelling to be heard over the expanding distance between them. "Your dads won't want to let us in, Wen. But they have to. Tell them they have to. We are not here to hurt you. We need your help to save the world. Please."

TWO

Eric

Small whitecaps dapple the water like little paintbrush strokes and quietly collapse against the rocky shoreline and the metal pipe posts of the cabin's functional but dilapidated dock. The wooden slats are bleached gray and warped, looking like fossilized bones, the rib cage of a fabled lake monster. Andrew promised to teach Wen how to fish for perch off the dock's edge before Eric could suggest everyone stay off the creaky, ill-kept structure. Eric suspects Wen will give up on fishing as soon as the first worm is impaled on a hook. If the worm guts, roiling squirms, and death throes won't do it, then she'll quit after she has to yank and tear a barbed hook out of a perch's button mouth. Then again, it's possible she'll love it and insist upon doing everything, including baiting the hook, herself. Her independence streak is so fierce as to be almost defiant. She has become so much like Andrew that it makes him love her and worry about her safety all the more. Late yesterday afternoon, as Wen changed into her bathing suit, Andrew rebuffed Eric's attempt to start a discussion about the rickety dock by sprinting across its length, the structure earthquaking under his feet, and then he cannonballed into the lake.

Eric and Andrew lounge on the elevated back deck overlooking the sprawling Gaudet Lake; deep and dark, its basin was gouged out by glaciers fifteen thousand years ago and ringed by a seemingly endless forest of pine, fir, and birch trees. Behind the forest, looming as distant and unreachable as the clouds, are the ancient humpbacks of the White Mountains in the south, the lake's natural fortress, both impenetrable and inescapable. The surrounding landscape is as spectacularly New England as it is alien to their everyday urban lives. There are a handful of cabins and camps on the lake, but none are visible from their deck. The only boat spied since their arrival was a yellow canoe gliding silently along the lake's far shore. The three of them wordlessly watched it fade from view, falling off the unseen edge of the world.

The nearest cabin to theirs is two miles farther down the one-time logging road. Earlier that morning, well before either Andrew or Wen were awake, Eric jogged down to the unoccupied cabin, which had been recently painted a dark blue and had white shutters and a pair of snowshoes decorating the white front door. He resisted an inexplicably strong urge to peer into the windows and explore the property. Only an irrational fear of being caught by the absent owners and then having to stammer through an embarrassing rationalization of his behavior turned him away.

Eric lies half reclined in a chaise longue under the bright light of the sun. He forgot to drape a towel over the chair and its weave of plastic bands sticks to his bare back. He is probably mere minutes away from a slight burn if he doesn't apply sunscreen. As a child he used to suffer through the stinging pain of sunburn on purpose so that he could later gross out his older sisters with his peeling skin. He'd carefully pry up large flakes and leave them attached to his body like miniature back and tail plates of a stegosaurus, his favorite dinosaur.

Andrew sits a few feet away from Eric, but not a patch of his pale skin is exposed to the sunlight. He is curled up with his legs folded on a bench seat under a nearly see-through umbrella that shades the old picnic table. The table sheds large strips of red stain. He wears baggy black shorts and a gray long-sleeve T-shirt adorned by Boston University's crest, and his long hair is pulled back and tucked into an army-green flat cap. Andrew is hunched over a collection of essays about twentieth-century South American writers and magical realism. Eric knows what the book is because, since arriving at the cabin, Andrew has told him three times what he's reading, and in the twenty minutes they've been on the deck, Andrew has read aloud two passages about Gabriel García Márquez. Eric read *One Hundred Years of Solitude* in college, but to his shame very little of that book has survived in his memory. That Andrew is not so subtly showing off and/or seeking Eric's approval is endearing and irritating in equal measure.

Eric reads and rereads the same paragraph of a novel that everyone is supposedly talking about this summer. It's a typical thriller involving a disappearance of a character, and he's already weary of the contrived and borderline absurd plot. But it's not the book's fault that he can't concentrate.

He says, "One of us should go see what Wen is up to." It's carefully worded and not a question to which Andrew can quickly say no. It's a statement; something he'll have to address directly.

"By one of us, do you mean me?"

"No." Eric says it in a way that he expects Andrew to be able to instantly translate as a *yes, of course, I wouldn't have said anything otherwise.* Eric doesn't know how he's become the hovering parent, the disciplinarian (God, how he hates that word), the one who obsesses over worst-case scenarios. Eric prides himself on being western-Pennsylvania friendly, easy to talk to, levelheaded, always willing to build toward consensus and compromise. The second youngest of nine children from a Catholic family, his ability to talk to and charm most everyone was how he survived his confusing teenage years and downright turbulent early twenties after he came out and his parents refused to pay for his final semester at the University of Pittsburgh. Eric's response was to couch surf with the help of many generous friends and work at a popular sandwich shop near campus for two years until he paid the remaining tuition and earned his degree. All the while he talked to his parents (mostly his mom) on the phone and remained confident they would *come around*. And they did. The day Eric received his diploma, his parents showed up at his friend's apartment in tears, apologizing, and they gave him a check equal to the amount of the college bill with a little extra thrown in, a check Eric promptly used to make a move up to Boston. Now a market analyst for Financeer, because of his obvious people skills he is occasionally called in to help mediate contentious meetings between administrators and his department director. Eric is laid-back in his approach to everything in his life, with the one exception of parenting. Andrew had to practically drag him out to the back deck instead of letting him remain inside, staring out the front windows and dutifully watching Wen playing alone in the yard.

Andrew doesn't look up from his book and says, "Bears. Wen is up to her neck in bears."

Eric drops his book and it claps loudly on the deck. "You are not funny." The owners left strict written instructions, all capital letters, to not leave any unsecured garbage bags outside because it would attract bears. There's a mini shedlike structure on the property for the sole purpose of housing and hiding trash. They are to bring trash to a town dump (which is only open to nonresidents on Tuesday, Thursday, and Saturday), a forty-minute drive away with a charge of two dollars a bag. They could've rented a property on popular Lake Winnipesaukee, a tourist hot spot in the southern/central part of the state, where Eric wouldn't be obsessing about bears (as much), instead of this beautiful but remote cabin, as lost in the woods as Goldilocks (more bears . . .), a stone's throw from the Canadian border. Eric sits up and rubs his bald head, which is hot to the touch, and most definitely sunburned.

Andrew says, "Yes, I am."

"You are not funny right now."

"I can yell to her from here. But that might spook the bears. Make them more likely to attack."

Eric laughs and says, "You are such a dick." He stands, walks to the deck railing, and stretches, pretending that he's looking out over the lake and that he is not going to walk inside the cabin or down the deck stairs and directly to the front yard.

"Maybe it'd be okay if some bears showed up. I like bears." Andrew closes his book. His dark brown eyes and smile are aren't-I-clever-and-cute big.

"She can come out back and search for grasshoppers." Eric gestures below the deck but there isn't much backyard at all, and what little they have is a mixture of sand, pine needles, mossy patches, and a small row of pine trees that yields to the shoreline. Eric twists his beard at the end of his chin, turns around, and says, "She probably needs a drink, or a snack, or more sunscreen."

"She's fine. Give her another five or ten minutes and then I'll go see her, or get her. She'll probably come looking for us before then, anyway. So sit, please. Stop worrying. Enjoy your sun. Or stand there and block it for me. Though you are getting a little pink. You burn even quicker than I do."

Eric plucks his white T-shirt with the team USA SOCCER logo from the picnic tabletop and puts it on. "I'm trying not to hover.

I'm trying to let her—" He pauses, leans against the deck railing, and folds his arms. "I'm trying to let her be."

"I know you are. And you're doing great."

"I hate feeling this way. I really don't like it."

"You need to stop beating yourself up. You're like the best dad in the world."

"Like? So I'm *almost* the best dad in the world."

Andrew laughs. "Hmm. Akin to, maybe."

"Can you be more specific as to my ranking? Put a percentile on it?"

"You know I'm not good with numbers, but you're near the pinnacle, the apex of best dads, the kind who earn the coffee mugs and T-shirts saying so." Andrew closes his book and is clearly enjoying teasing Eric.

Eric is losing the playful joust and his patience. He blurts out, "And you're one of those best dads, right?" even though he knows he isn't being fair. "Now I know what to get you for Christmas."

"Come on now, Eric. We're clearly tied for *like the best*."

"I think I prefer 'akin to.'"

"That's the spirit. But listen, even the best dads in the world worry and nag and fuck up, and you have to give yourself permission to fuck up and allow Wen to mess up on her own, too. Accept that none of us will ever be perfect." It's the start of a spiel that Andrew has given before, usually followed by references to their weeks-long discussions prior to adopting Wen, and how they talked about not giving in to the lizard-brained fear that rules too many parents and people in general, and Andrew would then switch into academic mode and quote studies that cite the importance of unsupervised play in a child's intellectual and emotional development. Eric isn't sure when Andrew became the whimsical, carefree sage who in his professional academic life is as persnickety and precise as an algorithm. But these are the roles they have fallen into since welcoming Wen into their lives. These are the roles they've embraced and find comforting in a way that acknowledges the wonderful, frightening, fulfilling, alienating, and all-consuming *what did we do to ourselves?* existential parental condition.

"Yeah, I know, I know. And I'm still going out front to see how she's doing—"

"Eric!"

"—only because I'm getting burned. I'm thirsty, and I'm bored. My book totally sucks." Eric walks to the sliding glass door that opens to the small kitchen.

Andrew sticks out both legs, blocking the door. "None shall pass."

"What is this, the world's hairiest toll bridge?"

"That's not very nice." Andrew doesn't move his legs and pretends to read his book. He obnoxiously licks a finger and turns a page.

Eric pinches some of Andrew's leg hair between his fingers and yanks quickly.

"Ow! You're such a bully." Andrew swipes at Eric with his book. Eric steps back and avoids getting hit initially, but Andrew lunges forward again and swats him in the back of his left leg.

"Don't hit me with magical realists!"

Eric slaps Andrew's hat brim down over his eyes and then snags the book out of midair while a laughing Andrew tries to hit him again. Andrew clamps down on Eric's arm and pulls him stumbling onto the picnic bench. The two of them wrestle for the book. They trade light, playful jabs, and then a warm kiss.

Andrew leans away, smirking like he won something, and says, "Okay, you can let go of the book now."

"Are you sure?" Eric tries to quickly yank it out of Andrew's hand.

"Don't—you'll tear off the cover. Let go so I can hit you with it again."

"I'm going to throw you and the book—"

The back slider opens with a rattling crash, loud enough that Eric instinctively looks for a shower of broken glass. Wen runs out onto the deck, talking at supersonic speed. She jumps back and forth through the doorway, inside to the cabin then out on the deck then back inside again. She looks around wildly like she's afraid to be outside, and she's still talking and now waving frantically at them: *come here, come inside.*

Andrew says, "Wen, slow down, honey."

Eric says, "What's wrong? Are you okay?"

She's not crying so she likely hasn't been stung by a wasp or physically hurt by anything. He briefly imagines a scenario in which Wen heard something rustling out in the woods and got spooked, but she's more than spooked. She's clearly frightened, and Eric's own alarm and panic rises.

Wen doesn't stop dancing between the deck and the cabin. She does, however, take care to enunciate and slow down. She says, "Come inside, now. Please come in. You have to. Hurry. There are people here and they want to come in and they want to talk to you and some of them scare me."

Wen

She doesn't answer any more questions until after she herds her confused, concerned dads inside the cabin. With the slider shut behind them, she places a sawed-off hockey stick in the frame so the glass door can't glide over the track even if the lock isn't latched. Daddy Andrew showed her how to do that last night before she went to bed.

She pushes her dads out of the kitchen and toward the locked front door. The common area, which is a living room space and kitchen, takes up almost the entirety of the cabin's interior. The walls are made of unstained wooden planks. Wen has already walked around most of the room, knocking and testing for loose ones. A map of the lake and forest, a framed mountain landscape at dusk, and a plaque with hand-carved loons hang haphazardly on the walls along with what look to be antique skis and poles and old baking soda and Moxie advertisements stamped onto sheets of tin, the kind of kitsch one can find at any general store in New Hampshire. A small sliver of a bathroom with the world's skinniest shower stall is to the kitchen's left. The showerhead leaks water more than it actually showers. Across from the back slider and to the right of the front door are the two rectangular bedrooms. Wen's room has bunk beds, the frame built into the walls. Wen has slept in both beds already and has decided she prefers the bottom bunk. To the right of the two bedrooms is the open mouth of a stairwell that spirals down into the basement. A short, thigh-high wrought-iron fence rings the perimeter of the stairwell landing. Next to that and up against the back wall are a stone-and-mortar fireplace and chimney. Squatting on the hearth is a woodburning stove, a small stack of firewood, and a rack of black pewter stove tools: minishovel, brush, tongs, and a poker. A long, army-green couch, the upholstery as prickly as a cactus, cuts a diagonal claim through the common area. Offset to its left is the puffy blue love seat paired with a spindly-legged end table ready to topple at the slightest nudge. A small lamp with a bright yellow lampshade rests on the end table like a toadstool. To the

left of the love seat and almost in the small kitchen is a rectangular table, an abandoned game of solitaire spread out on its top.
A dusty and cobweb-tinseled wagon wheel turned folksy chan-
delier hangs from the vaulted ceiling and between two wooden
beams wide enough to be footbridges. On the wall to their right
and directly across from the front door are a window and a flat-
screen television. The only modern appliance in the cabin (the
refrigerator and stove have to be older than both Andrew and
Eric), the television is tethered to a satellite dish, a lonely lump
of plastic stationed on the roof. The flat-screen is so out of place
as to be anachronistic. It seems impossible that it functions as intended and is less an accoutrement than it is a blackened window,
forever night beyond its glass with its sash permanently nailed
shut.

Their progress through the common room is slow and spas-
modic. Andrew and Eric continue to unleash a torrent of questions and pleas for Wen to respond. She tries to keep a tally in her
head but they are talking too fast and she can't possibly keep up,
and even if she could, she'd be attempting to answer their questions for days and days.

Wen tries her best, anyway. She speaks in clear and clipped
sentences.

"I don't know who they are.

Go look out the windows.

He says they want to talk.

There are four of them.

The big one is named Leonard.

He is very nice but started saying weird things.

He said we have to help save the world.

There isn't any car.

I think they walked here.

They're all sort of dressed the same.

Jeans and same kind of shirts but different colors.

I don't know.

They didn't say anything to me.

Only Leonard.

He said we had to choose something.

It sounded like something bad.

The others are carrying big and scary-looking tools.

Like scythes but not scythes.

I don't know.

They look homemade."

Her dads want to know more about the scary-looking tools. Wen hears her own words as a dull hum coming from some far-away place, as though she's outside of herself but not inside the cabin, and she's confused and thinking maybe she imagined their questions and imagined coming to get them and instead she's still standing out on the front lawn, frozen in place, spot-lighted by the sun, and the strangers with the awful things they carry are there and walking toward her.

Someone knocks on the front door. Seven knocks (Wen counts them); quiet, polite, and in rhythm. Leonard said seven wasn't always lucky.

Andrew and Eric split and flank the front door. Wen stays back, hovering near the table and the invisible line between the common room and the kitchen. Sunlight, relentless and unfor-giving, pours through the glass slider behind her. She curls her thumbs inside her fists and squeezes them, a nervous tick that has replaced chewing her hair. Two of her teachers at Chinese school have caught her doing the fist-thumb-squeeze in recent weeks and after her reassignment from what school calls the *emerg-ing group* to the *basics* classes where most of the other students are a year or two younger than she is. When Laoshi Quang, her Pinyin and grammar teacher, saw Wen's thumbs inside her fists, she smiled and gently unfolded Wen's hands without breaking from the writing lesson. Her history/culture teacher, Mr. Robert Lu (he lets all the younger kids call him Mr. Bob), asked if Wen was nervous and then told her a silly knock-knock joke so bad it was funny. Mr. Bob is nice but he also makes her want to cry; he's so nice he makes her feel guilty. Wen wants to stop going to the Chinese school. The work is difficult. She isn't picking up on the spoken words and written characters as quickly as the other students, almost all of whom have parents who are Chinese. She does not practice speaking nor does she do all her homework during the week. Wen can't articulate the following but she harbors an inchoate anger at her biological parents for giving her up, and she's angry at the country China itself that it is a place in which her parents would be allowed/forced to give her up. She also spends much of her class time daydreaming about all the fun Saturday things her regular-school friends get to do without her.

From outside: "Hey, hello. My name is Leonard. I'm here with some friends of mine. Hello, in there?" His voice is muffled by the front door but clear.

Andrew whispers to Eric, "Tell him to go away nicely. Probably just some religious freaks, right? Saving the world one pamphlet at a time."

Eric whispers back, "Probably. Probably. But Wen said they were carrying weird tools, something like . . . scythes, right?" He looks back at Wen and she nods her head.

"Christ . . ." Andrew pulls his cell phone out of his pocket, turns it on, and then puts it back in his pocket.

Wen wants to remind him cell phones don't work out here and didn't work when he tried to look up scythes yesterday. Her dads

chose this place because there would be no Wi-Fi or cell reception so they could unplug and it would just be the three of them
hanging out, swimming, talking, playing cards or board games
without any digital distractions. Andrew said that it would be
almost like camping, with a cabin instead of a tent. Wen wasn't
convinced of the merits of being unplugged, but she pretended to
be excited about cabin-camping. Her phone is stashed in one of
the wooden drawers beneath her bunk bed. She snapped pictures
of the lake, the wooden ceiling beams she'd give anything to
climb on/walk across, and her bunk bed when they arrived, but
she hasn't taken out her phone since. She isn't sure why Daddy
Andrew has his with him and so readily available in his pocket.
Has he been using it when he wasn't supposed to be? Were they
lying about no Wi-Fi or cell service?

Andrew sneaks up to one of the front windows on the left of
the door, peels back a corner of the curtain, and looks outside.
He reaches up and gently shuts the window and latches it. He
whispers, "The guy on the front stairs is frigging huge."

Eric is practically spinning in place in front of the door. He
finally says, "Hello. Hi, Leonard. We—"

Leonard interrupts. "Are you Daddy Andrew or Daddy Eric?
I met your delightful daughter, Wen, already. She's so smart,
thoughtful, kind. You should be very proud."

Andrew pulls his phone out again, checks it, swears, and
stuffs it back in his pocket like he's mad at it. He crouches, his
face almost touching the window glass in the lower right corner.
He says, "There are more people on his left, I think. Can't really
get a good look at them."

Eric, still in front of the door, is turned so he's facing Andrew.
He has his arms down by his side and he leans to his right until his
ear is only inches from the door. "This is Eric. Is there something

we can help you with? We weren't expecting any visitors. I don't want to sound rude, but we'd rather be left alone."

Leonard says, "I know, and I am sorry to intrude on your vacation. Such a beautiful spot, too. Never been to this lake before. Believe me, up until a few days ago, the four of us, we never thought we'd be here at this lake. The four of us never thought we'd be here to talk to you nice people. But we do need to talk with you, Eric, and with Andrew, and Wen, too. It's vital that we talk. I cannot stress that enough. I know you have no reason to, but you must trust me. I'm pretty sure Wen trusts me. I get the sense she's a very good judge of character."

Eric looks back at Wen and his expression is blank, unreadable, but she wonders if he's blaming her for all this somehow. Maybe this, whatever this is going to be, is her fault because instead of running inside as soon as Leonard and his big friendly smile showed up, she stayed and talked to him. She talked to a stranger when she wasn't supposed to and anything that happens after that is because of her.

Eric says, "We're talking now, Leonard, and we're listening. What do you want?"

Andrew, his face still in the window, scuttles over to Eric and whisper-talks some more, but Wen thinks he's plenty loud enough for Leonard to hear through the door. "There's a woman carrying something; looks like a hoe and shovel mixed together. Why the fuck is she carrying that?"

Eric asks through the door, "Who else is out there with you?"

Leonard says, "My friends Sabrina, Adriane, and Redmond. The four of us are here because we're trying to help save—save a whole bunch of people. But we need your help to do that. Help isn't even the right word. We can't do anything to help anyone without you. Please believe me. Would you mind letting us in?

We just want to talk, tell you more, explain, and speaking through the door is making a difficult conversation near impossible—"

As Leonard continues his filibuster, Eric slinks from the front door to the window on its right. He peels back a dusty lace curtain with two fingers, opening enough space for sunlight to shine on his forehead. After a brief look, he hisses and jumps back and away from the window. "What are they carrying? What are those things?"

Andrew swaps windows for the new view. Eric returns to the front door, facing it, staring at the wood. His hands are on the top of his head as though he's trying to keep it from flying away from his body.

Andrew is past being subtle with his peering out the window. He throws the curtain over his head. He leaks a terrified groan, a sound that turns Wen's knees into rubber bands and shakes the foundation of her once permanent state of belief that she is safe whenever she is with her dads.

Wen says, "I'm sorry . . ." under her breath. She can't explain why she is sorry, but she is.

Andrew slams the window shut, locks it, then staggers behind Eric and looks around the cabin with eyes as wide and deep as wells.

Eric asks, "What are they carrying? Could you see? Why are they here?"

Andrew says, "I—I don't know, but we're not waiting around. I'm calling the police. Now."

"How long will it take for them to get out here?"

Andrew doesn't answer and jogs through the room and to the beige landline phone hanging on the wooden frame outline of the kitchen, adjacent to the fridge.

Wen climbs into the love seat and crouches so that only her

head floats over its back. She says to Eric, "Tell them to go away again. Please make them go away."

Eric nods at Wen and says loudly to the four outside, "Listen, I'm sure you're all very nice, but we're not comfortable letting strangers into our cabin. I'm going to have to ask you to please leave the property."

Andrew loudly replaces the phone in its cradle, then lifts it out and presses it to his ear, and repeats the cycle. "Fuck! Fuck! Fuck! There's no dial tone. I don't understand—"

Eric turns around. "What do you mean? Is it plugged in? Check the connection, maybe it's loose. There was a dial tone yesterday. I checked as soon as we walked in." It's true. He did. Wen checked the phone right after him, too, and she wrapped herself in the long, springy cord until Eric told her not to mess with it, that it wasn't a toy. He checked the phone again after she was untangled.

Andrew lifts the phone off the wall and inspects a translucent cord connected to the jack. He removes it and plugs it back in, then takes the phone out of its cradle. "I checked and I'm checking again but it's not working. It's not—"

Another man's voice, this one deeper and older sounding than Leonard's friendly lilt. What he says has a hint of glee to it, as though what he's saying is a terrifically funny joke you won't get until later, or the kind of joke that is only funny to the teller, which is the worst kind.

"We're not leaving until after you let us in and we have our little chat."

Wen imagines the man saying it while he's staring through the door and cabin walls and looking right at her and his hands are wringing the thick wooden handle of his weapon. She has decided it is a weapon, something only a bad person or an orc would dare construct and carry.

Outside the cabin there's a rush of harsh whispers descending upon the not-Leonard man who spoke. Maybe under different circumstances the four strangers might've sounded like a strong breeze rustling through the forest.

Leonard says, "Hey, I'm sorry. Redmond is as anxious and . . . passionate as we all are, and I can assure you his intentions are pure. I can only imagine how nervous you all are, and understandably so, at our arrival on your doorstep. This isn't easy for us, either. We've never been in this position before. No one has, ever, not in the history of humankind."

Eric responds, coolly, and without hesitation, "We've heard you, Leonard, and we've been very patient thus far. We're not interested." He pauses, runs a hand over his neatly trimmed beard, and adds, "We'd like you to leave now. It doesn't sound like any of you are in trouble or anything like that, and I'm sure you can find someone else to help you." As calm and as *Daddy Eric* as he's been before now, there's a fissure somewhere beneath his words, and it opens wide enough for Wen to tumble down into the hopeless dark.

Andrew must hear the same change in Eric's voice too as he sprints across the short expanse of the room, steps in front of Eric like he's shielding him, and yells, "We said no thank you! Leave now!" He shifts back and forth on the balls of his feet and pushes up his sleeves over his elbows.

From behind, Eric slowly curls an arm around his husband's chest and pulls him away from the door. Andrew doesn't resist.

There's no response from Leonard or from any of the others outside. The silence lasts long enough to feel hopeful (*maybe they are leaving*) and menacing (*maybe they are done with talking because they are ready to do something else*).

Leonard says, "I do not intend this to sound like a threat, Andrew. It is Andrew, right?" Leonard pauses. Andrew nods his head yes although there's no way Leonard can see him. "We aren't leaving until we get a chance to talk, face-to-face. What we have to do is too important. We cannot and will not leave until that happens. I am sorry but we can't change this situation. We have no choice. We all have no choice but to deal with it."

Eric says, "Well, you leave *us* no choice. We are calling the police. Right now." His confident, stentorian voice, the one that makes people listen and makes people want to talk to him and be with him, is gone. He sounds shrunken, diminished, and Wen is afraid she'll only ever hear this new voice.

Andrew reaches up and gently squeezes Eric's arm, the one still wrapped across his chest at the shoulders.

One of the women says, "Hey, hi, um, we know you can't do that. Call the police, I mean. No cell service out here, right? My phone hasn't worked since somewhere way out on the Daniel Webster Highway. I'm sorry but I had to cut your landline. I'm, um, I'm Sabrina, by the way." The awkwardness of her introduction is as chilling as the cutting of the landline admission.

Eric and Andrew slowly back away from the front door. If they keep going like this, they'll fall over the back of the couch.

Eric says to Andrew, "Did you check your cell phone?"

"No bars. Nothing. Fucking nothing."

Eric says, "Wen, can you get your phone, turn it on, and tell us if it works?"

Wen scoots off the love seat and instead of running to her room for her phone, she walks in front of her retreating dads. She screams at the front door, "Leave us alone, Leonard! You're scaring us! You're not my friend! Go away! Just go away!" She hopes she sounds in control and angry instead of frightened. She likes to believe that she has Daddy Eric's voice inside of her somewhere.

Eric and Andrew step forward together and crouch down to Wen's level. They both hug her, squeezing her between them, and they say what are supposed to be soothing things. Eric's arm is sweaty on the back of her neck and Andrew is breathing fast, like he's been racing her around the cabin. Wen doesn't listen to her dads and instead strains to hear Leonard's response.

Leonard says, "I know, and I'm sorry, Wen. I am. I truly am. And I am your friend. No matter what happens. But we can't leave. Not yet. Please tell your dads to open the door. Everything will be easier if they do."

Andrew shouts, "You don't get to talk to her!"

As Eric is shushing her, Wen yells again, "Why do you have those scary weapons with you? Why do you need those?"

Leonard says, "They are not weapons, Wen. They are—tools. If you open the door now, we'll drop them on the ground and leave them outside. And—please believe me—I promise they are not weapons."

The other man yells, "Don't worry. They're not for you."

Her dads quickly confer, speaking so quickly and in hushed, grunting tones Wen can't tell who is saying what:

"'They are not for you?'"

"What the fuck does that mean?"

"I—I have no idea."

"What the hell is going on?"

"No phones."

"Check the cell again."

"What are we going to do?"

"I don't know. Stay calm."

"We're not letting them in here."

"No. We're not."

"No way."

The man named Redmond, the one who sounds like he's enjoying this, he shouts, "Yo! Hey!"

Andrew and Eric stop talking.

Redmond says, "Just do as Leonard says. Open the goddamn door. We're coming in either way."

Andrew yells over Wen's head, "The fuck you are! I have a gun!"

Her dads drop Wen from the group hug. She stumbles and almost falls to the hardwood. They were holding her so tightly between them, they lifted her off the floor. Neither of them noticed.

Andrew

Eric says, "What are you doing?"

Andrew ignores him and shouts, "I'm not just talking shit!"

Andrew's father used to say *anyone who says they're not talking shit has a mouthful.* Clay Meriwether (never "Daddy," only later in life did "Hey, Dad" have an honest ring of affection) was a mechanic/handyman from central Vermont. One morning there was a woman named Donna waiting outside the garage affixed to Clay's parents' old farmhouse. She lived on a commune in the microtown of Jamaica and she had a beat-up Datsun (that wasn't hers) the color of a banana bruise. Clay worked on the car for two weeks and for free, and they got married four months later. A true odd couple: Donna, a vegetarian since her early twenties, keeps a small garden at the house and sells some (but never enough) of what she grows, and she used to read palms and auras and now is practicing holistic healing as her *gig* (her word); Clay, despite being in his early seventies, is still a full-time handyman and an avid hunter on most weekends, and while he's softened his political stances in some ways (and hardened in others) he's generally as conservative as Donna is not. Both Donna and Clay have always been voracious readers, and their shared favorite authors include Tom Robbins, Daphne du Maurier, and Walter Mosley. Donna and Clay always got along and they never left Vermont. Although nostalgia has dulled the edges of growing up in near isolation at the family farmhouse, Andrew couldn't leave Vermont fast enough, and he managed to do so at age eighteen.

Eric pulls Andrew away from the front door, more urgently this time, grabbing and pulling his right arm, and he says, "No, don't. Stop, wait a—"

Andrew doesn't stop. He's so scared and angry, and though he's never pointed a gun at a person in the almost thirty years he's been on-and-off-and-then-on-again handling and shooting firearms, he imagines opening the door and pointing the little, unblinking black eye of the barrel at the forehead of the mostly formless shapes of Leonard or Redmond or whoever shows first. No, it's Redmond he imagines as the target. In the glimpse out of the window Andrew saw Redmond in his obnoxious red shirt, his squat, stocky build, his linebacker stance dripping macho bravura, that always-burning fuel of violence and calamity. In his head, Andrew points the gun at him, the guy who looks and sounds like so many of the hate-filled, ignorant cavemen he's had to deal with his whole life. Whenever Andrew is in a public place he is aware of their eyes and ears. That he is made to feel like he needs to make accommodations or adjustments to how he acts, to who he is in order to be left alone, to be safe, fills him with shame, guilt, fear, and anger. This Redmond might as well be a cipher, a stand-in, a representative for all of *them*: good ole boys, frat boys, card-carrying members of the old boys' network, hate-the-sin-love-the-sinner God-fearin' boys; they're all of the same species. When Redmond speaks, he sounds so familiar; even if they haven't met before, they have. Andrew would have no trouble pointing the gun at Redmond and he may even delight in watching the fear glaze over his dumb, animal eyes. If only Andrew actually had the gun on him.

He says, "Taurus snub-nosed .38 special. If you try to break in here, you're going to have some problems." Andrew gives his voice as much of an edge as he can muster, which maybe sounds like the-schoolteacher-is-upset, but in his own ears, he sounds too much like a stereotype of a comic book nerd. His voice isn't Eric's slow, calm baritone of reason and authority. Andrew heard Eric before he first saw him. They met at a mutual friend's BBQ, fifty people crammed into a comically small, square-shaped, postage-stamp backyard. The partygoers' *excuse mes* and *pardon mes* were the jokes that never got old. Andrew was part of a small ring of friends and coworkers, laughing at something, he no longer remembers at what, but he remembers laughing, and he remembers it as a pleasantly drunk, slightly unhinged, completely happy laugh. Then he heard Eric talking, no, *orating* behind him about some European soccer team and their outlandishly expensive player transfers. That voice of his vibrated at some golden frequency, rising above the giddy and tipsy chatter of the blissful summer revelers. Andrew couldn't have cared less about soccer, but he thought, *Who is that?*

Leonard says, "Please. Don't do—"

Redmond interrupts. "Show us what you got. Put it in the

window, dude." His inflection on "dude" is both dismissive and threatening.

"You'll see it when I point it at you."

Eric sidles next to Andrew and whispers in his ear, "Did you actually bring it? Do you have it?"

In their apartment, Andrew keeps the gun locked in a notebook-sized safe on a shelf in their closet. The safe is new. He bought it eight months ago. Battery powered, he can open it with a touchpad combination or the new biometric palm-print reader, and if the battery dies, there's a safety key.

Andrew grew up with guns. His father used to take him out hunting all the time, whether Andrew wanted to or not. When he was ten, his father gave him a .22 Huntington rifle. Andrew didn't enjoy hunting or shooting animals (though he shot two deer and more than his fair share of squirrels), but he liked target shooting, and he spent a good chunk of his early teen years shooting at a withered gray tree stump about one thousand paces behind the farmhouse. When Andrew moved to Boston, he renounced all things Vermont, including guns. After the attack in that bar near the Boston Garden thirteen years ago, Andrew took self-defense and boxing classes, which helped him to feel more empowered and the nightmares stopped occurring as frequently and his general anxiety decreased to near normal levels (whatever those were), but it wasn't enough. Within a year of the attack Andrew got his Massachusetts gun license/firearm identification and joined a shooting range. Eric strongly resisted having a gun in their apartment initially and they'd had the gun talk a second and third time before and after adopting Wen. Andrew insisted he wasn't reacting or giving in to fear. He'd explained to Eric that the attack left him feeling unmoored; the beer bottle smashing into the back of his head broke off some part of himself that had yet to return. Shooting a gun was a part of who Andrew was as a child and teen and maybe if he could reclaim that small bit of who he once was, he'd feel more whole. Andrew knew he wasn't explaining himself very well, but he also knew it sounded better than admitting his squeezing the trigger once a month at the range while imagining the silhouette on the paper target as his attacker felt so damned good and right.

Andrew says, "Yes and no."

"What do you mean?"

"The safe is in the side panel storage compartment, in the SUV." Andrew bringing the gun was an impulse decision made only minutes before leaving for the cabin. Eric and Wen were down the street getting coffee and donuts for the ride and Andrew took a last walk through the condo, making sure they weren't forgetting anything important. It suddenly occurred to Andrew the gun was important. During their week on the lake Eric would worry about bears and wild animals, and Andrew would worry about being in the sticks of not-so-socially-liberal New Hampshire. Andrew briefly imagined a pair of don't-tread-on-me types seeing him, Eric, and Wen buying food at a supermarket and then following them out to the parking lot spewing epithets and threats, or maybe the fucking rednecks would follow them out to their remote cabin to actualize their homophobia and hatred in more than words. Andrew chastised himself for imagining and dwelling on worst-case scenarios (but that didn't mean it wouldn't or couldn't happen; he knew this from experience) and he hummed "Dueling Banjos" in an attempt to make himself feel silly for wanting to bring the gun. It didn't work and he stashed the safe in the side panel. Andrew didn't tell Eric he was bringing the gun, and he knew he wasn't being fair, but he didn't want to have to deal with that conversation. Eric has been

as understanding as he possibly can about Andrew's gun own-
ership. Still, he would not have been happy at all about the gun
coming with them on vacation. Even though they already had a
long family talk about the gun and safe being off-limits to Wen, it
would've made Eric even more neurotic about her playing unsupervised in the cabin and he would've obsessed over scenarios in
which she finds the safe and somehow opens it.

Redmond says, "Hey, come on, now. We all like show-and-tell
out here. No? Nothing? That's what I thought. Lying through his
teeth. He doesn't—"

Leonard shouts, "That's enough!" his voice deep, percussive,
slightly unhinged, as shocking as an explosion of dog barks from
a once-presumed empty house. Wen whimpers and slaps her
hands over her ears. Andrew is reminded that as threatening and
Cro-Magnon as Redmond sounds and looks, this guy Leonard
standing a foot or two away on the other side of that door is a big
fucking boy.

Leonard says, "I'm sorry for yelling, and I'm not yelling at you
or your family. That was directed at Redmond." There's a beat of
silence that is almost as terrifying as anything that's been said to
this point. "There's no need for a gun, Andrew. We are not here
to—to harm any of you. We just need to talk face-to-face. I think
I've said all that I can say while we're out here. So I'm coming in
now, okay?"

The doorknob twists and the bolted door rattles in the frame.
Andrew, Eric, and Wen watch and say nothing and do nothing as
though Leonard's abrupt segue into attempted entry is the chess
equivalent of saying "checkmate."

Andrew breaks through their collective stupor and yells, "No,
not okay!"

Eric throws his body against the door. He says into the darkly stained wood, "We've been very understanding and we've asked you nicely to leave us alone. Go away." He adds, running out of breath, although he instantly regrets saying it, "You're scaring Wen." Then he turns to Andrew and says quickly through gritted teeth, "What do we do? What do we do?"

Leonard says, "Please, just open the door."

"Fuck off! Go away!" Andrew pulls his green hat tighter onto his head and spins himself in circles. He doesn't know what to do.

Wen is sitting on the floor, leaning against the back of the couch. She covers her eyes and screams "Go away, Leonard! You are not my friend!" repeatedly.

The woman in the black button-down shirt peers into the window to the left of the front door. She sees Andrew and raps on the screen with the wooden end of her tool like a child tapping on the glass of an aquarium. She disappears and says something to the rest of the group. There's a quick and hushed discussion outside, and a red shape blurs past the window on the other side of the door. Andrew thinks he can hear Redmond's plodding steps tracing the exterior of the cabin, heading toward the back deck.

Leonard is still talking. Since shouting at Redmond, his voice hasn't again raised or changed pitch; he might as well be a recording. His evenness and manners are proof of their collective madness. "We are not here to hurt you. We need your help to make things right, to save what must be saved. Only you can help us. You can start by opening the door . . ."

Andrew sprints to the front windows and pulls the threadbare, see-through curtains closed. He then vaults into the kitchen and pulls the dark blue curtain, as thick as a winter blanket, across the glass slider, eclipsing most of the sunlight. The space below the slider frame and above the curtain rod glows radioactive light as does the window above the kitchen sink. The rest of the cabin darkens.

Wen carefully turns on the small lamp with the buttercup-yellow lampshade on the end table. She stands trapped in its spotlight, holding her closed fists, with her thumbs curled up safely inside, against her mouth.

Andrew goes over to Wen and hugs her. She doesn't hug back. He reaches behind him, to the wall between the kitchen and bathroom, and he flicks on the wagon wheel ceiling light. Only four of the six bulbs work. He anticipates Wen asking him if everything will be okay, and if she does, he'll do what any good parent would do; he'll lie to her.

Wen says, "I'm scared."

"We can be scared together, all right?"

She nods. "They're coming in?"

"They might try."

He kisses the top of Wen's head. His lips and mouth are dry. He takes off his hat and places it on her head. It's too big for her but she doesn't take it off. She pulls the brim over her eyes and tucks as much of her hair as she can fit under the hat.

Eric says, "Andrew," and wanders into the common room. Leonard has stopped talking and stopped trying to open the front door. "Did they go away?"

Andrew knows it's a rhetorical, an I-have-to-say-something-or-scream kind of question. Of course they haven't gone away, not yet, and a part of him believes they will spend days, years, the rest of their lives trapped in this cabin, under siege. Andrew would rather hold on to that hellish image and dare not hope the others left because right now hope would be an intoxicant, a mind-duller; hope would be dangerous. Andrew plays along because Wen is listening and he plays along because he must. He says, "I think they're just trying to scare us, right? Too goddamn cowardly to actually—"

Heavy footsteps pound up the stairs that climb to the deck platform. Eric and Andrew eye the couch at the same time and Eric runs to the far end. Andrew momentarily considers telling Wen to hide in the bathroom and lock the door and don't come out no matter what. Instead he clears a path to the back slider, pushing the dinner table, the chairs, and love seat away from the couch, the legs scraping and rumbling across the hardwood floor before sliding onto the kitchen linoleum. Wen helps, too, moving the end table and lamp toward the bathroom.

"Good job, Wen."

Andrew and Eric lift the couch. It's an old sleeper sofa as heavy and unwieldy as a tank. Andrew shuffles to the slider, but Eric abruptly lowers his end, pitching Andrew back toward the common room. Eric says, "Wait, turn it around. We have to spin it around so the back goes against the glass."

Andrew wants to say, *Does it fucking matter?* If the others break the glass slider, what way the couch faces won't really stop them. He doesn't say anything even as it feels like a mistake, a panic move, a waste of precious time, and the two of them stutter-walk, grunt, and groan through a quick semicircle and drop the couch in front of the back slider. The guts of springs and metal framing crash and clang discordantly.

Andrew ducks into the kitchen and closes and latches the window above the sink. Are all the other windows closed? The ones in the bedrooms are big enough for someone to climb through. He opens drawers looking for knives, the biggest ones they have. They'll need knives, right? They'll need something. He says, "Make sure the bedroom windows are closed and covered."

"Oh, shit, hey—"

"What?"

"The basement stairs. What do we do about those?" That open rectangular hole in the floor and its stairs that circle and drain down below . . .

Leonard shouts from somewhere outside, no longer at the front door, but toward the bathroom/kitchen side. "Come on, guys, you can open the doors! Please don't do this! We're not trying to scare you! We're not here to harm you!"

"Cops are on the way, and if you set one foot in here, I'll shoot!" Andrew leaves the kitchen without taking anything with him. Eric stands in the middle of the room transfixed by the basement stairs.

Andrew jogs over and grabs Eric's arm. He whispers, "Is the basement door locked?"

"I don't know. Maybe not. Wen and I opened the door earlier, and we both went outside, and I—I don't remember if we locked it after. I don't think we did. The door might even be wide open."

"Should we go down and check?"

They gravitate to the emptied center of the common room. They listen. There might be the sound of someone walking lightly in the basement and there might not.

"Maybe." Eric looks around the cabin. "Or maybe we clog up the top, so even if they come in through the basement they can't come all the way up the stairs."

They carry the love seat over and Andrew already knows it's too light to be any kind of barrier. Maybe it's enough to slow a couple of them down if they were to come up through the basement and it would give him, Eric, and Wen enough time to flee the cabin through the front door and get to the SUV. They could fight off one or two of them on the way, too, he thinks, but not all four. The closer Andrew gets to the mouth of the stairs, the more anxiety hot-wires his system and he envisions hands shooting up out of the darkness and clutching their ankles to pull them down, down, down.

Eric says, "Here, tilt it toward me a little. We can wedge the feet inside the railing and the fence."

Andrew fears the love seat is too small and will tumble down the stairs, but it jams up against the railing a foot or so below the plane of the main room floor like Eric said it would. It's in there tight, too. Andrew runs back and grabs the kitchen table to add to the stopped-up staircase. Of course now he's thinking maybe they shouldn't block off a possible escape route. Plus there's all kinds of stuff in the basement they could use as weapons or barricades and now they can't get to any of it. Up here there isn't much with which to defend themselves, certainly not anything with the reach and menace of what the strangers are carrying.

Andrew places the table on top of the love seat. Two of the legs fit in the empty space between the wall, floor, and wrought-iron rail, and the other two legs are propped awkwardly on the love seat. He pushes down on the table hard enough that the middle of the table cracks and bends inward.

Eric goes to the hearth and the woodburning stove and plucks the pewter metal poker and tongs from the basket. He says, "Take this," and gives Andrew the poker.

The metal is cold and, instead of emboldening, it feels as useless as a handful of sand. He looks around the room for something, anything else but sees only the brittle museum-piece skis and poles and other useless kitsch on the walls.

Eric retrieves the tin mesh basket of fire logs and drops it next to the staircase.

"What are you doing with those?"

"We can—I don't know—hit them with the logs?" He points

at the bin like the log defense is self-explanatory. He mimes throwing logs down the stairs and then tries to hide a dawning sheepish smile.

"Right. Hell yeah, we're gonna hit 'em with logs."

Andrew and Eric fall into bright, quick bursts of we-shouldn't-be-laughing laughter. Tears ring Andrew's eyes as fear and the numbness of this irreality momentarily give way to absurdity.

Eric wipes his face and composes himself quicker than Andrew does. "Hey, Wen. Come on over with us, okay, honey?"

She doesn't ask what is so funny and she walks mechanically across the room, her eyes focused on the furniture-topped basement stairs.

Andrew pulls Eric close and whispers so that Wen won't hear him. "If they really try to come in here, I say we make a run for the SUV. Right out the front door. I'll go out first and hold them up so you and Wen can make it. If I don't get to the SUV with you, you two leave anyway and get help." Andrew reaches in his pocket for the keys.

Eric says, "No. Stop it. Don't give those to me. If we leave, we all leave together."

Wen tugs on Eric's arm and asks, "Daddy, can I have something to hold, too?"

The back deck reverberates with footsteps. One of the four is walking loudly, purposefully.

"Daddy, can I have something, please?"

"Yes. Yes, you can." Andrew quickly goes to the woodburning stove and returns with the minishovel.

Wen holds it like a softball bat and takes a practice swing. She spins around on her back heel and Andrew has to sidestep to dodge being inadvertently hit in the knee. Neither Andrew nor Eric tells her to be careful.

Andrew twists the poker in his hands. There has to be something else they can do. He says, "What about the knives? In the kitchen. We should grab some knives."

Eric sighs. "Are we really going to—"

"Yes, we really might have to."

"Have to what—"

The screen door slider to the deck that too easily jumps out of the track (Wen has already knocked it out of the doorframe twice) whooshes open.

Redmond calls out, "You really should get someone to fix the screen, guys! Wouldn't want you to lose any money on your deposit. Be good boys, let us in, and we'll fix it for you, yeah? Won't even charge you." The blue curtain obscures the view of the deck and Redmond, but it is not enough to keep them hidden and safe.

Wen shouts, "Go away!"

"That's what I thought." Redmond knocks shave-and-a-haircut on the glass door.

There's the unmistakable sound of movement in the basement: sliding and shuffling across the cement floor and the creak and low-frequency taps of feet trying not to be heard on wooden stairs.

Redmond says singsong, "That's supposed to be the signal knock. No matter." Something crashes and protrudes through the glass slider, bowing out the curtain away from the deck and over the barricade couch, a large blue fist thrusting defiantly into the kitchen before disappearing. A second then third blow pulls the curtain and rod off the wide doorframe. Sunlight flashes atomic bright in the cabin and Redmond is a hulking shadow in the Oppenheimer glare. He hacks at the rest of the glass door with the sledgehammer end of his makeshift weapon. He grunts, crouches, and rams shoulder-first into the couch, shoving it into the kitchen. Broken glass crackles and grinds under his heels and under the couch's stubby peg legs.

Andrew does the math: Redmond is almost fully inside the kitchen and there's at least one of them in the basement, so there are only two of the others, at most, outside. He and Eric can take them on or get past them and to the SUV. He believes they can. They have to.

Andrew fishes the keys out and stuffs them into a pocket of Eric's shorts. "Come on, let's go!"

Eric doesn't argue and scoops Wen up and holds her so that they are chest to chest. She wraps her arms around his shoulders and buries her face into the side of his neck. Eric's left arm coils under her butt. He brandishes the not-all-that-threatening woodstove tongs in his free hand.

Andrew runs to the front door and there are more instant calculations and considerations and variables. How long before Redmond is inside the cabin and across the common room and to them? Does Andrew try to stop him, or waylay him long enough for Eric and Wen to get out the front door? Should he instead focus on the door, opening it quickly, smoothly, without hesitation, and then running outside to clear a path for Eric and Wen? If Andrew were first to the SUV and first to his gun, then he wouldn't have any trouble keeping the others off them as they drove out of here. But what if he can't get to the SUV and what if Eric and Wen can't make it, either? Do they sprint madly down the road or scatter into the woods like spooked rabbits? Maybe they could run out behind the cabin and to the lake. The others wouldn't expect that, would they? He and Eric are both excellent swimmers. They could swim across the lake with Wen in tow if they had to. They could make it—

Andrew only has eyes for the door and the latch bolt and twist lock in the doorknob. He is not looking at Redmond and doesn't know if that man is past the couch obstacle. He does not look back to Eric and Wen, who are at least two steps behind. Andrew is running too fast to stop and he crashes into the door, knocking the poker out of his hand and to the floor. He picks it up.

Eric shouts from behind. "Andrew!"

The woman in the off-white shirt looms in the bedroom doorway to his right, holding her long-staffed weapon and its bizarre and curled-over shovel head pointed out into the room. Andrew has an Escher-esque view beyond her, into the bedroom he and Eric are sharing, and to the wide-open window through which she gained entry.

She says, "Please stop. It doesn't have to be like this."

Still barreling toward the front door, Eric pivots, opening his right shoulder, and swings the tongs at the woman. His first swipe makes solid contact, pinging off the pointed blade of her weapon, which she drops. He teeters and almost falls but follows up with another swing and hits her left shoulder. It's a glancing blow but enough to make her cry out, drop to her knees, and briefly clutch her arm. She quickly recovers, picks up her weapon, and jabs it at Eric's legs. There isn't much oomph behind her strike but it's well placed. She connects, somewhere below his knees and then the odd blade and wooden handle get caught up between his ankles. Eric trips and as he falls he twists his face and chest away from the floor, presumably so he doesn't land on top of Wen. With the added torque, his fall speeds up, he lands awkwardly on his back, and his head bounces off the floor, making a nauseating soft and hollow sound. His body goes limp, arms twitching and open. Wen rolls off his chest and slides into Andrew's feet. She scrambles back to Eric and screams his name. Eric's eyes are closed, his empty arms retracted so his elbows are on his chest, his forearms hovering above him, and his hands wilt inward, looking gnarled, arthritic.

Andrew yells Eric's name and yells Wen's name, too, and then he's just yelling. His back is against the front door and *get the gun get the gun get the gun* is an emergency-broadcast-system alert in his head but he can't open the door and he can't leave.

He tightens his grip on the poker and swings wildly in the direction of the woman in the white shirt. She creeps along the floor closer to Eric and Wen.

The woman holds her weapon out in Andrew's direction, but defensively. Her hands and arms shake as though the thing weighs two hundred pounds. She says, "Let me help him. I'm a nurse. He's hurt."

"Get the fuck away from them! Don't touch them!"

He lunges at her and strikes the blade of her weapon with the poker. Metal on metal clangs like a blacksmith's strike and vibrations run up through his hand and numb his forearm. He keeps swinging and she scoots away, backward toward the bedroom.

Andrew drops to a knee next to Eric's head. Eric's eyelids flutter and he drunkenly moves his arms and attempts to sit up, rolling and rocking like a turtle flipped onto his shell.

Wen has both arms wrapped around Eric's right arm, and she pulls him, saying, "Get up! We have to go, Daddy!"

Everything speeds up and collapses in on Andrew.

The kitchen table and love seat bubble up from the suddenly volcanic basement stairwell and spill out into the common room. Leonard follows, an ash cloud billowing into the cabin. He's enormous, bigger than a god. Unlike the others, he carries no weapon.

The sun shines mercilessly through the shattered glass slider doors. Redmond is a squat, silhouetted goblin, holding his bulky staff like a picket sign. He grunts and giggles his way past kitchen chairs and the end table, knocking over the little yellow lamp, snuffing out its weak light. He says, "Sorry about the mess. We'll clean it up. Promise. Now let's take it easy there, Zorro, yeah? Stop waving that thing around before someone gets—"

Andrew launches at Redmond. He swings the poker high, aiming for the man's head. Redmond is slow to react but he manages to duck behind the mass-of-shovel-and-trowel-blades end of the weapon. The poker gets caught in the spaces between the irregularly arranged hand tools. Redmond drops that end of the weapon, holding the wooden handle parallel to the floor, levering the poker out of Andrew's grasp. It clangs to the hardwood and skitters out of reach.

With Redmond's hands down by his waist, Andrew doesn't hesitate. He throws two quick punches. The first, a right hand, connects with Redmond's fleshy nose and draws a squirt of blood. The second jab, a sharp left, slams into his jaw, and Andrew cuts open the skin of his knuckles on teeth. Staggered, Redmond drops his weapon, checks his nose for blood, and his eyelids flutter like moth wings. Andrew doesn't let Redmond create space or opportunity to get his hands back up. Andrew goes in tight and works the body, punching Redmond in the ribs with two rights, and a left to the stomach, which goes soft like a sail with no wind, and an uppercut to the bottom of his chin that clicks his jaw shut. A hard punch to the solar plexus whooshes the rest of the air out.

Redmond is roughly the same height as Andrew, but he's a thick, beefy guy, probably outweighing him by more than fifty pounds. As many shots as Andrew is expertly landing, he knows it'll take a lot more to get Redmond to go down and to keep him down. So Andrew keeps hitting him.

Redmond has his arms up trying to protect himself, but he's

either too slow or has been knocked into being too slow to fend off the blur of blows. Blood gouts from his nose and leaks from his split lip but he doesn't go down. He absorbs the punishment as though in atonement.

"Daddy, stop hitting the man! Stop it! Stop it!"

Andrew stops and he backs away on sea legs, exhausted and gasping for breath. His knuckles are swollen and bloodied.

Redmond takes a shaky backward step and sits heavily on the couch he pushed away from the slider doors. The springs inside the couch reprise their dissonant chord.

Leonard stands in the middle of the common room, holding Wen in the crook of one arm. She looks so small, she could be a ribbon on his chest. Wen has her hands balled up in fists that way she does (with the thumbs inside) and she holds those fists against her mouth. She isn't wearing Andrew's hat anymore.

The woman in the black button-down shirt stands next to Leonard and Wen. She reaches across Leonard and pats Wen's leg and says, "Shh, you'll be okay. It'll be okay." Andrew doesn't know where she came from or how she got inside the cabin.

Eric is on the floor, sitting up. His eyes are wide in what would be a hammy pantomime of surprise if there were any life or light in his blank stare.

The woman in the white shirt kneels before Eric. She peers into one eye and then the other, examining him. She has a hand resting on his shoulder and she talks in a low voice. He responds with slight nods and confused, pained looks.

Leonard says, "Wen is right, Andrew. That's enough. That's enough."

LET'S MAKE A DEAL

THREE

Eric

Eric was a striker for his high school soccer team. He wasn't the most skilled player but his coach always made it a point to praise him for being fearless when going after headers, particularly off corners and direct kicks. Most of the team's set pieces were designed to get Eric a free run at volleys into the box. In mid-September of his senior season he knocked heads with a burly defensive back as they both went for a ball bending toward the far post. He doesn't remember the forty minutes of game play preceding the collision. The collision itself he remembers as a snapshot, a still photo of the green grass and chalk lines and other players frozen in athletic poses staged by some secret hand and the blue sky decorated with bright, cartoonish, white stars. Eric missed two weeks of practice and games after the concussion. He forced his way back onto the field before he was ready with the hope that he could help the team earn a trip to the state tournament. They didn't make it. For the rest of that season, after each header, Eric had a high-pitched ringing in his ears that would fade over time like the volume was slowly turned down but not all the way off.

His ears are not ringing now. His headache isn't a sharp pain and is instead an insistent pressure radiating out from the back of his skull, lodging against his forehead, throbbing in sync with his heartbeat. The sunlight pouring through the shattered slider doors is an assault under which he withers and cannot escape. Eric lowers his head and turns away from the light despite how much it hurts to move his head in the slightest. Even squinting is painful as it feels like he's pushing his eyes back into his head where there is simply no more room for anything. The damned light finds its way through closed eyelids, anyway, creating a blotchy red mapping of his torture.

The woman in the white shirt is behind him, cleaning up the cut on the back of his bald head. She says, "Try not to move. Almost done."

The light in the cabin mercifully dims as the late-afternoon sun hides behind clouds. Unable to walk out onto the back deck, Eric has no way of knowing how long the cloud relief will last. Waves of nausea rise and fall and his view of the cabin has a haze, as though he's looking through a dirty window.

Eric is sitting in a kitchen chair. His legs are tied to the chair's wooden legs with white rope about a quarter inch thick. His hands and arms are bound behind his back, and by the feel of it, they used the same rope or cord with the wrapping thickest around his wrists. He wiggles his fingers and attempts to flex and bend his wrists, but it all somehow increases the pressure in his head.

Andrew is similarly restrained in a chair offset to Eric's right. Andrew's head is down and his long hair obscures his face. His chest rises and falls evenly, straining against the loops of rope that affix his torso to the chair backing. Eric cannot remember if anyone struck or attacked Andrew, and he does not remember how they got to be anchored to the chairs. He remembers running for the door and falling and then seeing the ceiling from an impossible distance below.

He doesn't know if Andrew has already begged and pleaded with the others to leave them alone, to let them go. He doesn't know if Andrew and the others have come to some sort of bargain or agreement. Did Andrew give in, surrender? Andrew hasn't surrendered to anyone or anything in his life and it's a big part of why Eric loves him. He remembers jagged pieces of the whispered conversation they had by the barricaded basement stairs and laughing at hitting the others with logs and how Andrew was willing to stay behind in order to get Eric and Wen to the SUV. Eric wants to ask Andrew a question, but he's afraid to ask the wrong one.

Wen is unrestrained. She sits on the floor between Eric and Andrew, her legs crossed atop a pile of pillows and blankets scavenged from one of the bedrooms. The three of them fill the area where the couch had once occupied the common room.

The couch is now up against the far wall, below the flat-screen TV. Redmond is the gargoyle of the couch, perched, slouched forward, grunting and muttering to himself. He dabs his nose and swollen lips with a white kitchen hand towel, checking for blood.

The woman in the black shirt is on the deck, readjusting the screen door slider in its frame. It won't stay in the track and she says, "Goddammit," each time it falls out and in an accent that is not of New England.

Leonard is in the kitchen, sweeping broken glass into a metal dustpan. He dumps the debris into the garbage. The high-pitched frequency of grinding and breaking glass is as loud as a crumbling skyscraper, and the noise overstresses the hardware in Eric's head.

Wen's favorite show, *Steven Universe,* is on the TV, playing a few feet above Redmond's head. The TV's volume is too much for Eric. He has asked multiple times that they turn it down, and Leonard did as was asked the first two times but has since only pretended to turn down the volume, picking up the remote and pointing it at the TV, but no red volume bar then shows on the screen.

The woman in the white shirt finishes taping a pad of folded-up paper towels to the back of Eric's head. She says, "I don't think you need stitches, but it's a pretty nasty cut back there." The scalp on the back of his head is numb. He wants to feel the dressing with his fingers, verify its physical existence, but cannot.

With the sunlight still cowering behind clouds, the pressure in his head lowers out of the code-red range. Eric looks down at Wen. He wants her to talk to him, to say something, anything. He says, "Hey, Wen. I'm finally a match, you know?" He twists his head and shows off the bandaging. "Like I belong with you guys now. This isn't like, um, me shaving. It's going to be real now." He isn't explaining himself well. He means to say he'll now have a scar on his head just like Wen and Andrew have on theirs.

Wen doesn't speak and she keeps her eyes on the TV. Scooting over closer to Eric, she leans her head against his legs.

That Eric will now have a real, legit scar fills him with unexpected happiness, and he laughs, but then he thinks about the next time he shaves and how Wen won't need to inspect his bald head for nicks and fake scars that always fade away in a matter of hours. The scar will already be there, red and permanent. Losing that odd little post-head-shaving ritual with Wen is suddenly the saddest thing he can think of and his odd laughter morphs into a grotesque mix of manic, percussive cackles and uncontrollable, chest-heaving sobs. Having recently (and obsessively) read about the many, often undiagnosed concussive blows football and soccer players suffer, Eric is able to recall that having wild, unpredictable emotional swings is a symptom of a severe concussion, but it doesn't help and doesn't stop his tears.

The woman behind him pats his shoulder and shushes him, saying, "It's okay. You'll be all right."

Leonard leaves the dustpan on the floor next to the plastic garbage bin and leans the straw broom against the refrigerator. He asks, "Is Eric cleaned up?"

She says, "He's cleaned up, yeah, but severely concussed."

"Awake?"

"Yes, mostly."

The two of them continue a quick and clinical discussion of Eric's condition like he isn't there. Andrew whispers Eric's name. Eric tries to give Andrew a smile, to let him know that he's okay, but he's still crying.

Leonard tiptoes in from the kitchen and to the center of the common room. For a big man, he moves gracefully, but the floorboards betray him and creak under his weight. He bends from his great height and plants his hands on his knees. "Hi, Eric. Are you feeling better? Oh, Wen, I'm sorry." Leonard deftly sidesteps to Eric's left to keep from blocking Wen's view of the TV. He says to Wen, "I've never watched this show before but I like it. And it seems like a very you show."

Eric says, "What does that mean?" He sounds so loud to himself. Is he shouting?

Leonard clasps his hands together. "The characters are, well, you know, smart, and, um, good—"

Redmond, still on the couch, laughs and shakes his head.

Leonard gives Redmond a dark look and then crouches down so that his head is below Eric's. This guy is young and he is someone who will always look young until the one day he doesn't. "I get the sense the show teaches, or explores, empathy and tolerance."

Redmond says, "Makes me feel all squishy inside."

Andrew says, "Empathy and tolerance. Is that what you're here to talk about now that you have the queers tied up?"

Leonard stands up and says, "Andrew, I assure you that we're not here with hate or prejudice in our hearts. Not at all. That's, um, that's not us, not who we are."

The others speak at the same time as Leonard. The woman behind Eric squeezes his shoulders and talks, but he only hears some of what she says. "—not one homophobic bone in my body." The woman in the black shirt calls out from the deck/kitchen area, "I don't hate anybody, just this friggin' screen slider."

Leonard drones on. "Not who I am. You have to believe me on that. We are not here because—"

Andrew says, "Because we're fags?"

Leonard blushes, like a teen trapped in a lie. He stammers, sounding less and less confident with each syllable. "I know how this looks and I understand you thinking that. I really do. But I promise you that's not why we're here."

Andrew isn't looking at Leonard but at Redmond, who stares back at him with a cracked leer. He says, "You promise me, huh?"

"Yes, I do. We all promise, Andrew. We're just normal people like you, and we were thrown into this—this extraordinary situation. I want you to know that. We didn't choose this. We're here because, just like you, we have to be. We have no choice."

Andrew says, "There's always a choice."

"Yes, okay, you're right, Andrew. There's always a choice. Some choices are more difficult than others. We choose to be here because it's the only way we can help." Leonard looks at a thick, black-banded wristwatch with a white face as large as a sundial. "Hey, everyone come in here, please. It's almost time." He holds a hand out, wiggles his fingers in a come-here gesture.

Andrew asks, "Time for what? You don't need us tied up. You're here to talk so we'll talk. All right?" He struggles against his restraints, pulling his legs up hard enough to make the chair jump in place. No one tells him to stop.

The woman in the white shirt steps out from behind Eric and stands next to Leonard. The woman in black walks in from the deck and slowly closes the screen door. Her care is overexaggerated and she says, "If it falls out again, I'm going to stab it dead."

Redmond says, "Tsk, tsk, such violent language."

She gives Redmond the finger, then says to Wen, "Hey, sorry. Poor choice of words and finger."

The woman in the off-white shirt—or pearl, at least compared to the bright, starched-looking white of Leonard's shirt—steps up and says. "Hi, Eric, Wen, and Andrew. My name is Sabrina." She smiles and waves at Wen. She's young, too, younger than Eric's and Andrew's almost forty, anyway, and thin but broad shouldered. Her brown hair is between a bob cut and shoulder length, and curly at the ends. Freckles dust across the bridge of a long nose that dives deeply beneath her large, egg-shaped brown eyes. "I live in Southern California. You can tell by my tan, right?" She smiles, and it disappears immediately. She folds her hands behind her back and looks up at the ceiling as she says the rest. "I live in a town you've probably never heard of. I've been a post-op nurse for almost five years and was planning to go back to school to become a nurse practitioner. I, um, used most of my savings to come out to New Hampshire, to come here to talk with you guys." She rubs her face with both hands and says, "I have a little half sister back home, my dad remarried like ten years ago, and, Wen, you kind of remind me of her."

Wen shakes her head no and continues watching *Steven Universe*.

Sabrina walks behind Leonard, turns away from everyone, and holds a hand to her forehead and then down to her mouth.

Leonard pats her shoulder once and says, "Thank you, Sabrina. Right, so as I think you know already, my name is Leonard. I'm good at catching grasshoppers, right, Wen?" He pauses, waits, and Wen nods. Leonard tilts his head and smiles. Andrew spasms in his chair against the restraints. Eric knows that Andrew wants to thrash this man for that smile and for making their daughter nod her head the way she did. "I live just outside of Chicago. I help run an after-school sports program at an elementary school, and I bartend, too. I love working with kids but the after-school program isn't full-time yet and doesn't pay a ton." He pauses again, like he forgot the next line in a script. Sabrina, as far as Eric can figure, was telling the truth. He isn't sure about Leonard. "I haven't been to a cabin like this since my parents took me to the Lake of the Woods, which is up in Minnesota if you've never heard of it. Kind of a famous spot. We used to go there every summer. I read the Tim O'Brien book that was set on the lake in high school but didn't like it very much."

Andrew says, "It's a brilliant novel. One of my favorites."

Eric almost starts crying again because he loves Andrew for not being able to help himself.

Leonard says, "Yeah, but it's too dark and sad for me. Maybe it would've been different if it wasn't set at my favorite place. This is a beautiful spot, here, too." Leonard closes his eyes, like he's lost in the reverie of prayer. "I've always wanted to end up in a place like this."

Redmond starts in, almost cutting off Leonard. "Okay. Me? Am I next? Hi there, my name is Redmond and I like long walks on the beach and I like beer." He laughs long and loud at his own joke. The other three give him a look that glances off him to somewhere else in the room, anywhere else that isn't Redmond. It's a shared look communicating clearly they don't like him.

Leonard speaks in a voice that Eric imagines he uses with the kids in his after-school program, real or imagined. "This is important. We already discussed this. They deserve to know who we are."

Redmond jabs a hand toward Leonard as he speaks, "You're so concerned what they think and feel when it doesn't matter, not one bit." He points that punctuating hand at Andrew and Eric. "No offense, fellas," then back at Leonard, "And it doesn't change what it is we have to do and it doesn't change what they are going to have to do. So let's stop pretending any of this bullshit matters and just get to it."

Leonard says, "When you say stuff like this and sound how you sound, you scare them, and make it less likely they'll believe us and cooperate."

"I don't know, *Leonard*." Redmond says his name like he's teasing, mocking him somehow. "Have you considered that breaking in, tying them to chairs, and then us standing here like a bunch of freaks, cleaning up, making house, grinning like dick-holes, and now introducing ourselves like we're all at a goddamned family reunion or something, is what's scaring them?"

"This is how it's supposed to be."

"Ah, yes, right. I guess I didn't get that particular memo."

"No, I guess you didn't."

"Of course you're the only one who did," Redmond mumbles, a pouting child who isn't getting his way.

Sabrina says, "What are you talking about? We already told you that Adriane and I got the same message, too."

Redmond's wide face flushes to the color of his shirt. "Whatever. It still doesn't make—"

Leonard takes a hard, floor-shaking step toward Redmond and the couch.

Redmond jumps up and raises hey-I-surrender hands. "Okay, okay, my turn it is. Hey, I'm the local boy. Live in beautiful Medford, Massachusetts." He exaggerates a Boston accent with the long *aaaah* sound in the front. "I work for the gas company making sure houses and apartment buildings don't blow up. I'm single, if you can believe that. Sabrina and Adriane don't seem to care, though. Ha ha, right? I've done some time, as they say. I did a lot of, uh, *questionable* stuff when I was young and stupid, but I'm much better now. And I mean that sincerely." He pauses, presses the towel to his lip, and then holds his arm out straight to his right and drops the towel. It parachutes to the couch. "You know, my father used to beat the shit out of me, like Andrew just did. Would you believe me if I said I never deserved it? I wish I could go back in time and give the kid-me this thing." He picks up the oar with the sledgehammer and trowel/shovel blades Q-tipping each end, shakes it, like he's sizing it up for a mighty swing. He looks at Andrew, leans the weapon against the couch, and says, "Christ, guy, all my front teeth are loose, still bleeding. Remind me not to fuck with you again. But I knew you were lying about having a gun. So fucking obvious in so many ways that you didn't have one. The funny part is—"

Leonard shouts, "Redmond!"

"Yeah, yeah, fine. So how's all that?" He holds his arms out wide. "Me in thirty seconds. Damaged goods but I have a heart of gold; here to help save the world and all that. Can I get a hug now, Adriane?"

Adriane walks past Redmond to the center of the room and

says, "I'd rather work on that screen door for eternity." She claps her hands and says, "I'm always the last one. I know this is so weird but—"

Eric says, "Okay, hold on a second. We get that you guys are part of some group and it sounds like you want to"—his pause becomes a stammer—"er, what, fix things? Help?"

Andrew says, "Eric, you don't have to—"

"No, I'm okay, a little scrambled, but I want to say this." He takes two deep breaths and prays a silent please-God-get-us-out-of-this-safely complete with an Amen. "If you're trying to recruit us, I mean, why else bother introducing yourselves to us, right?" Eric lets out a groan. He's frustrated with himself because he didn't intend to say the last part, to say exactly what he was thinking instead of sculpting his words into a pointed, purposeful statement. "If you're trying to recruit us, or what, change us, make us different?" He's again verbalizing what's in his head and not curating something a bit more politic. Eric is supposed to be the great communicator, builder of compromise and consensus. He can do this; he just needs to concentrate harder. "This, all this, isn't the way—"

Eric is cut off by the vengeful return of the sun. Its rays burn through the cabin and his head and fill the rotten world with hateful, damning light.

Wen

Wen has seen this episode of *Steven Universe* before. Steven is called away from his favorite TV show by Peridot's distress call. Steven and the Crystal Gems rush to the dangerous communications hub to take apart what Peridot had rebuilt without their knowing. Two of the gems, Pearl and Garnet, merge together (Amethyst is sad and feels left out) and form Sardonyx, a magician who also carries a war hammer, a long thin pole with two giant cube-shaped fists at the end. Steven and Sardonyx break the hub apart. But the hub is restored the next day and the day after and they keep having to return to tear the hub down. Pearl eventually admits she is the one who keeps rebuilding the hub because she loves how it feels to merge with Garnet and become the powerful Sardonyx.

Eric's voice is soft and high pitched. "Can someone put the curtain back up? The big blue one. Over the slider."

Wen watches the show, but isn't really watching. She can both watch and not-watch at the same time. She's good at it because she secretly has two brains. One brain dreams of becoming Sardonyx and sweeping the four strangers into the garbage with her war hammer. With her other brain, she ignores the television and watches what's happening and listens to what is being said in the cabin. She pays close attention, and despite how dangerous everything feels, she can hide and stay safe inside this other brain, while scheming, plotting, waiting for a signal or message from either one of her dads to do whatever it is they'll need her to do.

Everyone is talking over one another.

"What's wrong with Eric?"

"When you have a concussion, you're extremely sensitive to light."

"There's nothing we can do about that now."

"He's only going to get better if he rests in a dark room or if we make it dark in here."

"I don't think we should move him until after we make our, um—"

"Our proposal?"

"Right."

"Yeah. Let's make a deal. Door number three, man, it's always door number three."

"You can't joke about this."

"I can and I have to."

"Because you're an asshole?"

"Because I'm scared shitless just like everyone else."

"He might need to be in a darkened room for days, not just a few hours."

Eric stirs as much as his tied-down body allows. Wen lifts her head away from his legs. He says, "You're not separating me from Wen and Andrew. I'll be fine."

He doesn't sound fine. Wen doesn't want to look at him because of how not-fine he sounds.

Andrew says, "Come on, just untie him. He's not going anywhere."

"I'll see what I can do with the curtain," Redmond says and walks into the kitchen and the slider door's frame.

Adriane says, "If you knock out that screen—"

"Yeah, I know, I get it. Do your intro thing so we can get this over with."

Andrew starts to say something, but Adriane interrupts and says, "We'll answer all of your questions real soon. Just let me get through this. I'll be quick." She moves differently than the others, a weird combination of hyper and slow.

There was one day during this past February school vacation week Daddy Eric worked from home. He spent most of the day on the phone, doodling on a cube of yellow sticky notes. Each doodle was a stick figure he penned in the lower right corner of a sheet. Its head had long stringy J's on each side, which was supposed to represent Wen's hair. He spent hours drawing the same figure over and over again, one per individual sticky note. He was finished drawing at the same time he proclaimed his work-day completed. She asked him what it was and he said he made a cartoon. He showed her how to flip the notes, bending the pad and using his thumb to let the individual sheets tick by. The stick figure waved, did some deep knee bends, three jumping jacks with her arms blurring over the stick-figure head, and then she jumped in the air and flew back and forth across the yellow pages like a superhero.

The herky-jerky way the minimovie stick-figure Wen moved is how Adriane moves. It makes Wen want to watch her closely.

"So, yeah, I'm Adriane. I've been a lot of things but right now, or before I came up here, I was a line cook at a Mexican restaurant in Dupont Circle, D.C. I could show you my forearms covered in burn marks." Her hands are alive, flapping around, crashing into each other, sock puppets in a Punch and Judy show. There's a thick black ring on the thumb of her right hand and she twists it or checks to see if it's still there after all the hand waving. She talks with a papery rasp that pitches her voice, making it sound lower and higher at the same time. Wen decides that this is how all people who live in Washington, D.C., talk.

"What else? Um, I have two cats, and you'd love them, Wen. Their names are Riff and Raff." Adriane's hair is longer than Sabrina's and much darker. Probably fake darker. Her eyebrows are thin and arched, encroaching on her forehead. She looks like the youngest of the four from a distance, but the oldest when she's close up because of crinkle lines that show around her mouth and eyes. "Do you like cats, Wen?"

"You don't have to answer her," Andrew says, and he says it like he'd be mad at her if she did.

She answers in her head. *Yes, I like all animals.*

Leonard turns off the television, tosses the remote control onto the couch, and checks his watch again. "Sorry, Wen. Maybe I'll put it back on later."

The room darkens as the sun continues to play hide-and-seek. Shade blankets the deck and seems to act as soundproofing for the surrounding forest, muffling bird chirps and insect wings.

Redmond stands dumbly in front of the slider doors with the heading of the curtain in his hands, the rest pooling around his feet and ankles. His fingers are lost inside the thick loops through which the rod is supposed to pass.

"Forget the curtain. It's time," Leonard says.

Redmond doesn't respond with a joke. He drops the curtain, walks back into the center of the room, and stands with the others. The four of them make a line across the room. Seeing them together in their button-down shirts and jeans makes Wen afraid all over again. How they are dressed must mean something important but no one has explained why and maybe they'll never explain why.

Andrew says, "Wait, hold on, time for what? Keep talking to us. We'll listen. We are listening . . ."

Leonard smiles weakly. "Wen asked me earlier if the four of us were friends. I did not lie to her then and I will not lie to you now, not ever. I don't know if I can say that Sabrina, Adriane, and Redmond are my friends exactly. But I trust in them and I believe in them. They're regular everyday people like me—"

Andrew mutters but loud enough to be heard, "Fucking hell, someone save us from all the everyday people." His pleading tone from a moment ago disappears, and he sounds angry, like Professor Daddy, which is what she and Eric teasingly call him when he lectures about minor infractions that include abandoning glasses of water or juice boxes on the windowsills, leaving cereal bowls half filled with milk next to the kitchen sink, and not replacing the toilet paper roll after one is spun down to the cardboard tube.

Leonard stammers and fumbles through "—and regular just like you."

Redmond laughs.

Leonard twists left and right as though looking to fellow actors who have forgotten a line or cue. "Let me start by telling you the four of us didn't meet each other in person for the first time until this morning."

The three others nod. Sabrina has her arms crossed, and she swirls tiny circles on the floor with a foot. Redmond has his hands behind his back and his jaw clenched tight. Adriane's face swaps into and out of an odd smile or a snarl and a wince at a punch she sees coming.

"Look, Leonard, just let us go and we won't call the police or anything, we won't, okay? I promise . . ."

"As you've heard, we're all from different parts of the country and we didn't know each other before"—Leonard holds his arms out—"before this. We didn't even know that each other existed before last Monday. 11:50 P.M. I know the exact time my life changed forever. That's when I first got the message. They got the message, too. The same message. We were called and are united by a common vision, which has now become a command we cannot ignore."

Andrew thrashes around in his chair.

Eric says, "Stop, just stop, please. Please, God, whatever this is. Stop . . ."

Wen wishes she had the small shovel in her hands. She wishes the TV were still on. She wishes she could stop shaking. She gets up and scrambles behind Andrew's chair.

"Wen, I'm sorry, I really am, but it's important that you hear this, too. What you decide is as important as what your dads decide."

Andrew shouts, "Don't talk to her! Don't say anything to her!"

Eric calls out to Wen and tells her that she'll be okay, that everything will be all right. The white wad of paper towel as big as a movie screen on the back of his head has a bright red bull's-eye. She feels terrible that she went behind Andrew's chair and not Eric's but she doesn't move.

Leonard says, "The four of us are here to prevent the apocalypse. We—and by *we* I mean everyone in this cabin—can stop it from happening but only with your help. In fact, it's more than help. Ultimately, whether the world ends or doesn't end is entirely up to you three. I know it's a horrible burden, believe me, I do. I didn't want to believe it, either, when I first got the message. I tried to ignore it." Leonard looks to the others and they nod their heads, and the world's quietest *yes* escapes from someone's mouth. "I didn't want it to be true. But I was quickly made to see it was the truth and this was what was going to happen whether or not I wanted it to, whether or not I thought it was fair."

"We are not going to listen to this," Eric says.

"The message is clear, and we are the messengers, or a mechanism through which the message must pass."

Leonard breaks the line of the four and steps forward, putting himself between Eric and Andrew. He's bigger than all the others combined and he's bigger than the cabin itself; a conflicting, confounding size that only a child could ever equate with innate, implacable gentleness. Wen remembers being held in his arms while Daddy Andrew fought with Redmond. To her shame, she remembers feeling safe.

Wen says, "Please leave us alone, Leonard. Please go away and I'll still be your friend."

Leonard blinks hard and rapidly and lets out a percussive, deep breath. He starts talking and as he talks, he doesn't look at Eric, Andrew, or Wen, despite having moved closer to them and crouching to their level.

Andrew

If Leonard again insists the four of them are regular, everyday people—as though *everyday people* have nothing but love in their hearts and are always reasonable and have never committed atrocities in the name of their self-proclaimed *everydayness*—Andrew is going to scream until he can't scream anymore. He gets it; of course they are regular people. That message (there are regular people and there are *others*) is loud, clear, and received to the point where Andrew is beginning to think he may have seen or met each one of them before, with the strongest, nagging don't-I-know-you? vibe coming from the loathsome Redmond.

Leonard says, "Your family must choose to willingly sacrifice one of your three in order to prevent the apocalypse. After you make what I know is an impossible choice, you must then kill whoever it is you choose. If you fail to make the choice or fail to follow through with the sacrifice, the world will end. The three of you will live but the rest of humanity, seven billion plus, will perish." Leonard's mannerless, reading-the-high-school-morning-announcements tone becomes the breathless impassioned entreaty of a zealot. "And you will only live long enough to witness the horror of the end of everything and be left to wander the devastated planet alone, permanently and cosmically alone."

Andrew anticipated some form of unhinged, hateful, quasi-fundamentalist-Christian, cult manifesto, but he did not expect

this. He is so flummoxed and terrified he has difficulty process-
ing exactly what Leonard is saying, and the implications and
permutations of possible future outcomes to be determined in
part by what he and Eric say and do next are as irretrievable as
the quarks of a smashed atom. Andrew briefly imagines he, Eric,
and Wen holding hands and walking through a postapocalyptic
landscape, specifically the blasted and burnt ruins of Cambridge
and Boston: ash-gray sky, Storrow Drive's footbridges collapsed
onto soot-topped cars, steel girders curled like a dead insect's
legs, buildings and brownstones reduced to brick piles of burning rubble, the Charles River black, motionless, and choked with
debris. He turns away from the image and away from Leonard,
twisting his head as far as it will go, but not enough so that he can
see Wen hiding behind his chair. He wants to tell her to cover
her ears and ignore Leonard's poisonous words even though he
knows it would be impossible for anyone to do so.

Eric says, "Leonard, you don't have to do this. You don't. This,
whatever this is, isn't you. It doesn't have to be. We haven't done
anything to deserve this."

Leonard still won't look directly at Andrew or Eric or Wen.
His gaze is somewhere over their heads, on a secret spot of the
cabin door, under their chairs, spying a shard of glass on the
kitchen linoleum that managed to escape his broom, the yellow
lamp lying crookedly on its side. "I agree that you haven't done
anything wrong or bad to deserve this burden. You haven't. I
can't make that clear enough. Perhaps you are being chosen, like
we were chosen, because you're strong enough to make the decision that needs to be made to stave off the ruination of humanity.
I think that's the way to look at this, Eric."

Despite the terror of this continuing assault and the pain and
discomfort with which Eric clearly suffers, he turns his head and

says to Andrew, "That's thoughtful of them to give us the proper way to look at this."

Andrew laughs the cynical, mocking one-note plosive of the death row inmate. Waves of love and pride for Eric surge with righteous anger and defiance, yet he knows feeling strong and emboldened isn't enough to rid his family of the four intruders. It's not enough to break him free from his chair.

"Please don't kill us," Wen whispers from behind Andrew. The quaver in her voice is the worst thing he's ever heard, without a close second. Andrew renews his struggles against the ropes. His wrists burn as he flexes, twists, and contorts.

Leonard drops to one knee and leans forward, finally making eye contact. "We are not going to kill you, Wen, and we aren't going to kill your parents. We aren't. Aside from what we had to do to enter the cabin and get you to listen to what we had to say, we are not going to lay another finger on any of you. That is a promise. We'll help make you as comfortable as you can be—but you have to stay here in the cabin with us—until you choose or the allotted time you have to choose runs out."

"And how long is—"

Leonard speaks over Eric, "Not long, not long at all. Time is running out on the world, on us. Look, we're not here to hurt you."

Redmond interrupts with, "If we wanted to hurt you, we would've used duct tape instead of rope. Believe me."

Leonard continues as though Redmond didn't speak. "You have to understand; we cannot and will not choose who is sacrificed for you and as importantly, we cannot act for you, either. It doesn't—it won't work that way. You must choose who is to be sacrificed and you must physically perform the act. Like I said, we are here to make sure the message is heard and understood."

Redmond says, "Hey, have one of them repeat all this back to you," and makes circular motions with his right hand.

Sabrina says, "Redmond, just shut up, all right?"

"What. I'm not being a wiseass. Have them prove they heard you, understood you, Leonard. We have to make sure they get what we're saying here, that we're serious. This is real, man. We're not making this shit up. Who would make something like this up?" Redmond talks fast and his Boston accent is clear and authentic unlike the exaggerated one from earlier.

Andrew ping-pongs from wanting to say the magic words that would defuse what's happening, to being compliant with the hope they'll leave Wen alone, if not him and Eric, to wanting to ensure the four of them hear and know his mocking, disdain, and hatred for who they are, for who they're choosing to be. He says, "We have to kill one of us or the world will end. We get it. And we already know our answer."

Adriane breaks from the line, reaches out, and taps Leonard's shoulder. "Let them take a minute to, I don't know, let it all sink in, get over the shock. This is pretty messed up, right?"

"Yeah, okay." Leonard nods his head, stands up, and backs away until he is between Sabrina and Redmond.

Sabrina steps forward and as she does so, it occurs to Andrew that this is how groups like theirs operate, how they brainwash, how they infect with their virulent, recursive beliefs, how they get what they want. The moment one member stops talking the next steps in to present the same concepts but spun slightly to sound less threatening, the original spiel repackaged inside a more palatable Trojan horse. The second speaker is friendlier than the first, more rational, and so is the third speaker, and the fourth, and the next and the next, and their bolus of ideologies begins to make sense and becomes familiar, becomes an affirmation of what was already there hidden inside your own head.

Sabrina says, "We wish it wasn't this way, but there's nothing we can do to change it. I know it all sounds crazy, batshit crazy, but you have to somehow trust us. We're going to trust you'll make the right decision, of course."

Andrew says, "Of course." He strains to reach out to Wen with his tied hands. His bruised, abraded knuckles and his swollen fingers throb. If he manages to touch her, pinch her shorts or shirt between his fingers, maybe she'll figure out he wants her to help untie the rope if she can do so without being seen by the others. Andrew brushes the back of his left hand against her. She scoots back and away from him quickly, as though startled. He wiggles his fat and laggard fingers, desperate to somehow communicate *untie me*. Her hands do not fall upon the ropes or on his wrists.

Leonard looks at his watch again and says, "I'm afraid we don't have much time before you have to choose. That's, um, our fault for taking so long to get in here, and then Eric's unfortunate injury that we did not want or intend to happen, not at all, I swear, and it put us behind where we wanted to be by now. So now we're running out—"

Andrew lifts his head, shakes the hair out of his eyes, and says, "We're not choosing anyone. We're not sacrificing anyone. Not now, not ever."

Leonard closes his eyes and is otherwise expressionless. Redmond laughs dismissively and folds his arms across his chest. Adriane bows her head and lets her arms fall to her side and dangle limply.

Sabrina clasps her hands together, her eyes widen, and her

mouth drops open, dumbfounded, heartbroken. "Even if it means the death of everyone else in the world?"

Andrew wants to believe there's an opening, a crack, through which he and Eric (it would've most certainly been Eric if he hadn't sustained a concussion) could talk the four out of whatever they have planned after he reiterates their answer to this lunacy is of course no. However, Andrew is not good at mollifying, at saying what people want to hear. He excels at saying what he wants people to hear. That is not the same as telling-it-like-it-is, a folksy descriptor that is spin for being an entitled asshole. It's more like he tells-it-like-it-should-be backed with an impeccably logical through-line. He has no trouble speaking in front of a lecture hall, from his position of authority and expert, and his students both fear and adore him for it. Department and faculty meetings are trickier for him to navigate without hurting feelings and angering misguided and perhaps well-intended colleagues.

Andrew opts for the unvarnished truth: "Yes. Even if I believed the world was at stake, which I don't, that's what it means. I would watch the world die a hundred times over before . . ." and he doesn't finish because he doesn't want to finish.

"Christ." Redmond returns to the couch and picks up his weapon, weighs it in his hands. "Fucking waste of time. They're never going to choose to do this. I don't blame 'em. Who would ever choose to—"

"Shut your goddamn mouth!" Adriane increases volume with each syllable. She storms around the room mumbling, "Oh, man. Oh, man, we're so screwed . . ."

Leonard says her name and reaches for her left elbow.

Adriane slaps him away and rubs her arms like she's freezing. She pivots, takes two quick steps to Eric, anchors her hands on the chair's armrests, and sticks her face only inches away from his. "We heard from Andrew. Come on, Eric, what do you say? Huh? You have to believe us."

Eric winces at her closeness and volume. He shakes his head slowly, side to side, his paper-towel dressing pad a limp white flag.

Wen mumbles, "Leave Daddy alone," from behind Andrew.

"He's going to say the same thing I said! Get out of his face!" He shakes the hair out of his eyes. Sitting as tall as he can with his pointed chin held up and out, he dares any one of the four to come as close to him as Adriane is to Eric. If one of them does, he'll head-butt the person at the bridge of their nose.

Adriane's panic twitches below her eyes and tugs at the corners of her mouth. "We're not fucking around. You don't think we're not sacrificing anything to be here? We dropped our lives and came all the way out there for this, man. Came out here for you. We had to. Unlike you, we had no choice. You have to believe us. You have to." She pushes off the armrests and straightens up.

Eric takes a deep breath and says, "We are not choosing anyone, we will never choose anyone. We will not hurt each other or anyone else. I cannot be more clear on that. We cannot be more clear. So that means you're going to let us go and then you're going to leave and then—"

Leonard claps his hands once, as loud as a slamming door. "Okay, you need to listen to this part, too. I've been shown exactly what will happen if you choose not to make a sacrifice. We've all been shown." He spreads his arms out wide across the cabin.

Adriane bites the back of her knuckles, shrinks away from Eric and off into the kitchen. She circles around her weapon.

"I've been made to watch the end, over and over. Since last Monday. It started as a nightmare and whenever I closed my eyes, the end was there, and as we got closer to this day, the visions started happening when I was awake. I couldn't escape it. I didn't want to believe it. I thought there might be something wrong with me but the visions were so strong and so specific, so real—" Leonard pauses and wipes his face. "Sabrina, Adriane, and Redmond all saw the same things, too. They saw the exact same things I was seeing. And we were led to each other and we were led here. I don't think you're getting that we don't want to be here, don't want any of this to happen, but we have no choice. The choice is yours."

Sabrina stands behind Leonard with her weapon in her hands. Andrew didn't see when she retrieved it. He tries to get his breathing under control; he cannot let fear totally shut him down. His stiff fingers renew their frantic waving at Wen and stretching toward the knots out of reach. Andrew considers arching his back and pushing off with the balls of his feet until he flips himself and the chair backward to crash to the floor. Maybe the fall would somehow loosen his restraints. The longest of shots, but it might be his only chance.

Andrew shouts to be heard over Leonard. The shouting doesn't stop Leonard from speaking.

"So you had an apocalyptic nightmare! So what? We've all had them—"

"First the cities will drown. No one living in cities will know it's coming—"

"That doesn't mean anything! You know that! You have to know that—"

"The ocean will swell and rise up into a great fist and pound all the buildings and people into the sand and then drag everything out to sea—"

"There is something wrong with you, all of you, if you believe this—"

"Then a terrible plague will descend and people will writhe with fever and mucus will fill their lungs—"

"This is psychotic, delusional! Did you try to get help? Let us go and we'll get you help—"

"The skies will fall and crash to the earth like pieces of glass. And then the final, everlasting darkness will descend over humanity and all the species of the earth—"

"You need help! This is fucking insane, all of this—"

"This is going to happen and we've been shown that only your sacrifice can stop it—"

"Shown by who? By what? Are you going to answer that?"

Leonard bows his head and doesn't say anything. Neither does Sabrina, Redmond, or Adriane.

That we-can-talk-them-out-of-this window is closed, if it ever was open.

Eric says, "Come on. Talk to us, tell us more about what you were shown. Who gave you the nightmares? Who told you about us? It doesn't make sense. Think about it for a second."

Leonard remains motionless. Sabrina and Redmond briefly make eye contact and then look away; actively and obviously looking anywhere else in the cabin but at each other. Adriane tightens her circle around her weapon. The only sound Andrew hears in the madness of silence is his own labored breathing.

Leonard lifts his head and says, "The choice has been made."

Redmond and Sabrina walk in front of Leonard, holding their weapons. They step in time, as trained soldiers might. Redmond twists his neck from side to side, the obnoxious tough-guy equivalent of cracking knuckles. Sabrina closes her eyes, inhales, and then adjusts her grip on the wooden staff, the strange curlicued shovel head held like a torch in the darkness.

Eric says, "Wait, stop, you don't have to do this." He strains and struggles in his chair, but there isn't much strength behind his efforts.

"Hey, you don't need those things. You said you couldn't hurt us." Andrew strains to pull his legs free, to peel his arms apart; they feel looser in his restraints but not close to free. He yells names and *no* and *stop* and he vibrates in his seat. He pushes up onto his toes, and the tipping point is close; one twitchy push-off and he'll fall over backward.

From behind him Adriane puts a hand on his shoulder and anchors him and the chair flush to the floor without any struggle at all. One hand and that's all the pressure needed to keep him pinned to where he is, no matter how much thrashing he does. He throws his head back, trying to hit her but he doesn't make contact.

Her hand leaves his shoulder and Wen screams, "Leave me alone!"

Andrew yells for Wen and twists to see where Adriane went, to see what she's doing. Legs suddenly appear in front of Andrew's face, kicking and waving as though attempting to swim up from a great depth. Adriane is lowering his daughter onto his lap.

"Don't touch her! Let her go!"

Wen twists free and hugs Andrew tightly around the neck. Her cheek is hot and wet against his. He says her name repeatedly and whispers into her ear that she has to leave, to run, to push the screen slider out and run onto the deck and run and run.

Redmond loudly bangs the sledgehammer end of his double-ended staff on the floor. Then he gives Leonard the weapon without an exchange of words. Their movements are choreographed, ritualized. Leonard flips the ends of the staff so that the arrangement of shovel and trowel blades is pointed at the floor.

Redmond scratches the back of his head and fidgets with his

empty hands. He kneels on the hardwood floor, making a triangle with Eric and Andrew.

He says, "Aw, fuck. Okay. Come on, come on, here we go,"
and claps his hands, wipes his face, laughs once, shakes his head,
and grunts like a weight lifter gearing up for an inhuman feat of
strength.

Andrew isn't whispering anymore. "Run, Wen, run!"

Wen shakes her head and says, "I can't."

Redmond abruptly quits his routine, stops moving, and stares
at Andrew with his head tilted.

Andrew maneuvers his face around Wen's head so he can see
this, whatever it is.

Redmond's face has drained of color, and sweat darkens his
receding hairline. He licks his cracked, bleeding lips and blinks
rapidly. He's scared and it makes him look younger. He could be
one of Andrew's students, hundreds or thousands of miles from
home, in his office to plead for an extension on a paper or for a better grade in the class to ensure he doesn't lose his performance-
based grant money.

Redmond reaches into the front pocket of his jeans and pulls
out something white. It practically glows as he unfolds it in front
of his red shirt. Larger than the dressing on the back of Eric's
head, it appears to be a swatch of thin cloth, ribbed or waffled
like thermal underwear. He lifts it high over his head, stretching
and extending his arms as far up as they will go.

Redmond winks at Andrew and grins, the kind that makes
any face ugly. Andrew has been the recipient of this version of
the smug, judgmental, nonverbal *fuck you* countless times, and
it nags at him that perhaps he's seen this smile on this particular
face before today.

Eric says, "Please God, just let us go, let us go," in a continuous loop.

Wen has stopped crying. "What is that? What is he doing?"

Andrew tells her not to watch.

Redmond pulls and stretches the material over his head, face, and halfway down his neck. It's formfitting, like a sock over a foot. The lump of his nose protrudes below his prominent brow and from between the uncanny valleys of his concave eye sockets. A star of red blooms in the cloth over his split lip. He drops his arms to his sides.

The sun breaks through the clouds, a promise that will one day be broken, and shines into the cabin via the deck, illuminating this reluctant summit. The players are momentarily as still as stone obelisks and their ancient shadows.

Although Redmond's face is concealed within the blank, white mask, Andrew feels the man's stare, and like all stares, it accrues mass with passing time.

Then, finally, there are two words.

"Thank you."

Eric

Eric's litany of *please-Gods* cuts out and he shrinks from the return of the sun like a vampire. His head is one of the old hot water radiators from their condo and it hisses with pain.

Redmond in the supplicant's eternal pose, awash in golden light, is transformed. The red of his shirt is no longer confined to the cloth and slicks into the air like oil in water. Red mists beyond the boundary of Redmond, forming an aura, as amorphous as a storm. There's a darker spot of red clinging stubbornly to his white mask, a different kind of promise; all will be red eventually.

Redmond says, "Thank you."

Sabrina, Leonard, and Adriane drift into the center of the cabin, creeping delicately, hunters stalking elusive, skittish prey. They form a half circle around Redmond, their gnarly, improvised staffs aloft.

Something shimmers in the nowhere between Redmond and the doorway to the deck. Like heat waves on summer-baked pavement, the shimmer is whiter and brighter than the surrounding solar light. Eric blinks and the strange refraction realigns, finds a focus, coalesces into a shape, a form, and for the briefest of moments there is an unmistakable contour of a head and shoulders, an outline of another person, a fourth (or another fourth) joining the semicircle encompassing Redmond.

Leonard and Adriane swap positions. They walk between Redmond and the deck, passing through that nowhere space, eclipsing the vision, wiping it out. It's gone, whatever it is, made of empty space and the whitest light. Eric does not think he saw another person coming in from outside, some secret member of their group, hiding and waiting until the right time to enter the cabin. The vision's near instant appearance and disappearance only amplifies the wrongness and unearthliness, filling Eric's head with the snow and crackle of a lost signal's static. He realizes what he saw is most certainly the result of his injury and misfiring synapses. Still, he's afraid to inspect too closely the memory of the experience; more than an instinctual fear of the inexplicable that cannot be verbalized, it's the bone-deep dread of discovery. What if the shimmer and its light did not come from his scrambled brain and was not a trick of the sun?

That question is followed by another that bubbles up and

does not present in his typical inner voice or manner. An ever-evolving mental life is impossible to fully detail, even by the owner, and one generally goes from day to day unquestioning one's own being or consciousness, with absolute faith in *this is who I am and this is how I think*. The follow-up question does not fit within Eric's secret mental code, does not use the unique parts of speech of his interior language; it is not of *him*. To Eric's horror, the question feels like an intrusion from a different mind or a terrifying answer to an unspoken prayer.

What if the shimmer's light came from the colder spaces of the infinite sky?

Wen

Nothing that has happened to this point is as scary or creepy as the kneeling and masked Redmond. The outline and contours of his hidden face fill her with the same mix of fascination and dread she felt when she stared at the human skull that was in her classroom. What if the mask is Redmond's new skin and underneath there is only the whiter white of bone? She imagines his face and head changing shape while hidden away and then Leonard ripping off the mask like a magician to reveal a grotesque, ravenous monster, the kind so terrible and ugly that just looking at it will kill you.

Redmond says, "Thank you." His puppet mouth opens and closes out of rhythm with the words, an amateur attempt at ventriloquism. The cloth through which he speaks is thin, but his voice sounds garbled, modulated. He shouldn't sound like he does. Wen covers her ears because she does not want to hear anything else he might say.

Adriane appears from behind Andrew's chair, floating like a patient ghost, and flanks Redmond's left side. The bramble of raking claws at the end of Adriane's weapon passes over her and Andrew's heads, close enough so Wen can count the tangles of claws and their individual sharpened points plaqued with rust and dirt. Adriane's face is blank; her facial muscles are rigid scaffolding for her skin.

Leonard stands behind Redmond, as stoic and still as a brick wall. Wen stares at Leonard, wanting and waiting for him to look at her. Despite everything, she hopes Leonard will show himself to be a good person, the person she thought he was when they were out in the front yard together. She considers waving at him but decides against trying to get his attention. He has the same blank, robot face Adriane has. Sabrina has the robot face, too. She drifts within arm's reach of Eric and settles to Redmond's right.

Wen darts her eyes around the room, memorizing everyone's position, where they stand and how they hold their staffs. She turns her head and twists her torso, almost falling off Andrew's lap. Poor Daddy Eric is alone. He alternates between being wide-eyed and squeezing his eyelids shut, exaggerated blinks like he has something stuck in his eyes and it won't go away. It appears he's looking above Redmond (not at him) and into the kitchen or out toward the deck. Wen looks out there, too, and then past the deck to the shimmering blue lake, which is a million miles away.

Wen sinks deeper into Daddy Andrew's lap and deeper inside herself. Should she go to Daddy Eric? Maybe walking over and simply kissing the back of his head will make him better. Then she'll talk to him and no one else, shake him if she has to, and tell him she can help if he would just tell her what to do. What are they going to do?

Maybe she should run like Daddy Andrew said, sprint through the room, dodge the turned-over furniture like a mouse through high grass, then onto the deck and outside and away. She can run fast. Her dads tell her that she is fast, so fast, all the time. And they tell her she is shifty. She knows their races are fixed for her to win, but Wen outlasting the catchers in their catch-me-if-you-can games until Eric and/or Andrew are bent over, hands on knees, gasping for air is legitimate. She is shifty. Wen loves that word. It means hard to catch. It means even better than fast; it's a smart fast.

Leonard and Adriane exchange positions: Adriane is stationed in front of the couch and directly behind Redmond; Leonard is now closer to the kitchen and parked to Redmond's left. The room is bright and quiet but for Andrew's heavy breathing. Wen rocks and tilts side to side with his expanding and then collapsing chest.

She knows she'd make it out of the cabin without getting caught if she was to run, but where would she run to? She doesn't want to accidentally get lost on the dirt roads that fork and branch away leading to nowhere or to worse places than here, and what if she has to ditch the road for the thick woods surrounding the cabin for miles and miles? Her dads were explicit in saying she could not go into these woods by herself under any circumstances because they might never find her again.

She blurts out, "Go away, all of you! And take off the mask and stop trying to scare us!" No one responds. None of the four, including the masked Redmond, look at her. Wen is terrified but she puts on her own mask, an angry face, the angriest one she has so that hers is not as blank and lifeless as the four others' faces.

She shifts her hips and slides her left leg off Andrew's lap. Her foot hovers a few inches above the floor as a brief test. No one moves to grab her, no one moves at all. She slides down farther until the toe of her sneaker kisses the hardwood. She waits. If no one notices, if no one says anything, she is going to run between Redmond and Leonard and then onto the deck. In her head, she is down the back stairs and running on the dirt road already, with long and shifty strides.

In one motion, Adriane lunges forward and swings her weapon. The raking claws whistle through the air.

Andrew

Even as Leonard and Adriane exchange positions in the common room, Andrew remains focused on and obsessed with Redmond: Why is he so familiar and why is he wearing that freak show of a mask and what can he see through it and why did he say, "Thank you," and why did he say it the way he said it—low, guttural, breathless, not angry but groveling and as fervent as an ecstatic?

Wen says, "Go away, all of you! And take off the mask and stop trying to scare us!" She no longer has her arms wrapped around Andrew's neck and she is not burrowed into his chest. Her weight is unbalanced on his lap. He tempers his efforts at pulling his legs and hands free from the ropes and chair for fear he'll jostle her and she'll fall awkwardly to the floor and get hurt.

She slowly leaks off his lap, to his left, and there's nothing he can do to readjust her position. He's about to say her name to jolt her into readjusting herself and staying put when it occurs to him that her sliding off is purposeful, and perhaps she's getting ready to make a run for it like he told her to. She methodically stretches toward the floor with one leg and he's now convinced she's considering a mad dash outside the cabin and beyond. He silently pleads with her to go now and it's all he can do to not say *go* out loud. She might not get another chance. If she does run, then one or two of them will go after her and that would buy him some time to work on loosening his restraints. Careful to not give away inadvertently an escape route by staring it down, Andrew surveys potential paths through the common room and possible roadblocks to the deck for Wen.

Andrew hears the movement first, a quick shuffle of feet coming from Redmond's direction. Andrew assumes the noise is Redmond scrambling onto his feet, but he has not moved. Redmond is still kneeling on the floor, his spine straight and masked head held high. Then there's a loud stomp on the floor behind Redmond. Adriane's right foot is forward, planted only inches behind Redmond's feet. Her hips pivot and she swings her staff. The sphere of raking claws comets through the air and the rusted metal crashes into the right side of Redmond's face.

He sways with the impact, but he recovers and straightens again and remains kneeling and upright. A slight but visible shiver ripples throughout his body. A high-pitched, animal whimper escapes from under his mask.

At the same time as the impact of the blow, Eric exhales a loud grunt, as though he is the one who is struck. Wen completes her slide off his lap and is standing next to Andrew and the chair. She turns so she is facing the front door and wraps her arms around Andrew's neck again. She doesn't scream or cry. Her mouth is next to his ear and her breathing is off rhythm, exhaling too soon after a sharp inhale, and then too long a pause between breaths, and after the pause, air rushes out like she's deflating.

Raking claw tips are caught, stuck in Redmond's mask and face. Adriane pulls on the handle of her weapon as though working an ax out from a deep gash in a tree. The white mask stretches, stubbornly hooked on one of the claws. The right side of Redmond's head turns as bright red as his shirt.

From Redmond's right, Sabrina crow-hops forward and swings her staff in a horizontal arc, the tapered and oddly curled shovel blade held sideways so as to be more bladelike. She's close enough to Andrew that he feels the whoosh of parting air. The thin edge of metal mashes into the front of Redmond's face, in the area of his nose and mouth, and there's a clang and scraping noise. Redmond collapses onto his side and loosens a wail, a liquid scream.

Adriane and Sabrina shower blow after blow upon Redmond. The abstract metal shapes at the ends of their handles rise and then strike downward like greedy bird heads. The women grunt with each swing and retrieval of their weapons. The metal configurations of the weapons chime and reverberate with contact, singing joyfully now that they are finally being used as their retrofitters intended. There are also hollow thuds and other sounds that are wet and wooden.

Redmond's guttural screams and squeals weaken and become less recognizably human. Wen's shallow, ragged breathing are Andrew's own breaths, if he is in fact breathing at all.

Redmond's mask remains in place despite the assault. Small puncture holes, black with blood, acne the white cloth, the whole of which has turned pink and red. The contents inside the mask have lost their original shape; the borders of his face and skull rupture and are amorphous.

His arms never once rise above his chest and shoulders to shield his head. His hands hang down to the tops of his thighs, and they flop and twitch as if attempting to break off and flee. His legs kick out and spasm, his shoes knocking a desperate SOS against the floor.

Leonard circles behind Redmond, maneuvering between Adriane and Sabrina, mindful of their backswings. He waits and watches, politely waiting for a turn. He widens the distance between his hands on the weapon's thick handle. A stress crack, a fault line in the wood, runs down the length of what was once a sun-bleached boat oar. He lifts the sledgehammer end into the dusty sunbeam above them all. He yells and powers the hammer down in a looping, accelerating trajectory, splitting the space between Adriane and Sabrina.

There's a tree-snapping-and-falling crack and crunch. Redmond's sternum and rib cage collapse under the weight and force of the anvil-sized block of metal, which punches clear through to the spine. The violence of the impact vibration radiates across the floor and up the frame of Andrew's chair. A plume of red sprays the rope and Andrew's bare legs below the knee. The blood is warm on his skin. Red graffitis the jeans and white and off-white shirts of Sabrina and Leonard. Redmond's limbs cease fluttering. The fingers of his open, pleading hands close into his palms.

Leonard retracts the sledgehammer and stumbles backward until he knocks into the couch. A crater in the middle of Redmond's chest fills with blood and it has an absurd depth, perhaps stretching beyond the floor and into the basement. More blood pools beneath his body and flows away, dowsing the cracks and grain of the hardwood floor. That his red shirt somehow remains fully buttoned and tucked into his jeans seems mocking and cruel. Jagged spears of bone peek through two of the gaps in the shirt between buttons.

Wen hasn't moved from her spot next to Andrew and still faces away from the carnage. Her odd breathing hasn't changed though she mixes in a nearly inaudible high-pitched moan or wheeze, like her throat and lungs are clogged. Her eyelashes brush against Andrew's ear when she blinks.

He whispers, "I love you, Wen. Don't look. Don't turn around, okay?"

Leonard drops the weapon, and it clatters heavily on the floor. He coughs through his closed mouth, puffing out his cheeks. He steps left, hesitates, and then steps back to the right, apparently unsure of where to go or what to do, until darting into the kitchen and throwing up into the sink. He turns the water on full blast, trying to drown out his puking.

Adriane's face is blank, but it's a different kind of blank. She still has her weapon raised. The ends of the raking claws drip thick, syrupy blood.

Color rushes into Sabrina's shocked face, making her cheeks ruddy, almost purple. She twists and tosses her weapon against the woodburning stove. With her back to Andrew and the others, she folds her hands behind her neck, shakes her head, and talks to herself. Andrew can't hear what she says.

Eric is slumped in his chair, eyes vacant and staring out to the deck and beyond. Andrew considers calling out his name and asking if he's okay. By the look of him, eyes glassy and in a half squint, Eric might be better off being lost and hiding inside his own head.

Andrew needs to regroup and focus on escaping from the chair. The ropes wrapped around his legs and wrists feel like they've tightened instead of loosening during his struggles.

Leonard returns from the kitchen and stands at the head of Redmond's body. He wipes his mouth on his sleeve. "Adriane, can you help out here?" He sways, unsteady on his feet. The cabin is a boat pitching in rough seas.

Adriane doesn't answer and blankly stares at Redmond's corpse.

"Adriane? Hey, Adriane?"

She moves and talks in slow motion. "Hey, yeah. What? I'm still here."

"Help me take Redmond outside."

Adriane gently places her weapon on the floor behind her, only a step from the bathroom doorway.

Leonard bends by Redmond's head and reaches out to dig his arms underneath the man's shoulders. Instead he straightens and walks around the body to Redmond's feet. He is only inches away from Andrew.

Andrew whispers, "Shhh," to Wen even though she isn't saying anything. He holds his breath, afraid that any sound or movement could trigger another frenzy of violence.

Leonard says, "I'm going to, um, pull him outside, onto the deck there. Grab a bedspread or something so we can cover him up. And can you open the screen for me? Maybe pull that chair and end table out of the way, too?"

Adriane whispers what Andrew thinks is, "This is all so fucked." She slides the little end table deeper into the kitchen, the wooden legs complaining as they are dragged over the linoleum. She stands up the small lamp, straightening the yellow lampshade, and turns the switch on and off, two, three, four times, and more. The little clicks don't result in any light.

"Adriane?"

"Yeah, sorry." She lifts back one of the remaining kitchen chairs and drops it in front of the refrigerator. Then she runs across the room into a bedroom and comes back out with a quilted and light-and-dark-blue-checkered bedspread, large enough to cover a wheat field. With the bedspread folded under her arm, Adriane kicks aside the balled-up curtain and slides open the screen to the deck, careful to keep it in the track.

Leonard says, "You might have to take it off. I need as much space as you can give me to get through."

As Adriane walks onto the deck with the screen slider held out in front of her like a shield, Leonard picks up Redmond's feet. He tries tucking a leg under each of his arms, but it's an awkward hold, and the legs drop out and hit the floor with a wet splat. The earthy and iron-tinted smell of blood and piss intensifies with the disturbance of the body, as though the legs are bellows pumping out tainted air. Leonard grabs fistfuls of Redmond's jeans cuffed around the ankle. With the legs reelevated, the smell further intensifies, and he whispers, "Oh, God," and breathes loudly through his mouth. He spins the body one hundred and eighty degrees so that the feet point to the deck. Leonard pauses and dry heaves once, dropping one leg to cover his mouth with the back of his hand. He says, "I'm okay, I got it," and he grabs the leg again, continuing to talk to himself throughout the whole process. He pedals backward hastily, dragging the body behind him, leaving a smeared trail of blood on the floor. Redmond's masked head wobbles and shakes like an overfilled water balloon.

Sabrina jogs into the bathroom and comes back out with an armload of towels. She sets the stack down on the floor to Andrew's right and spreads two towels (one is brown, the other a fraying and tattered Harry Potter towel featuring the cover of the first novel) over the blood on the floor. She stirs the towels around with her feet, halfheartedly mopping up the mess.

Leonard is on the deck and paused with Redmond's body half in and half out of the cabin. Hunched over, Leonard says, "Watch out," to Adriane. He lunges backward and the body goes with him, passing over the glass slider's metal tracking in the doorway and thunking down onto the deck. The wooden planks knock and echo with the body-relocation effort until Leonard parks Redmond up against the banister railing opposite the doorway and past the picnic table; the body is not out of sight from the interior of the cabin. Leonard inspects his hands and his red-smeared shirt and pants, and then looks at his watch twice. The first peek is autonomic, a reflex. The second look lasts longer and is a conscious attempt at determining the time. It occurs to Andrew that Leonard has been obsessively checking his watch ever since the four of them entered the cabin.

Adriane covers the body with the blue blanket, tugging and pulling the corners over Redmond's legs. The blanket tents over his feet and its extra length pools over his head and against the railing. Picking the screen slider back up (which has seen better days; the wire mesh is misshapen and sags near the corners of the warped frame), she speaks and gestures with motions of her head at the body and then inside the cabin.

Leonard says something and he, too, points inside the cabin, and then he turns and walks away from both Adriane and the body. He pauses and says, "I don't want to look at him, either." As he ducks into the kitchen the sunlight dies. How quickly it becomes dark inside the cabin alarms Andrew, and he can't help but imagine the light inside and outside continuing to dim until there is no light at all.

Eric

Leonard stands in the same area of the common room where Eric saw whatever it was he thought he saw in the moments before the attack on Redmond: an amorphous image hovering in the air, a bas-relief made of light and outlined in more jagged light, which became a head and shoulders, then a full figure in a swirl of glint and glare. He wants to dismiss it as an illusion, a result or symptom of his injury, but in his memory, the figure animates before disappearing; it turns inexorably to face him.

Did Andrew or Wen or any of the others see the figure, too? No one reacted like they did.

To Eric's right, Andrew shivers like he is freezing. Wen stands on Andrew's left, arms around his neck. She is in profile to Eric, facing the front door. Her eyes are open and they don't blink often enough. Did Wen watch the death of Redmond? Eric can't remember if she was looking when Adriane first swung her weapon. Had she turned away before that? He thinks so but he can't be sure. Did she see the figure made of light? Is she seeing it now in front of the door and staring back at her?

"I'm truly sorry that had to happen and that you had to see it." Leonard's voice wavers and has active fault lines. He stares at his hands, opens them and closes them. "But we had no choice. We have no choice." His apparent sincerity, or his sincere belief in his own words, is appalling and frightening. Eric believes for the first time that they will never leave this cabin alive and prays silently.

When there is no response to his apology and explanation, Leonard slumps and shuffles to the couch. He paws around the cushions and finds the remote control. He turns on the television and Wen's *Steven Universe* winks back on, filling the black screen on the wall. Eric recognizes the episode as having seen it before, but he does not remember what is going to happen next or later. Is it an episode he watched previously this summer or is it the same episode that was on earlier, before Leonard turned off the

TV? Had everything happened in fifteen minutes? Ten minutes? Less? Eric doesn't know.

He doesn't know what time it is or how long the four have been inside the cabin and he can't remember when or how he was tied to his chair. He fears that he is forgetting other stuff, too, the most important stuff. Because of the concussion, he is also exhausted and is having trouble keeping his head up and eyes open.

With her show back on, Wen turns around. She stands unnaturally straight and wooden, her body devoid of the kinetic energy with which she normally emanates. Her thumbs are again inside her fists and held against her mouth.

Andrew says, "Wen, don't look outside."

Wen shakes her head no. Eric isn't sure if the *no* is defiance or an agreement or a meaningless automatic response.

Sabrina carries the kitchen trash bin to the middle of the floor. She wipes her hands on her jeans as though her hands have already handled the towels and are covered in blood. She bends and lifts the sludgy, blood-soaked towels off the floor, and drops them heavily into the bin and two black flies spin into the air like whorls of smoke.

With Redmond's body outdoors and now the towels disposed of, the smell in the room improves enough that inhaling through his nose doesn't totally flip his stomach. The floor is still slick with blood; it'll never be clean again. Previously invisible gouges in the wood are angry slashes, scars that won't heal. Floorboards are tinted red in a trail leading to the deck. Taking the two remaining towels from the stack she brought out of the bathroom, Sabrina spreads them over the floor, end to end. She doesn't mop or push the towels around; they're left to be rugs. Then she covers the towels with the slider curtain. The flies briefly crawl on the curtain and then flit away disappointed.

Leonard says, "I'm sorry, Wen, but I'm going to change the channel, okay? Just for a little bit, and then I'll put it back. I promise. You're doing so good, you know that? So brave. Your parents must be so proud."

Andrew says, "Go fuck yourself." His voice goes from child-who-can't-find-his-parents to full-on righteously angry Andrew in the span of three words.

Leonard holds the remote close to his face, his hands trembling. He pauses the show with Steven Universe smiling, his plump fist raised triumphantly above his head.

Eric looks outside at the shaded deck, and the covered body against the railing. A strong breeze ripples through the folds and edges of the checkered blue cloth. That charmingly homey and homely bedspread was half of an apartment-warming gift from his parents when he and Andrew moved in together more than fifteen years ago. The other half of the apartment-warming gift wasn't quite as charming: a golden framed placard that read, "God bless this home and all who enter," writ in a looping gothic script above prayer hands pressed together. Eric couldn't decide if the framed blessing was a rider, a parental compromise between no-gift and gift. Eric wasn't opposed to the blessing's sentiment (as tacky as its presentation was) but Andrew ranted like only the deeply offended could. He and Andrew tossed the placard and repurposed the frame. Eric insisted on keeping and using the bedspread for their guest room should his parents visit and stay over. Mom and Dad never set foot in their first apartment. They made their maiden visit to Cambridge and the condo shortly after they adopted Wen, and in the years since, they have visited four more times. For those keeping score, Andrew's parents drive down from Vermont to visit once every two months. Eric keeps score. His mom and dad have yet to sleep in the condo's guest room and have instead stayed in a hotel, insisting they didn't want to be a bother, didn't want to get in the way. Mom said it so warmly and with such regret, Eric believed it to be true. While Mom acted as spokesperson, Dad would break off eye contact, slump his shoulders, and drop his head like a scolded dog only now reminded of a bad deed, but one he doesn't regret. It was like watching Dad—this graying and diminishing version of the man who was once as big and strong as Paul Bunyan—remember he wasn't supposed to be enjoying himself in their company as much as he was. Andrew once asked Eric what he was thinking as he stood at the bay window while his parents left the building and ducked into an idling cab two stories below. Eric said, "I'm happy and proud they're here." He paused and Andrew hugged him from behind. "And I'm sad. Infinitely sad."

Eric lifts his drooped head and swims up from the warm waters of reverie. Did he fall asleep or pass out, and for how long was he out? He looks around the cabin nervously, and everyone seems to be in the same place they were moments before. He blurts out, "Let's stop this now, right? We can get you help. We can. I promise. Let us go and we can get you help. Nothing more has to happen. It can end now. You can end it now." Eric sighs at himself. He doesn't mean it the way it might sound to them; he shouldn't be using the words *end it now*.

Leonard impatiently shakes his head, brushing Eric off. He looks at his wristwatch and says, "Please watch the TV. It'll be on soon."

The screen blips over to a cable news network. It's some mid-afternoon business talking-head kind of show according to the guide bar at the bottom of the screen. Instead of news, a supplemental health coverage commercial for seniors is being broadcast. The pitch comes from a onetime famous actress who speaks plaintively into the camera.

Andrew asks, "What will be on soon?"

"What you need to see."

"Is it your favorite show? You just can't miss it, right? I've seen you check your watch every five minutes since you broke into our cabin. Well, it must be a great show. I know I can't wait. What's it rated? We don't let Wen just watch anything, you know. Maybe you should've set the DVR."

Andrew is pushing too hard and gearing up to push harder. Eric says, "Okay, okay, easy, Andrew." Eric appreciates that Andrew hasn't shut down and isn't giving up talking them out of this, but Christ, they bludgeoned one of their own to death, an act that is as confounding as it is horrifying. What is clear to Eric is the level of violence to which they've committed will not be verbally wiseassed away. Perhaps Andrew senses a weakening or flagging of their will to see whatever this is through given how obviously shaken they are in the aftermath of Redmond's ritualized attack and death. Eric doesn't see it. He sees zealots, fully engaged with their cause. Further, their squeamishness likely means it'll be easier for them to abdicate any sense of personal responsibility and continue to attribute their actions to the as-of-yet unattributed source of their professed apocalyptic visions and murderous commands.

Unbidden and unwanted, questions from a corner in a forgotten chamber inside Eric's head: *Did they see the same figure of light I saw? Have they seen it before they came here to us? Did they see it when they closed their eyes, when they dreamed their Armageddon dreams?*

Two more commercials run. One is for a cleaning product that cannot be purchased in stores, and the other is a seizure-inducing promo for the network's prime-time political round table. Everyone in the cabin remains quiet throughout the inanity of shouted slogans and loud exclamations as though this is their very own sponsored intermission. The news program returns with a blizzard of garish color that hurts Eric's head. The infinite news ticker at the bottom of the screen scrolls by with blurry data blips about refugees, unemployment, the death of a beloved celebrity, and the Dow Jones average being down. BREAKING NEWS in large red font bullies the main screen, overlaying the red-white-and-blue-adorned newsroom. A finely pressed news-caster in a finely pressed suit stands in the lower right corner of the screen. He gravely welcomes everyone back for their con-tinuing coverage of a 7.9-magnitude earthquake centered in the Aleutian Islands, which struck more than four hours ago.

The Aleutians are a chain of volcanic islands stretching across the Bering Sea, with some of the islands belonging to both Alaska and, at its western extremes, Russia. Eric and Andrew researched booking an Alaskan cruise that would navigate by some of the larger islands but they gave up when the opportunity to adopt a child materialized quicker than they'd planned.

The U.S. National Tsunami Warning Center has issued a cautionary advisory to British Columbia, Canada, and over one thousand miles of coast along the American Pacific Northwest including the cities of Seattle and Portland. However, the Pa-cific Tsunami Warning Center issued its strongest warning to the islands of Hawaii. Residents and tourists on the north-facing coastlines are under a mandatory evacuation order and are to seek higher ground immediately.

Andrew says, "Is this what we're supposed to see?"

"It is. You don't get it yet?"

"No. I don't."

"I explained to all of you that if you didn't choose to make a sacrifice, the oceans will rise and cities will drown. I used those exact words: the cities will drown." Leonard slowly and loudly enunciates and points at the television. His patient tone and calm demeanor he employs whenever addressing Andrew, Wen, or Eric cracks and anger oozes out. Or is it panic? It's difficult to tell the difference. "You remember me telling you that, right? You said you understood what I was telling you."

Eric vaguely recalls Leonard saying something about drowning cities along with a list of other threats, but he doesn't remember them.

Andrew says, "Yes, I remember, but this doesn't mean anything, this—"

"No! No more." He points the remote control at Andrew. "I've been very patient with you but now you have to watch and listen." Leonard closes his eyes, shakes his head, and shrugs his shoulders as if to say *I'm trying my best to make everything go smoothly.* He points at the TV again. "I shouldn't yell, I know you're scared of me, of us, but please. Watch."

The network cuts to an interviewer and interviewee digitally separated on the screen. The woman on the right is a spokesperson for the Pacific Tsunami Warning Center. She explains that there are nearly two dozen tsunami detection buoys in the Northern Pacific, with a cluster tracing the perimeter of the northern Ring of Fire, which is only a hundred miles or so from the epicenter of this earthquake. The data they've received points to a sizable wave of fifteen to twenty feet in height headed south toward the Hawaiian islands. The newscaster cuts in to announce that a tsunami has made landfall. As the audio of the interview continues, its video is banished to the lower right corner. A feed from a beach resort on the Hawaiian island of Kauai fills the center of the screen. It's unclear if this is live or taped. In Hawaii it's a bright, beautiful day. Small tufts of clouds are afterthoughts in the wide sky. The sand is golden and the palm leaves are green. The hotel pool is crystal blue and empty. The resort has already been evacuated. A swell of water gray with foam and sand, speckled with dark soil, palm fronds, and other debris, rushes up the length of the beach, overwhelms the pool and courtyard, swallowing chairs and tables, pushing into cabanas and the hotel's lower-level rooms. The channel cuts to other videos from smaller towns and from the less-traveled and populated Northwestern or Leeward Islands; the greedy waves capsize small boats, swamp marinas, wipe out decks and docks, and wash out seaside roads.

While acknowledging beach erosion and the damage to property will be extensive, the spokesperson talks about the success of their early warning detection system as they had plenty of lead time to evacuate the coasts and low-lying areas of the affected Hawaiian islands. It's early but no injuries or fatalities have been reported.

Andrew says, "Hey—"

Eric interrupts with, "Don't. Just don't," because he knows what Andrew wants to say, is going to say.

Andrew grits his teeth, shakes the hair out of his eyes, and says it, anyway. "This is some doomsday you have going there. So how about you let us go now?"

Leonard doesn't respond.

"Let Eric and Wen go, at least. I'll stay and we can discuss apocalyptic themes and cultural traumas of the twenty-first century all you want. Just let them go."

Adriane hurries into the bathroom, shuts the door, and turns the sink on full blast. There are lower sounds buried under the rush of water. Eric can't tell if she's crying and/or talking to herself.

Sabrina says, "I don't understand. This isn't—" She stops in midsentence, walks over to Leonard's side of the room, and taps his arm. "Leonard?"

"I know, but keep watching. We're supposed to keep watching."

Eric says, "How long?"

"Until we see what we're supposed to see. Until we see what was shown to us." Leonard sounds unsure, even desperate. He chances a quick look at Eric and then Andrew before intently staring at the TV again, willing it to play the images in his head, whatever they are.

The station replays the flooding of the resort, which is the most dramatic footage to have aired. The talking heads repeat the same numbers and timelines. Eric is about to ask if they can change the channel back to a show for Wen when there's a rough cut away from the various Hawaiian video feeds to the lead broadcaster. He doesn't say anything and has a finger in his ear. He doesn't know he's on-air. He recovers and announces that a second massive earthquake has struck in the Pacific, registering at 8.6 on the Richter scale. The epicenter is only seventy miles off the coast of Oregon in what's called the Cascadia Subduction Zone, an area scientists have long feared would produce a catastrophic earthquake.

Leonard shouts, "This is it! This is it!" He turns and for a moment he has an I-got-exactly-what-I-wanted-for-my-birthday smile on his face, which quickly landslides into the pained look of a reluctant witness. "You didn't stop it from happening and you could've. You were supposed to make a sacrifice. When you didn't, we were forced to make one for you, and now, the consequences. You could've stopped this—"

Sabrina is standing and facing the TV. She says, "No, no, no..."

Adriane explodes out of the bathroom, her face red and dripping wet. "It's happening? Is it really fucking happening? Oh, Jesus God . . ."

Leonard continues talking to Eric, Andrew, and Wen, but he watches the screen. His eyes shimmer with tears. He says, "I'm sorry, that's not fair of me. Of course I mean to say *we*, not you. *We* could've stopped it but we didn't. We failed. We are in this together. All of us. I'm sorry. This is hard, this is impossible; I keep saying that but it's true. And we didn't stop this. We're too late."

Sabrina, Adriane, and Leonard talk and they ask questions; some are rhetorical and some are impossible to answer. They share reactions, looks, and nods of support, nonverbal confirmation that what is happening on the rectangular, one-inch-thick screen is real. Eric strains to block them out and hear what is being said on the news but the cabin is all shouts and exclamations, everything muddying in the echo chamber of his throbbing head.

The room pauses to take a collective breath long enough for one of the seismologists to posit the earthquake in the Aleutian Islands triggered this second quake, which lasted for almost five minutes. Given the proximity of the epicenter, people along the coast will only have minutes to seek higher ground before a tsunami reaches shore. Given the size and duration of the quake, damaged infrastructure and buildings will make it difficult to impossible in some low-lying areas for any sort of mass evacuation to occur in time. Another scientist estimates a tsunami triggered by a quake of this magnitude and proximity to shore as being anywhere from twenty to fifty feet tall, and the wave would be kilometers long so that the initial and sudden surge in sea level would continue for the entire length and duration of that wave, pushing all that water inland. She suggests residents immediately seek areas that are eighty to one hundred feet above sea level; the fifty-foot-tall bluffs along the coastline likely won't be a safe enough height.

The lead newscaster interrupts the split-screen discussion, announcing a tsunami has indeed struck the Oregon shoreline and they have video footage from Cannon Beach. He warns the images they are about to show are disturbing.

The video plays; a shaky, handheld wide shot of the beach, which is dotted with large rocks jutting out like shark fins from its flat sand and shallow low-tide water. The rocks are as black as shadow, giving them an uncanny, otherworldly feel, like looking at frozen pieces of space-time. One rock dwarfs the others, looming in the center of the shot, big enough to be its own mountain, big enough that it should sink through the sand and to the center of the earth.

Adriane says, "Shit, that's *The Goonies* rock! Remember that movie?" She smiles widely and stares at Eric and Andrew, apparently waiting for some sort of response or validation from them. "Come on, you've all seen that movie, yeah? The kid solves a clue with that big fucking rock or the rocks around it."

"It's called Haystack Rock," Sabrina says. "Almost two hundred fifty feet tall. I was there last summer. My best friend from college lives in Portland. It's a beautiful spot."

A blast of wind crackles through the speakers. There are people still on the beach, some of them a great distance away and some at the rocks and the eerily receded water. They are small digital avatars of actual people, blips of bathing suit colors on blurry legs. A guy off-camera, impossible to tell how far away he is, shouts, "Come on. Let's go." The owner of the smartphone, a woman, says, "I know. Okay, we're going. We're going. I promise." But she isn't going. She and the camera stay in their same spot.

Adriane walks into the middle of the room, points at the TV, and says, "Holy shit, this is what I saw."

Leonard nods his head and narrows his eyes, but in an exaggerated manner, as though he's pretending to listen, pretending to deeply consider what she says.

Sabrina backs away from the TV and mumbles something Eric thinks is, "Not what I saw."

Adriane laughs. "I saw this exact fucking thing and I thought I was crazy, you know, because of *The Goonies* rock. I really did. There was one night last week I stayed up all night drinking black tea and I was out of milk but I kept drinking it because I didn't want to go back asleep and see the goddamn *Goonies* rock get swamped again." She looks excitedly around the room. "Only crazy people keep having tidal wave nightmares with people getting swallowed up at the fucking *Goonies* rock, right?" She laughs again, demonstrating what her going crazy would sound like. "Love that stupid movie. Still do. No matter what people say about it now."

As Adriane talks there's shouting on and off the screen, and a flash of an angry guy wearing black sunglasses and a white tank top. The camera finally starts moving away from Haystack Rock, which slowly recedes into the horizon, a horizon growing in height and coming toward the camera. There are faraway, small-in-volume screams that sound canned, and loud ones that are close, that could be in the cabin with them, and there are cries and shouts of *run* and *help*. A blue wall rises, its darker blue frosted with white contrasts with the indifference of the light blue sky. Those small digital blips of people down by the rocks are running but they are slow. Some of the small blips are smaller than others.

Sabrina walks in front of Wen, blocking her view of the TV.

"Do you want to play in your room instead of watching this? Did you bring any toys? I'd like to see them. Will you show me?"

Leonard says, "Sabrina, not now. You know they have to see—"

She snaps at him. "Nope. Wen doesn't. She does not have to see anything more."

"Sabrina . . ."

"She's seen enough, don't you think? You can let them watch. Fine. But she's done. I'm done. And I'm taking her out of here. Come on, Wen. Show me your room and your toys, please." She tries a smile, but it crumbles, unable to hold up the rest of her face. She reaches out a hand toward Wen.

Shouts and screams coming from the TV speakers grow louder as if making up for lost horrors.

Eric says, "Maybe that's a good idea, Wen." He says it before thinking and wishes he could take it back as soon as he says it.

Wen says, "No! I'm staying," shakes her head violently, and leans into Andrew.

"You're not going anywhere. I love you," Andrew says. "What's happening on TV doesn't prove or mean anything. But don't watch. Okay?"

Haystack Rock shrinks into the rising ocean, momentarily fulfilling a geological pledge made eons ago. The shark fin rocks are gone. The people-blips who were running up the beach are gone and so is most of the beach.

The sunlight flashes brightly into the cabin again and Eric is washed away.

FOUR

Andrew and Eric

After Sabrina takes the remote and finally changes the channel from the coverage of the devastating northern Pacific earthquake and tsunami to the Cartoon Network, Andrew suggests Wen sit with Eric. He says it's because Eric needs some Wen-time right now, which is true, but Andrew also wants to be left alone to work at the restraints without her leaning on or otherwise drawing attention to him.

Wen watches *Adventure Time* while sitting cross-legged on top of Eric's feet. In this episode Lumpy Space Princess argues with her parents and screams about a spilled can of beans. *Adventure Time* will later become other cartoons, some Andrew and Eric have seen before and some they haven't.

During a commercial, Leonard says to them, "You will be given the same choice again. This choice is a gift. Not all gifts are easy to accept. The most important gifts are often the ones we wish with all our hearts to refuse. Tomorrow morning you can make the difficult, selfless choice of sacrifice and save the world. Or you can again choose for the clock to move another minute closer to permanent midnight like it did this afternoon. For the rest of today and tonight, we'll tend to your needs within reason, and we'll otherwise leave you be, let you reflect and talk it over with each other." He repeats this, without pause. The retelling matches word for word, inflection for inflection.

Further shaken by the horrific and uncannily prophesied images broadcast on the news, and their sounds—the immutable roar of the surging ocean, the screams crackling through the speakers, tin-canned and somehow more authentic because their volume and desperation could not be reproduced digitally without modulation—and with the last of the fading afternoon's sunlight forcing his eyes closed, Eric again worries at the memory of the figure in light he did or didn't see.

Andrew says, "We don't need to wait until tomorrow morning and we're never going to change our minds."

Leonard retreats into the kitchen. He opens the refrigerator and cabinets. He asks if anyone is hungry. No one answers. He says, "I'm going to grill up the chicken in a little bit. We all need to eat. You have to eat. No one makes good decisions when they are hungry."

Sabrina asks if anyone has seen a mop and/or floor cleaner. She roots around under the kitchen sink and emerges with a plastic bottle of amber liquid. She soon finds a yellow bucket and a large green sponge in the cellar. She scrubs the bloodstained floor with mixed results.

Adriane stacks the three homemade weapons next to the woodburning stove. She spends more than an hour cleaning them with warm water, a dab of dishwashing detergent, and hand towels. After, she rescues the kitchen table from the edge of the basement stairs and puts it back in its old spot. One of the legs is bent and loose, making the table wobbly. She jams the book Eric was reading—the one about a kid going missing—under the leg for stability. It's not the right size. She tries again with Andrew's book of critical essays and it's a better fit.

Andrew and Eric remain tied to their chairs throughout the afternoon and into early evening. The only constants are the cartoons and the flurry of cabin cleaning and kitchen prep. They do not speak other than to check in with Wen: "Are you hungry? Are you okay? Do you need to go to the bathroom? Do you want to nap? Take a break from watching TV? You just tell us, okay? We love you." They mostly retreat inside their heads; panic and their varying discomforts from injuries and the physical trial of a constant sitting position within restraints interrupt their inner dialogues, their increasingly hopeless plans and fantasies of escape.

The sun sinks into the forest beyond the front door of the west-facing cabin. The gaudy glow of the television screen is the only source of light until the three others turn on the lamps and light fixtures. The wagon wheel bulbs above their heads are tinted yellow with age. Cobwebs link the bulbs and the spokes of the wooden frame.

The weaker artificial light is trapped inside the cabin. It quickly grows too dark outside to see Redmond from within the glow of the common room. The color and the topography of the blanket cover for his body are not visible and there's only a vague sense of something there, dumbly occupying space on the deck. It's as though he isn't there at all, like a decaying cultural memory of a deep, dark historical past (a *something* that happened to someone else; those someone elses are always so hapless, aren't they?), one we actively wish to forget even as we claim to acknowledge the danger of forgetting.

Leonard announces he is going to turn on the grill and cook the chicken. He says it like he's reading the first steps of the how-to manual for the bizarre evening ahead. He walks over to Wen and gently plucks her from Eric's feet. She does not resist. Andrew and Eric shout and tell Leonard to leave her alone, to not touch her, responses as automatic as they are feckless. Leonard says she will be fine and she is just going to sit with him on the couch while her dads use the bathroom to wash up for dinner. Then he asks Wen if them going to the bathroom is a good idea, and shouldn't everyone wash their hands before they eat? She is adrift on Leonard's lap, positioned like a ventriloquist's dummy. She squirms and slouches, obviously trying to slide off his lap. He readjusts her. He tells Andrew and Eric that they will not try anything stupid while their legs are untied. He says, "We've reached a critical point, the point of no return, and you must cooperate." It's less what he says but how he says it. Adriane retrieves the dual-ended weapon, the largest one, the one that cratered Redmond's chest, and leans it against the couch next to Leonard and Wen.

Sabrina and Adriane untie Andrew's legs first. Andrew makes a joke about needing more than his feet to go to the bathroom. Sabrina says she will help and, "I'm a nurse and I've seen it all." Standing up from the chair is difficult and his nearly forty-year-old legs are practically numb; a painful rush of pins and needles swarms his lower extremities. Eric has the same experience when he first stands, and he has to move slower as the act of standing fuzzes his head with light and heat. Both men, their hands tied behind their backs, have a turn at shuffling feebly into the bathroom. The door remains open with Adriane standing in the doorway as a guard. They are positioned in front of the toilet and suffer the indignity of Sabrina loosening their shorts and underwear to allow them to urinate.

Leonard keeps a one-sided dialogue going about him and Wen having a nice visit together on the couch. He asks her questions. He pretends she answers him to continue the conversation.

Both men, at certain points during their odyssey to and from the bathroom, consider running and/or bashing themselves into Sabrina and/or kicking Adriane. Both men decide this isn't the time, not while the others are at their most vigilant. They do not want to believe Leonard would hurt Wen despite his clearly being more than capable of extreme violence. They rationalize an escape attempt will make more sense the next time they are allowed to use the bathroom. Having coordinated this successful, uneventful maiden trip, the three others can't help but slacken their guard just a little bit the next time, or the time after that.

After they are returned and retied to their chairs, they notice the ropes wound around their hands and wrists have slackened, or perhaps that's wishful thinking. No, their bodies' change of position and leverage, their movement, their walking across the cabin and reshaping themselves into the tighter space of the bathroom alongside Sabrina has to have loosened the ropes. They can feel it.

Leonard clumsily washes and preps the boneless chicken breasts before Adriane takes over. She forgoes the deck floodlighting (insisting she doesn't need it, yelling at Leonard until he shuts the exterior lights off) and works in the near total dark. She says the grill sucks and she can't be judged by what such an inferior product produces. The smell is simply exquisite, and Sabrina says so with a smile on her face as she prepares a large bowl of garden salad. Leonard sets the kitchen table: four plates, four forks, and four plastic cups. Adriane ducks through the broken sliders with a platter of steaming, grilled meat, warning the room with, "Watch out. Hot stuff," and she barks at Leonard to shut the screen door behind her before they let in every moth and mosquito in New Hampshire. There is already a gaggle of winged insects swarming the wagon wheel light fixture, their bodies relentlessly pinging against the bulbs. Eric spies two thick, black flies (wondering if they are the same ones he saw earlier) and when they smack into a bulb, Eric is convinced the wagon wheel sways with the impact. Their buzzing is a low hum, like a chant.

Leonard takes Wen's hand, and with a small, gentle tug, she stands and follows him to the kitchen table. She sits on the far side, next to Leonard and facing her parents. Sabrina made her a cup of chocolate milk with chocolate kisses she melted in the microwave. On Wen's plate are a small pile of bite-sized pieces of chicken and a minisalad composed of lettuce, two cherry tomatoes, and three cucumber wheels. Wen holds one cucumber slice up and looks at Andrew and Eric. The rind was peeled off, the way she likes it.

Andrew says, "Go ahead. You can eat."

She eats everything on her plate, grim and determined to complete the task. She will later leave the table with a faint chocolate milk mustache coloring her lip.

The three others are seated at the table. Leonard and Sabrina praise Adriane for how moist the chicken is. Single-word *delicious* declaratives and *I didn't think I was hungry* are passed around the table along with the pepper, BBQ sauce, and raspberry balsamic dressing. Busy knives and forks clink and scrape on the plates.

Andrew seethes, boiling with incredulity and despair. How can the others simply engage in go-through-the-dinner-motions as though nothing is wrong? How do they so easily ignore the horror of what has happened and the expanding horror of what is happening and what will happen?

Adriane mumbles about how a beer would hit the spot and then laughs. No one else laughs with her.

Andrew says, "Hey, go ahead, help yourselves to the twelve-pack in the bottom drawer of the fridge. Make sure to recycle after."

Adriane says, "Really?" and looks at Sabrina and Leonard for a reaction. "Nah, that's all right." She raises her glass of water. "Maybe some other time." She takes a big sip and wipes her face with both hands.

Eric notices that none of the others said grace or a prayer before the meal. He anticipated and hoped they would. If they said grace he might've learned about what god they believe is the source of their visions and is ultimately the motivation behind them being here. Maybe Eric would've been able to use that information to better engage them in a conversation about their faith and possibly persuade them into letting his family go. He was so sure that grace was going to happen, Eric thinks he might've zoned out and missed it, or the prayer happened and he witnessed it and promptly forgot it because of his concussion. That he hasn't even spied one of the others performing a quick, furtive sign of the cross, doesn't make sense to him.

After they finish eating, Leonard asks Wen to help with dinner for her dads. He says it's a superimportant job. "I don't think they'll eat without you."

Wen wordlessly agrees to help. She stands in front of Eric with a fork in her hand. Leonard carries over a plate of cut-up chicken and a leaf-pile of salad. Sabrina patiently details a set of instructions for all to follow. Wen spears a piece of chicken on a plastic fork and holds it in front of Eric's face. He opens his mouth only wide enough to let the chicken pass through. It's lukewarm. He doesn't linger, doesn't allow himself the luxury of taste, and chews and swallows quickly. Wen doesn't talk, doesn't ask if he wants chicken again next or a cherry tomato. She doesn't look at his eyes, only his mouth. She doesn't stop feeding him until Eric says, "That's enough for me, sweetie. Thank you." She puts the fork on the plate and then holds up a cup of water.

Andrew wants to tell the others to fuck off, that he doesn't want anything from them. He imagines accepting the first bite and spitting it into one of their faces. But when his daughter stands in front of him, so intently doing her job, he loses his resolve and eats everything that is offered.

Postdinner there's cleanup and more cartoons on the television. Sabrina plays game after game of solitaire at the kitchen table. Adriane disinterestedly flips through the book Eric brought and goes out onto the front stoop to smoke cigarettes. She asks if anyone has a jigsaw puzzle. She says that's what her mom always used to do when they went on vacation.

Leonard asks Wen questions about what she's watching. If it's a yes or no question, she answers ("Do you like this show?" Yes "Have you seen this one before?" No). Any question inviting a more detailed response yields a shrug or a thousand-yard stare.

Eric is exhausted and has a difficult time keeping his eyes open. He attempts to get the others talking about the visions (avoiding explicit references to God and the Bible because of his own growing unease), the why of the apocalyptic choice, the why of the whole thing, but none of them bite. Sabrina says, "We'll talk about it tomorrow after you and your family have slept on it."

Andrew tries a different tact, periodically asking to be untied, successive requests becoming more elaborate and ridiculous: "How about you untie me so I can fix the kitchen table leg? I notice the playing cards sliding off the edge there, and really, the table shouldn't be propped up on magical realists. You know, there's a lumberyard not too far away and I can go pick up some wood, whittle it into a new leg in no time. I guess I'd have to stop somewhere and get some white paint, but that's not a big deal. I don't mind. I'd already be out." Andrew figures if they take him less seriously because of his barrage of increasingly untenable requests, all the better for when he makes the serious attempt at breaking free, and then to the SUV and his gun.

Leonard announces, "It's getting late. We could all use the rest. And we'll be up with the sun." He gathers the towels and curtain off the floor. Then the three others drag the mattresses out of the bedrooms. There's enough space for the queen-size to be sandwiched between two singles from the bunk beds. With the television turned off and Wen already changed into pajamas and having washed up and brushed her teeth, Andrew and Eric are again taken to the bathroom separately. Wen sits with Leonard on the couch next to the sledgehammer weapon.

Adriane repositions Andrew's and Eric's chairs to either side of the front door. Their shoulders brush against the wall as their arms are slipped behind the chair backs. Sabrina and Adriane tie the men's legs to the chair legs and Sabrina apologizes, saying they can't trust that the two of them will sleep on the mattresses and remain tied. She says they'll try to make sleeping while sitting up as comfortable as possible.

It's going to be a cold night in the cabin. The temperature has already dropped into the high fifties. Adriane builds a fire in the woodburning stove but the heat rapidly dissipates through the porous screen slider. Thin blankets are pulled over Andrew's and Eric's chests and tucked between their shoulders and the wall, pillows stuffed behind their heads and necks.

Andrew doesn't say anything and is confident he'll be able to break free from the ropes after the others are asleep. Eric is spent and the warm, soft pillow enveloping his head is a potent soporific. He's in a half-awake, half-asleep state before the lights are turned out.

Andrew and Eric are allowed a good-night kiss with Wen. They smile and repeatedly say her name with every known inflection, attempting to let her know they will still protect her and keep her safe despite all evidence to the contrary. They tell her she is brave and doing so well and they love her more than anything in the world. She has seen so much and heard so much and done so much; they do not dare imagine reliving the events of this day through the prism of Wen. She is nonresponsive, an automaton following a basic program of breathing, blinks, and sluggish limb movements. Wen is funneled to the queen-sized mattress without struggle or fuss. She lies down, burrowing into the blankets, taking up as little space as possible, adrift on the sea of foam. Leonard proffers her stuffed-animal pig (Corey, her favorite) and she pulls it into her chest with all the enthusiasm of a student accepting a math test from her teacher.

Sabrina and Adriane crawl onto the smaller bunk mattresses. Leonard stretches out on the couch.

No one moves or adjusts their resting positions for hours, seemingly. Andrew remains awake and quietly struggles to loosen the ropes on his hands and wrists, which have gone numb from being pinned behind his back for so long. It's cold, still, and quiet in the cabin but for the occasional crackle and hiss from the woodburning stove. The bathroom light is the only light on and the door is shut so there is only a weak yellow glow tracing its outline. Outside, a cloudless night sky and a bright crescent moon lord over the lake. Andrew can now see Redmond's covered body on the deck just fine. He can't help but wonder if he stays up all night will he see a wild animal (are there any other kind?) crawl up the deck stairs and investigate what's underneath the blanket.

Unable to make any progress with the ropes, he whispers, "Eric. Hey, are you awake? Eric? Hey—"

Adriane says, "There are people trying to sleep."

"Keep trying, and you fuckers aren't people. I'm going to talk to my husband," Andrew says in a stern talking voice that might as well be a shout in the nocturnal silence and calm.

Eric says, "I'm awake now."

Eric and Andrew share a rapid-fire whispered conversation. Eric is murky with sleep and doubt. Andrew is manic and self-aware that his desperation is apparent, as audible as a creaking door in an empty house.

"Are you okay, Eric? Are you feeling any better?"

"Yeah, a little better, I think. My brain doesn't feel three sizes too small for my skull anymore. Maybe one size."

"I know you're not feeling great, and I wanted to make sure you noticed the first earthquake, the one up near Alaska, happened four hours before they turned on the TV."

"Was it that long?"

"Yes, that's what they said on the news. Remember? Hawaii had all that lead time to evacuate. Remember the empty resort?"

"Okay, I guess, yeah, that sounds right."

"It is right. Trust me on that. And did you see how often Leonard checked his watch?"

"Maybe. I can't really remember. I think so."

"He checked it like one thousand times. I saw some of the others checking the time, too. Which means the time was important to them. They didn't start any of it until the time was right. Leonard even said something about the time being right. He did. He definitely did."

"Yeah, okay, I think I remember that. You know they can hear us even though we're whispering, right?"

Sabrina says, "Yeah, um, we can hear you and—"

"I know and I don't care. I'm not talking to any of you. So, they knew about the first earthquake and Hawaii tsunami before they came out to the cabin. Think about it. They didn't get any visions or prophecies; they knew about the Alaska quake and of the imminent tsunami before they got here. They had that shit in their pockets with them when they came out here."

"Sure. Makes sense. Why are you telling me this?"

"Because I know you and I don't want you to be—to be spooked by them lying about getting visions and predicting the earthquake and the apocalypse."

Leonard says, "That's enough, guys. Please—"

Andrew and Eric continue as though no one else is speaking, no one else is there.

"You really think I believe them?"

"No. I don't know. I just wanted to make sure, with your bad fall and everything, that you could see what they were doing, how they targeted us and how they're trying to break us down and manipulate us. How they knew about the earthquake before they came to the cabin, and how that second earthquake was just a coincidence, set off by the first one, right? And how all the *Goonies* bullshit was bullshit. And you saw how they reacted when the second earthquake hit, like they won the fucking lottery and—"

"Oh my God, you do think I might believe them. Are you serious with this?"

There's a hesitation, an empty space filled with silent words. "No, I don't think that. I'm sorry, don't get mad. I'm not trying to make you mad. Please, I'm sorry. I'm just scared, and I wanted to make sure that, you know . . ."

"Yeah, I know. Don't worry about me. I don't believe them."

"I know you don't. I know you don't."

"I don't."

Sabrina says, "That's enough. Please. We all need to sleep."

"Hey, Eric?"

"Still here."

"I'm sorry, and I love you."

"I love you, too."

There's another beat of silence that both men want to fill but don't know how they possibly could. Then Andrew says, "Hey, can you guys untie me? I want to keep the fire in the stove going all night. Don't worry, I won't fall asleep on the job. I promise. And I'll go outside and gather more wood—"

Adriane says, "Shut up or we'll shut you up. Put, like, gags over your mouth or something."

Leonard says, "Easy, Adriane. It's okay. Everyone is good, everyone is fine. We can all go back to sleep now." Leonard prattles on in a low voice and Sabrina joins in with empty we-won't-hurt-you avowals.

Eric is stung by Andrew thinking that he might, even in the smallest of ways, believe the others are telling some version of the truth. It stings because Andrew would be more than a little correct in thinking that. Eric's fear gives way temporarily to shame and anger, and it leaks out as he says, "If any of you attempt to put something over my mouth, I'll bite your fingers off." Then he silently prays for God to help them.

Wen

In Wen's bedroom back home there's a night-light plugged into the wall across from her bed. It has a simple white bulb that isn't shaped like a cartoon character or a comic book hero or an animal or the moon or anything in particular. She likes it that way;

she doesn't want any funny shapes because funny shapes make scary shadows. In addition to the night-light, she insists the hallway light stay on as well, and the bathroom light, too, with the door open. Her parents have tried to wean her off sleeping with lights on, explaining her still-growing brain needs the dark for proper rest. Wen once told them she doesn't want her brain growing too fast for her head, anyway. Sometimes, after she falls asleep, one of her parents shuts off the bathroom light, the hall light, or (gasp!) both. She thinks it must be Daddy Eric because he always complains about her and Daddy Andrew leaving lights on everywhere in the condo, wasting electricity, but she has yet to catch him in the act. Shutting off the bathroom light is a grievous betrayal and it once angered her enough to announce at the breakfast table that she will have a terrible day. When her parents asked why, she dramatically pouted and said, "You know why," and then couldn't hide her snarky smirk in the brightness of the kitchen.

Wen is sitting up on the mattress without the memory of waking. She looks around, moving only her eyes at first; she doesn't move her head until she's convinced everyone else is asleep. It's dark, but less dark than it should be with almost no lights on in the cabin. The bathroom light doesn't count as being on because the door is shut.

She wonders if anything happened while she was asleep. She wonders if it's possible she slept through an entire day and it's now the next night instead of the same one.

Wen slips out of her blankets and crawls to the edge of the mattress. If this were another evening under different circumstances, she would jump mattress to mattress, pretending they were rafts in a vast, cold sea, or the mattresses were rocks stubbornly maintaining their lifesaving heft and shape within a bubbling lava flow. Instead, she's careful to not disturb Sabrina (she sleeps on her back with her arms over her head, dangling off the mattress, her mouth open slightly) and Adriane (she sleeps rolled up into a ball, like she's hiding because she's mad at everyone in the room; only the top half of her head sticks out from under her blanket, exposed to the cool night air).

To her left are the screen slider and deck. The blanket covering Redmond ripples in a breeze like it's considering a transformation into a wing and flying away. She wonders what Redmond looks like now. Is he all broken and mashed up, squished like a stepped-on caterpillar, or does he look the same as he did before but like he is sleeping? She's never seen a dead body before. She has asked adults what a dead body looks like and the only one who somewhat answered her was Daddy Andrew. He told her a dead body looked like the person but not like them at the same time because there was something missing. She joked, "Like a nose or an ear?" and he laughed. Wen never felt more proud of herself as when she made one of her dads laugh. She asked him to explain what he meant, and Daddy Andrew pretended (she knew he was pretending and she hated when he did this to her) with loud *hmm*s, a finger tapping his lips, chin rubs, and other I-don't-really-want-to-answer-this stalling tactics. She thought he was never going to explain further, but she played it smart. She didn't press, didn't whine, didn't demand. She waited him out. She waited until he shrank down a little under her stare, and he smiled the *you-win* smile. He said that the dead bodies he saw reminded him of slightly deflated birthday balloons, ones that hung around limply a day or two after the party. She didn't like the answer and wanted to ask him more, but he said, "Don't tell Eric we were talking about dead bodies, all right?"

Wen doesn't think Redmond would look like a balloon. Even

though she didn't see any of it, she knows they hit him repeatedly with the weapons, and she did see all the blood after and she could smell it. She heard him screaming. She heard it all and she can hear it now if she lets herself, those awful, hollow thumps and the final, wet crack that shook the floor and her legs. But what if it sounded worse than it was and he just got hurt badly and was knocked out like Daddy Eric? What if Redmond is alive and he wakes up? What if he's awake now and waiting for someone to come outside, or he's waiting for her to make a run for it and he'll reach out and grab her and pull her underneath the blanket and she'll be stuck there with him forever?

She whispers, "No," to make herself look away from the deck and Redmond. She crawls on all fours to the end table pushed up against the wall next to the bathroom. The yellow lamp looks black, like it's its own shadow. She reaches up and tries to turn it on. Two, three clicks of the spinning switch, and it doesn't work.

"Hey, Wen." It's Leonard. "What's up?"

He sounds like he's right behind her, and his shadow is heavier than a lead blanket, the kind they put over her chest for when she had x-rays, and she freezes with her hand on the lamp, willing herself to fade into the darkness of the night room.

Leonard is not right behind her. He sits up on the couch. The springs groan under his weight. He asks, "Do you have to go to the bathroom?"

Wen shakes her head.

He says, "It's okay."

Nothing is okay. She knows this. Wen shouldn't say anything to him; she knows this, too, but she can't help it. She whispers, "I want a light. I always go to sleep with a light on."

He says, "Come back to bed, and I'll tell you why we didn't leave one on for you."

There's an echo inside of her, coming from far enough away that the speaker cannot be identified. It might be her voice, it might be one or both of her dads, or a mix, or someone else entirely. This voice repeats what Daddy Andrew said to her earlier. The voice tells her to run, to go onto the deck and never mind about Redmond because he's not getting up ever again. *Run now. Go outside and run and hide. Don't be afraid of the dark out there. Be afraid of what's happening inside and what will happen inside.* It says, *This is your only chance now now now now.*

She can't, and in her head, she tells the voice she's sorry.

Wen stands up, moving like a sunrise. She considers sitting with one of her dads but they are both asleep, their heads slumped forward. She walks the short distance back to her mattress and disappears under the blankets, remaining with her head covered. Her pillow is cold against her face.

Leonard says, "We didn't leave any lights on because it's better for Eric's head. He needs sleep and he needs it dark for his head to get better."

Why do adults keep telling her that dark makes heads better? She thinks they're lying and that they lie way more than any kid ever does. Wen flips over and faces Leonard. He has his blanket pulled up to his chin so he's only a big head. She says, "How do you know?"

"Sabrina told me and she's a nurse. The light hurts his head so after he sleeps in the dark he'll feel much better in the morning."

"He will?"

"Yes, I promise."

Another lie, but it's one she wants to believe.

She says, "Then you'll make us choose again."

"I won't make you, but I will ask. I have to."

"Please don't."

"I'm sorry. But I have to."

"I can't be friends with you."

"I know, and I'm sorry. I have no choice."

"Who is making you?"

"What do you mean?"

"Who is making you do this to us?"

"God." Leonard says the one-syllable word sheepishly and he has a strange look on his face. Speaking the word aloud brings him both great relief and terror.

There's a boy at Wen's school who talked about God all the time and insisted that his god was a he. That boy was annoying and Wen avoided playing with him whenever she could. Daddy Andrew makes it a point to tell her about all kinds of religions and gods from around the world. There are so many it's confusing, but she enjoys listening to the different stories even if some of them frighten her. She knows that Daddy Eric believes in a god and that he even goes to church by himself sometimes on Sunday mornings. He doesn't invite Wen or Daddy Andrew to go with him and he doesn't seem to like to talk about his god or religion so she doesn't ever ask him. It's almost like it's this secret Daddy Eric keeps under his bed instead of the old pictures. Wen isn't sure what she believes in and sometimes that fills her with anxiety and a desire to simply choose a random religion like someone might choose to become a fan of a sports team because of the mascot or the color of the uniform.

She says, "I don't believe you. Why do you keep lying to me?"

"It's the truth."

"I think you're wrong."

"I wish I was. I wish more than anything."

"Why would God make you do this?"

Leonard sighs and shifts around under his blanket. "I'm not

sure. I'm not. That's the truth, Wen. It's something I've thought a lot about, but I can't do anything to change it, if that makes sense."

Wen blinks, and sudden and surprising tears fall from her eyes. She says, "It doesn't make sense."

"I don't think it's supposed to. We're not supposed to make sense of it. We're just supposed to do."

"Your god is a killer then."

"Wen, no. It's not like—"

"And if we don't choose, then something else bad is going to happen, like another terrible earthquake?"

"Not another earthquake, but yes, something very bad."

"And a lot of people will die?"

"People will die."

"I don't believe you and I wish you would stop making this all up."

"I can promise you one thing, Wen."

"What."

"Your parents won't ever choose to sacrifice you. I know they won't and I wouldn't let them do anything to you. I would stop them. I would protect you if I had to. That's my promise. You shouldn't be worried about that."

"Sacrifice means die, right?"

"Yes, but one of your dads will be saving the rest of the world, Wen. Think about how many people out there—"

"I don't want any of us to die. Ever." Wen sinks back under the blanket, covering her head. Leonard whispers her name, trying to coax her back out. She can't help but imagine her dads as saggy balloons stuck in this cabin and never able to float away.

She makes a deal with this killer-god of Leonard's, a god she doesn't believe is real but is very much frightened of. She has this image of his god as all the black empty space between stars when you look up at the night sky, and this god of collected blankness is big enough to swallow the moon, the earth, the sun, the Milky Way, and big enough it couldn't possibly care about anyone or anything. Still, she asks this god if she and her parents can please leave the cabin, can they please go home and be safe, and if it lets them, she promises she won't ever complain about sleeping in the dark with the lights off ever again.

Eric

In the morning the others scurry around the kitchen making placemats out of paper towels and setting glasses and mugs on the table. They are purposeful, determined, and clearly anxious. The surreal, relaxed-family-on-vacation vibe from last night's dinner is gone. If one of them was to accidentally brush up against the other, there'd be a bright and loud static-electric spark, which would then set off an explosion.

Sabrina asks them all twice if they want coffee and how much. She obsessively glances out the small window above the sink to the deck, from which wafts a putrid, tangy, many-days-old garbage smell.

Leonard checks his watch, claps his hands together, and says, "Okay," to himself.

Adriane stacks buttered, browned toast onto a plate and she shoos and mutters at the stubborn gaggle of flies buzzing the food, "Get out. Get the fuck out."

Wen sits at the kitchen table with the others but doesn't speak to anyone. She looks down into her lap and her hands are clenched into fists, her thumbs cocooned inside.

Andrew tells her it's all right to eat. Wen doesn't eat or drink anything, even when offered chocolate milk. Andrew tells her if she doesn't feel like eating right now that's okay, too. Eric adds, "Whatever you want to do," which, given their current circumstances, is an unintentionally cruel thing to say.

Wen deflates and sags into the kitchen chair so only the top of her head is visible above the table. Andrew and Eric loudly refuse offers of toast and water in solidarity.

Eric's head doesn't hurt like it did the day before, though he is far from fully recovered from his concussion. His head is an overstuffed washing machine, wobbling off its track in the spin cycle. The room is too brightly lit when it isn't bright for anyone else. His throat is dry and he regrets not drinking water when offered. He's exhausted and struggles to remain awake even as the rest of his body screams and begs to be released from the prison of its sitting position. His arms and legs ache although the restraints have perceptibly slackened over the long night. He's now able to pull his hands apart so they are no longer touching and he can stretch his lower legs a centimeter or two away from the chair; small but significant progress. He wonders if the ropes around Andrew have loosened as well.

After the hurried breakfast, Sabrina checks Eric's dressing and wound. She says it doesn't look great and perhaps could've used a few stitches after all, but it isn't infected. The others carry the blankets and mattresses out of the common room. They move quickly and efficiently, stagehands making short work of a scene change. Leonard drags Andrew, still tied to the chair, away from the front door and into the center of the room. The wooden chair legs scrape and screech across the floor, as percussive as a passing tractor trailer on a highway, leaving gouged parallel lines in the wood.

When Leonard comes for Eric and his chair, Eric says, "No, please, dragging me like that will not be good for my head. I'm feeling better but not that much better. Untie my legs and I'll walk. I promise I'll be good." Eric is an inept liar and always has been.

Leonard towers above, as large and solemn as an Easter Island statue. He says, "Sorry, not yet." He retucks his white shirt into his jeans, then bends and reaches for the chair's armrests.

"Hey, let's pick him up, carry him instead. We can help you. We need him to be thinking clearly, more clearly than he was thinking yesterday, right?" Sabrina jogs over and stands next to Eric and his chair. Adriane comes over, too.

Leonard says, "We don't have much time," but he acquiesces after a brief negotiation. The three of them lift Eric and his chair a few inches off the ground. He wobbles and pitches as they readjust, overcorrect, and shuffle-carry him. Eric considers twisting or leaning all his weight to one side so they might drop him for no strategic reason other than he can for the moment control what will happen to him. They set him down with Andrew to his right, the same area of the room in which he was moored yesterday. Having been returned to this spot is more than a little demoralizing, and it's as though Eric's dizziness and low-grade nausea is the result of time travel.

Wen is on the couch. Eric didn't witness her relocation from the kitchen table. Did she walk there on her own or was she carried, too? A blanket is pulled over her legs. Andrew is trying to get her attention and asks if she is cold, if she's all right, if she wants to sit with him or Eric. She doesn't answer and stares ahead blankly as though witnessing the horror awaiting their near futures.

The others pace around the room, searching for something

they forgot to prepare properly. They circle like carrion birds, squawking and muttering. Each asks the others how they feel and if they're ready. One of them says, "I can't believe we have to go through this again," and another one says, "I know," and another, "This is so hard," and another, "I don't know if I can," and another, "You can," and another, "We can and we must," and another, "This isn't like a bad dream but I wish it was," and another, "It's real, the realest thing I've ever done," and another, "Let's just get it over with," and another, "We have to do it right," and another, "We owe it to them," and another, "Give them a chance to save us all."

Their positioning within the room shifts on some unseen, unheard cue. Adriane steps up between Eric and Andrew. Leonard and Sabrina retreat into the background.

Leonard says, "I didn't do a very good job of, um, presenting the choice, yesterday." Leonard looks at his watch and then looks everywhere else in the room but at Wen. "You'll be great, Adriane. I know it."

Adriane rolls her eyes and says, "Gee, thanks, boss. So, yeah, here we are again."

Leonard and Sabrina gather the same weaponized wooden staffs they used the day before. They are held with purpose, with the confidence of already having been wielded properly and successfully.

Adriane is empty-handed. Propped against the woodburning stove, her cleaned weapon is a rustic decoration, something from an alternate bygone era, impractical as it is improbable.

Adriane says, "We"—she pauses to look over her shoulder at Sabrina, who nods encouragement—"are here to present you with the same choice you had yesterday."

Eric says, "Look, we're powerless here. It's you three that have a choice, and a chance to do the right thing and let us go. You know letting us go is the right thing to do. You all seem like nice people who honestly don't want to be doing what you're doing. And the good news is you do not have to do this, any of this." Eric feels more in control, feels more like himself, and the nagging echo of the vision of the figure in light he saw yesterday is more easily dismissed as a hallucination, or perhaps a visual symptom of an acute ocular migraine, something that he has suffered in the past.

Adriane twitches and rubs her arms, clearly uncomfortable speaking for the group. "No, we do have to. We don't have a choice. Not like you. Even if we wanted to let you go, we can't. It wouldn't fly, man. We wouldn't be allowed to."

Eric focuses on Adriane's fidgeting, empty hands, and with her weapon across the room, it occurs to him that she is next. He almost says aloud *you will be next*. If he, Andrew, and Wen again choose not to sacrifice any one of themselves, then the other two will kill Adriane ritualistically with their weapons like they killed Redmond yesterday. Does he have it correct? It feels right but it doesn't make any sense and at some point they would have to stop killing each other, wouldn't they?

"So you guys have the same choice to make, and you have to make it now, same as yesterday. Same deal, right? I mean, you saw what happened on the West Coast." Adriane points at the television, her outstretched arm reflected in the black screen. "How could you not believe us after watching all those people drown? We told you it was coming and when you didn't make the choice, all those people died and died screaming, how could you see that and not—"

Andrew screams, "For fuck's sake," and thrashes around in his chair. "None of that had anything to do with us or you."

Eric says, "Purely a coincidence." The lack of conviction in his voice is obvious, so obvious the three others look at him as though they're seeing him for the first time, as though they've made a discovery.

Andrew says, "No, it was not a coincidence. It wasn't. You knew the Alaskan earthquake had happened already, before you came out to the cabin, and there was the tsunami warning and you planned your little visit here accordingly—"

Sabrina says, "That's not true."

"—so tell us what's going to be on TV this morning? I know it's almost time for something Leonard wants to see because he keeps checking his watch, just like he did yesterday. You know, I never realized the end of the world would be kept to such a tight, regimented *TV Guide* schedule. This is enough! This is insane! You're all insane!"

Adriane shouts, "You need to calm right the fuck down and think for a second!"

Sabrina leans forward and speaks to Eric, as to his shame, he's now been identified as the one who might believe them. "Even if we knew about the earthquake in the hours before we came here, why and how did we end up even coming here in the first place? I mean, how did the four of us strangers from different parts of the country know to randomly meet in the Middle of Nowhere, New Hampshire? It was because we had visions, were sent here, were told to—"

Andrew shouts over her, "So you're admitting you knew about the earthquake before you got to the cabin!"

"Yes. I mean, no, no that's not what I'm saying at all."

Adriane says, "It doesn't matter. You have another chance to stop more people from dying by making the choice. You and us and everyone on the fucking planet will run out of chances if you don't choose to save us." Her eyes are wide, incredulous. She can't believe she isn't being believed. "If you choose to sacrifice one of you, then the world doesn't end. That's it. It's that simple. I can't tell you any other way. Fuck—"

Leonard says, "Easy . . ."

Adriane continues on ranting. "No charts and graphs or Power-Points or, what, a fucking puppet show—" She cuts out and holds pleading hands out toward Eric.

He feels all the eyes of the room on him, including Andrew's and Wen's. He says, "There is no choice. We will never choose to sacrifice one of ourselves, no matter what. Period. Look, I know this is hard to hear but you three are suffering from some kind of a shared delusion, and delusions are powerful things . . ."

Adriane says, "Oh, Christ, we're fucked. We're all fucked," and throws her hands up.

Wen says from the couch, "Leonard told me it's God making them do this." Her speaking for the first time that morning freezes all the adults in place, like they were playing a game of Red Light Green Light.

Andrew asks, "When did he tell you that?"

"In the middle of the night. I woke up and he was awake, too."

Andrew says, "Well, he's wrong. They're doing this. No one and nothing else but them, and I know Leonard likes to act like your friend but if he really was, he'd let us all go." Andrew glowers at Leonard, who doesn't rebut.

Wen doesn't say anything else. She opens and closes her legs under the blanket, flapping them like butterfly wings.

"God wouldn't do this." Less confident in the declarative than his words would indicate, Eric says it hurriedly, as one might when uttering a perceived truth about a future event while simultaneously worrying about being a jinx. In the same mental breath, he silently prays to God that they be freed from this ordeal unharmed. If pressed, Eric would identify himself as Catholic; he once said to a coworker that he was a "cautious Catholic." He goes to church once or twice a month. Sometimes he attends Mass on Sundays, and sometimes, when he is feeling particularly stressed, he'll go early on a weekday before work. Although he often struggles with the message and the messenger, the rote prayers and songs memorized so long ago as to have their own elaborately decorated memory palaces, the waxy cardboard taste of the host, and even the smell of dust, candles, and incense are a comfort, a balm. No Christmas Catholic—only attending church for the big holidays—is he, and he would stop going to church altogether before becoming one. In the weeks preceding Wen's adoption, Eric reluctantly agreed (though the avowed agnostic Andrew doesn't know how reluctantly) with Andrew that they would not have Wen baptized and not force her to adhere to any religion. Wen would be able to choose a religion when she was older and when the choice was hers alone. Eric knew that was the same as saying that Wen would be brought up without any religion at all. It nags at him on occasion, as he feels like he's keeping an important part of himself from Wen, but he hasn't once protested the family decision, nor has he secretly proselytized.

A warm breeze flows into the cabin through the screen slider, which wobbles and vibrates in its track, bringing with it the stronger-by-the-minute garbage smell that isn't really garbage. Andrew catches Eric's eye and nods at him. Is he telling him he did a good job? Does he know something? Are Andrew's ropes even looser than his and he's telling him to be ready? The sunlight flashes and Eric turns away, fearful of being exposed to the light again when he might not be ready.

Adriane walks to Sabrina and asks what are they going to do? Sabrina whispers something out of earshot. Adriane drops her head and covers her face with her hands.

Leonard fills himself up with air. He says, "Sacrifices are required and will be made, one way or another, whether we like it or—"

Andrew jolts and spasms like he is stung by a bee. He shouts, "Jesus Christ! Holy shit—" spewing a mess of profanities.

Eric asks, "What? What happened? Are you okay?" Is Andrew acting? Is this part of a plan to get one of them over to his chair so he can do . . . Do what?

Andrew is wild-eyed and breathing deeply, like he's fighting off the urge to throw up. "Oh, fucking hell, Eric, it was him. Fucking Redmond! It was him! It was him! I knew these guys were nothing but a fringe group of homophobic nutbags here to . . . Oh, shit, Eric. Shit, shit . . ."

Leonard, Sabrina, and Adriane back away from Andrew and share confused, what-now? looks.

"Slow down, slow down. Talk to me." Eric, momentarily forgetting about the chair and the ropes, tries to stand and walk to Andrew. He full-body flexes against his restraints and rebounds heavily back into the chair, which sends a dagger of pain through the center of his head. The rope binding his hands is looser than it was minutes ago with the bulk of the wound knot having slid lower down his wrists, almost to the tops of his palms. He's confident he can squirm his hands free but he isn't sure how long it would take and how obvious the effort would be to his captors.

Andrew shouts at the others. "Redmond isn't his name! You assholes using fake names, too? Did God tell you to do that?"

Adriane still has her hands over her face. "What the hell is he talking about?"

Sabrina says, "No, none of us are using fake names. Same for you guys, right?" Adriane and Leonard say, "Yeah," and "Of course." She looks distrustful of Andrew, afraid of him and what he's saying.

"That dead guy out there, the one you killed. His name is Jeff O'Bannon."

"Jeff O'Bannon?" Eric repeats the man's name out loud and then says it many more times in his creaky head. It's a name he knows, or a name he should know and should be able to put a face to or summon a dossier of significance for.

"He's the guy who attacked me in the bar, Eric! It's him!"

Andrew

A hockey bar by name, the Penalty Box was a hard-drinking dive eschewing the ironic, hipster faux charm that might now be associated with the term *dive bar*. On the corner of Causeway Street, across from North Station and the Boston Garden, the bar was on the first floor of a brick-and-cement, two-story rectangular shoebox of no recognizable architectural style beyond industrial. It had one square front window next to a cavelike entrance chiseled out of the brick, above which perched a yellow sign with thick black letters. It was generally patronized by mean drunks, people spending their last dollars or loose change, or amateur-hour assholes fluttering in pre- and post-Bruins and Celtics games. In the late 1990s, the tiny room above the Penalty Box, called the Upstairs Lounge, was a local music hot spot and used to host what were called "pill dance parties" every Friday night. Eighty or so people would jam into the dark and grimy room with a DJ playing Britpop. Pre-Eric, Andrew and a small group of friends attended the dances religiously for an almost five-year run, including after they moved the pill dances from the Upstairs Lounge to a new venue in Allston.

In November of 2005, Andrew and his friend Ritchie decided to go to the Penalty Box (the Upstairs Lounge having been long shuttered up) after ditching a Celtics game early for a glass or two of nostalgia. The bar was half full with the green shirts of other Celtics game attendees who had given up on the home team as they were down by twenty-five points early in the fourth quarter. Andrew had on a twenty-year-old Robert Parish tank top that was too small for him over a white long-sleeve T-shirt. Ritchie had a new Paul Pierce jersey on even though he spent most of the game complaining about the player's shot selection and perceived lack of foot speed.

In the intervening years, Andrew has curated a carefully pieced together timeline of nonevents prior to his attack: He and Ritchie were in the Penalty Box for less than ten minutes. Andrew made a beeline for the bar upon entering and ordered two Sam Adams drafts. He doesn't remember seeing Jeff O'Bannon or his two friends sitting at the bar, which was where they were according to the police report and testimony. Andrew carried the two beers over to Ritchie, who was near the entrance and talking to a middle-aged woman wearing a Bruins hoodie and jeans. Tall and rail thin, she was loudly drunk, and when she wasn't wiping greasy hair out of her face, her hummingbird hands were all over Ritchie's arms, shoulders, and back, and Ritchie couldn't have been more amused or pleased. Andrew doesn't remember her name. He gave Ritchie a beer and they clinked their plastic cups. The woman told Ritchie he looked like Ricardo Montalbán when he didn't look anything like him. She told Ritchie that Andrew was cute but not as cute as he was. She laughed at her own joke but there was a lag between, so he couldn't be sure why she was laughing. Andrew pretended to be offended at his second-class cuteness status. She asked Ritchie to dance even though there wasn't any music playing, only the TV audio of Mike Gorman and Tommy Heinsohn calling the blowout game in muted, eulogistic tones. Andrew egged Ritchie on, telling him to go ahead and dance. Ritchie said things like, "I don't know. My quads are sore from my run this morning. Maybe. I have an inner-ear problem and I get dizzy if I spin around. I'm thinking about it. I'm missing the baby toe on my left foot so I always list to the right. Sounds like fun, but . . ." She interjected with "oh yeahs" and more pleas for a dance and now a beer, as her demands increased with the extended negotiating. Andrew thought she was pleased to simply have this conversation continue. Ritchie wasn't flustered in the least (like Andrew would've been) and started to ask her questions ("So, where are you from? Come here often? Will the Celtics ever be good again?"). Ritchie clearly enjoyed building the suspense of will-he-or-won't-he. Then Andrew remembers Ritchie asking, "What was the name of the last guy you danced with in here?" She smiled and waved a hand in the general direction of the opposite side of the room like her previous dance partner was still there and she said, "That fucking guy, his name was Milton" (Andrew interjected, "Like the city?"). "Yeah. He was no fun. Wouldn't let me feel him up." The three of them shared a big laugh, and then O'Bannon was behind Andrew, over his left shoulder, and he said, "Faggot," and it wasn't a wild, out-of-control shout, and it wasn't slurred or sloppy. It was clear, concise, and dismissive, a one-word statement of argument and justification. Andrew turned to his left, toward the speaker whose face he would not see in person until the two of them were in the same courtroom. As he turned, O'Bannon smashed a beer

bottle on his head, the impact and follow-through cutting a gash
that needed almost thirty stitches to close. Andrew remembers
hearing the smash of glass, but there was no pain, and instead a
flash of cold on his head and neck, and then he was looking at
the floor, which began getting closer very quickly. He remembers lying facedown with his eyes closed and people shouting.
He doesn't remember getting into the ambulance, but he remembers insisting upon sitting up during the ride. He remembers the
inexplicable feeling of shame upon seeing Eric for the first time
at the hospital. When Eric said, "Oh my God, what happened to
you?" Andrew whispered, "I don't know . . ." and stopped so he
wouldn't say *I don't know what I did.* O'Bannon later pled guilty
and told the court he was drunk and not thinking clearly and
that Andrew had accidentally spilled a beer on one of his friends
(which was patently false), and they then were looking for a fight
and his friends egged him on, and he said repeatedly that that
wasn't him, wasn't who he was.

Andrew thought about the attack before every boxing lesson
and workout, before each trip to the shooting range. For the first
couple of years postattack, when he couldn't sleep, he internet-
searched his attacker's name and he'd spend hours digging into
the digital lives of other people named Jeff O'Bannon. After ex-
hausting the information on his O'Bannon (and that's how he
thought of the man, as belonging to him like a disease might),
Andrew read about an O'Bannon who lived in Los Angeles and
worked in the art department for major Hollywood movies, and
there was the one who was a middle-school social science teacher
in New Mexico and hosted a Looney Tunes viewing party for
his students the first Friday of every month. Andrew spent one
night poring through the 1940 government census and finding a
twenty-five-year-old Jeff O'Bannon who had a wife, three kids,

and his mother living in their Mississippi home. Later that night, Eric woke to find Andrew asleep in the desk chair, and he gently led him back to bed.

Andrew has long since quit those internet searches and he doesn't look over his shoulder in public places as frequently and as urgently as he once did, though the hypervigilance will never go away completely. In unguarded moments, he'll still pick and worry at why he was attacked. Well, he knows why, the hate-filled *why* was made painfully clear, but why did O'Bannon choose Andrew? How did O'Bannon know Andrew was gay and by proxy that Ritchie was not? If Ritchie had been standing with his back to the bar, would he have been the one who was attacked? Had O'Bannon simply made a terrible, lucky guess? (O'Bannon maintained in court his *faggot* wasn't why he attacked Andrew and it didn't mean he thought Andrew was gay; it was a word he and his buddies used all the time and it didn't mean anything to them and the slur didn't and wasn't supposed to mean what it actually meant.) Had O'Bannon seen Andrew outside or even inside the Boston Garden and then followed him to the bar, his dumb, ravenous hate fueled by Andrew's visage, the way he talked, the way he walked or smiled or laughed or shook his head or blinked his eyes? Did O'Bannon first see Andrew when he walked to the bar and ordered the beers? Did he look at Andrew and instantly see whatever it was he saw? Was Andrew like a bright orange flame to O'Bannon, burning only to invite his violence? Did O'Bannon patiently observe and deliberate and plan and have doubts that he overcame with a grunt and a swing of a glass bottle? As galling as Andrew's being somehow read and then classified by that fucking loser as an other, a thing, was that Andrew, at least for one night, was then marked as a victim.

Andrew says, "It's him. He buzzed his head. He's older and

more than fifty pounds heavier, and that bloated up his face and everything, so I didn't see it right away, but Christ it's him. Redmond is Jeff O'Bannon. You know who I'm talking about, right?"

"Yes, of course. Yes." Eric furrows his brow and Andrew can't tell if Eric remembers O'Bannon and/or recognizes Redmond is the same guy. "Um, okay, you might be right."

"Might be?"

"I mean, I don't see it but—"

"How can you not see it?"

"—but if you say it's him, then it's him. I believe you." Eric won't meet Andrew's eyes.

Andrew sighs. "Dammit, I'm telling you it's him. I would know, Eric."

"Yes, yes, of course you would."

Adriane says, "Hey, guys? We don't have time for this? We need you to make the choice?" Her statements are questions.

"Wait, hold on," Sabrina says, and her weapon wilts in her hands. "What are you saying Redmond did?"

Andrew says, "Going on thirteen years ago I was in a Boston bar with a friend and your guy—totally unprovoked—snuck up behind me, called me a faggot, and smashed a bottle over my head, knocking me out and cutting me open." Andrew spies Wen watching him. Her empty expression breaks open as she flinches and blinks hard twice.

Adriane says, "Oh shit . . ."

Sabrina exhales sharply, distending her cheeks.

Adriane says, "Hey, you're not, you know, making that up, to get us to—?" She stops talking as though the question mark is worth a thousand more words.

He considers telling them to take a good look at his scar that runs from the base of his skull down the back of his neck, but he doesn't want to risk their closer inspection now that his hands are finally loose enough within the ropes to wriggle free. He spent his waking hours in the dark last night flexing and unflexing his fingers, twisting and bending his wrists. It's no longer a question of if he can free his hands, but when should he?

Andrew says, "I'm not lying or making any of this up. And Redmond is the guy who attacked me. I've never been more sure of anything in my life. How about one of you go out to the deck and find his wallet, his license, and read his name? It'll be Jeff O'Bannon."

Sabrina says, "I'm not calling you a liar, Andrew. I believe you're not making up the getting assaulted—"

"He does have that nasty-ass scar on the back of his neck," Adriane says, pointing at Andrew, and backs away from him to stand between the others.

Leonard's shoulders are slumped. Some unseen great weight is pushing him down. "Andrew, you told Wen your scar was from getting hit with a baseball bat when you were a kid."

"Huh? Wait. How—?" Andrew sputters and looks at Wen. She doesn't look back, as immobile and blank faced as a mannequin. He doesn't know what to say to her other than he's sorry, he's sorry for everything in the world.

Leonard says, "Wen told me. So which one of you is telling the truth?"

"Both of us. I'm telling you what happened *and* what she told you is what I told her." Andrew says to Wen, "I didn't want you to know that a terrible, awful person did this to me. I didn't want you to know there were those kinds of people out there." Andrew makes sure to dramatically glare at each of the three others before continuing. "Not yet, anyway." He'd planned on telling her the truth about his scar when she was older, when she could understand. He'd irrationally hoped he could somehow put off indefinitely the future day on which she would recognize cruelty, ignorance, and injustice were the struts and pillars of the social order, as unavoidable and inevitable as the weather.

Leonard says, "I get it and I don't blame you at all. And listen, I believe you're not making it up. But isn't it possible that Redmond only resembles—"

"No. It's him. I guarantee it." Andrew can see that ratty, skinny weasel he watched squirm in the courtroom, grow older and bulk up before his eyes, transforming into the troll-like Redmond. There is no doubt. He will not allow for it.

Andrew closes his hands into fists, clenching some of the rope, hopefully giving the appearance his restraints are still tight and secure should one of them walk behind him.

Adriane says in a lowered voice, like she's trying it out, "I guess Redmond got his then."

Sabrina groans and goes chest to chest with Leonard. "Fuck. Fuck! Jesus, Leonard, did you know this, any of this about Redmond?"

"What? No. No, of course not. And I'm not calling Andrew a liar but maybe it's not—"

"What do you know about him?"

"I know as much as you do. I know him as well as I know you two. And I thought—we really don't have time for this." He pauses and Sabrina doesn't move, doesn't release him. "I thought like you thought: he was rough around the edges and stuff but was basically a good guy."

"Seriously? It was pretty obvious he wasn't. At best he was an obnoxious dick," Adriane says.

Sabrina says, "You and him were there on the message board before I found it, before Adriane got there—"

"A message board?" Andrew shouts and he means it to sound like an aha accusation or vindication. A fucking online message board. Maybe the others aren't religious lunatics and maybe they are, but they are certainly regular, nondenominational lunatics with—as Eric had phrased earlier—a shared delusion. Andrew recalls reading about a uniquely twenty-first-century mental-health crisis with a growing population of people suffering from clinically paranoid, psychotic delusions deciding to ignore professional help and cut themselves off from friends and family. These people are instead seeking emotional support online where they have found hundreds, even thousands, of like-minded people (many of whom refer to themselves as "targeted individuals" or "TIs") on social media and yes, on message boards. Online, the delusion sufferer is not told what she is experiencing is a chemical lie or the result of misfiring synapses and she is not accused of being crazy. The online groups reinforce and validate the delusions because the same thing is happening to them. There was a man who recently shot and killed three people on an army base in Louisiana; he had been part of a large online group of TIs who blogged and posted YouTube videos explaining how a shadow government was stalking them and using mind-control weapons in an attempt to destroy their lives.

Andrew wonders if proving to the three intruders that Redmond isn't who they thought he might be, that he isn't like them, isn't one of them—*them* being some quasi-pious, noble group of would-be humanity savers—would allow doubt to create cracks and fissures spidering through the group delusion? All three of them are clearly unnerved by the bar-attack accusation, and Sabrina and Adriane appear to be openly struggling with what they've done and whatever it is they are supposed to do next. Doubt is good, right? Or will it make them more desperate and dangerous, more likely to become violent and lash out in defense of their beliefs? Andrew loosens his fists and lets the rope out of his clenched fingers for a moment, double-checking that he will indeed be able to free his hands.

Sabrina says, "Yes, a message board." Then to Leonard, "How long were you—?"

Leonard says, "I set it up, like one of my visions told me to, and Redmond was the first to get there but he was there only, like, a few hours before you. We didn't talk about anything you couldn't read yourselves after you joined. And he never said anything outright hateful."

"Did you and him talk on the phone or anything?"

"No, never."

Adriane says, "Redmond was the one who first said he had the vision of the name of the lake and the town."

Leonard asks, "Maybe, okay, I guess so, but what are you saying? What are you implying?"

Eric, who has been conspicuously silent, raises his voice to interrupt, and winces as he does so. "She's implying that your Redmond picked out this place purposefully."

Andrew adds, "And he picked it out because Redmond knew we were going to be here. Or most importantly to him, that I was going to be here."

Leonard says, "That's impossible. Even if—how could he find that out? It's not like that. We all had the visions. Sabrina, Adriane, me: we saw this cabin, too. You saw it, didn't you? You both said you did."

Sabrina and Adriane nod their heads affirmative and then peel away from Leonard's orbit and away from each other, spreading into the room.

Leonard says, "We saw the lake, this little red cabin. We saw where this place was." He pauses and points at the front door. "I saw the dirt road and the front of the cabin; I even saw the grain of the wood on the front door. It was like I'd known it my whole life, and I knew there would be a family here, a very special one. And the family would have to make the choice, would have to make a sacrifice to save us all." He ping-pongs between looking at Sabrina and Adriane. "Now don't let it get all turned around. I know, this sucks, all of it, and I'm sick to my stomach over it. But we'll all get past it because the suffering here is not eternal. It's a test. We were chosen and we're being tested. All of us. You, too, Andrew, Eric, and Wen, and if we don't pass this most difficult and important of all tests, the world is going to end.

"And as far as Redmond goes. Maybe"—he turns and holds a hand out to Andrew—"maybe it's not him. You said yourself thirteen years have passed and he's, what, more than fifty pounds heavier?"

"I know it's him! I'm not—"

"I know, I know, and maybe it is him. I don't know if Redmond is his real name or not, and I don't mean to belittle what happened to you, but does it matter in terms of what we have to do here?"

Sabrina goes red-faced and shouts, "Of course it matters! If I had known he'd done that to Andrew or to anyone, I wouldn't have—" She stops.

Eric says, "You wouldn't have what?"

"I was going to say that I wouldn't have come here. But it's not true because I didn't choose to come here. This is not my choice. I—I already tried to ignore the visions and messages and I tried to stay home and I tried not to come out here and it didn't work. The day before I was supposed to fly out I didn't set my alarm or pack or do anything to get ready. I didn't even tell work I was going to be out. And then it was the next morning and there I was sitting in a cab halfway to LAX."

Adriane says, "Same," and laughs an odd little laugh, high pitched and chittering. "Isn't this a fucking pickle?"

Eric says, "You don't want to be here, so let us go. You don't have to do this anymore. You know you don't."

Sabrina lifts her weapon, recalibrating, reconsidering. It rises like a buoy in an ocean swell.

"Sabrina," Leonard says, "I know you are not who O'Bannon was—regardless if Redmond is the same guy—and Adriane is not O'Bannon, and I am not O'Bannon. We were called to be here as a force of good. I know this to be true. I feel it in my cells. I think you do, too. I said it before, we are not here with hate or judgment in our hearts. We're here with love for everyone, for all humankind. We're willing to sacrifice our own lives in the hope that we might save everyone else."

Eric says, "No," repeatedly, and then, "Just let us go. Please? Let us go . . ."

Andrew stares hard at Eric and Eric stares back. Can Andrew somehow communicate that the ropes are loose around his wrists with a look?

Leonard says, "I only said it doesn't matter if Redmond was Andrew's attacker because what any of us might've done in the past will not change this moment or what happens next. The past, all of our pasts, will be wiped away. What matters is we're here now and why we're here. What matters is passing this test. We were chosen, all of us, for a reason. That is what matters and I'm not going to question that. We can't."

Eric says, "No, you should be questioning it. That's exactly what you should be doing."

Andrew says, "Don't you recognize how wrong this is? Look

at us tied up here. Really look at us. Is this right or normal? Is this what young nurses, chefs, and guys right out of college do on the weekends? How about you go have a look at the guy you mashed to a pulp out on the deck, tell me that's not wrong." He regrets mentioning their killing Redmond/O'Bannon, as though not speaking of the act prevents them from more killing.

Leonard says, "If you and Eric can find a way to make the right choice, sacrifice one of yourselves, then the world will live and that means Wen will live, too. Don't you want her to—"

Eric says, "Enough, that's enough. Stop talking. I can't, just stop . . ."

The room goes quiet, as though the silence is planned, allotted. Outside the cabin, unseen birds chirp and sing their evolutionary songs as the sun creeps higher in the blue morning sky that keeps watch over the lake and its still, dark, and cold water. Andrew knows he must make a move to escape from the chair soon. But with hands that are stiff and numb, he doesn't know if he'll be able to untie his legs before the others descend upon him.

Sabrina coughs. "I think we're running out of time."

"It's me running out of fucking time." Adriane bends forward, and each percussive sob is leaden with grief, a hidden scream. "We have to do something to get them to choose and choose now."

Leonard says, "I know. We're trying—"

"Try more! Try fucking harder! Threaten to hurt one of them, bust a knee, take off a finger, something. Not seriously hurt them, but enough to know this is serious!"

"Adriane!" Sabrina steps between her and Andrew and Eric.

Andrew's sour and curdling stomach plummets through the floor, to the center of the shrinking earth, as his traitorous head fills with images of them cutting off Eric's fingers or Wen's, one by one. He looks at Wen and she remains huddled on the couch, half covered by a blanket. She has shut down. Perhaps she's in shock.

"It'll be the only way!" Adriane is full-throat yelling. "We have to get this shit done! They'll just wait us out until all of us die if we don't!"

Leonard strides forward, a rolling boulder filling a narrowing cave. "We can't let you hurt them. You know we can't. It's not allowed."

"Fuckin' easy for you to say. You're not next, are you? I don't want my body stuffed under a blanket and stacked next to that piece of shit out there. I don't want to die!"

Sabrina crouches and calmly says, "They'll believe us. They will."

"No, they don't, and they won't. Not ever."

"Shh, they will. You'll see. They will."

Adriane's words come in clipped bursts between hitching inhales. "The worst part is I knew I was dead as soon as I started seeing all this shit. I knew I was dead already."

Adriane is still bent over and crying. Sabrina crouches and whispers and cajoles. Leonard checks his watch, and while he utters vague reassurances to them, he has the resigned, desperate, and committed look of a person who knows everything is going poorly and will continue to go poorly no matter what.

Adriane straightens up, pushes Sabrina and Leonard away, and wipes the tears off her cheeks violently. "Okay. I'm okay. I lost it, but I'm good." She takes two steps toward Eric and Andrew. "Hey, so you know I'm dead meat—"

Leonard says, "Adriane, you can't—"

She turns on Leonard and snarls at him. "Shut your fucking mouth. It's my turn. It's up to me and I'm going to do it my way.

All right? Is that all right?" She doesn't give Leonard or Sabrina a chance to respond. "So what's it going to be? Another calamity like the earthquakes and tsunamis and hundreds, thousands more people dying, this time by plague. That'll be fun, yeah? Plus the bonus of the unpleasant sight of little old me getting bashed like a piñata. Or will you stop it all from happening and sacrifice one of yourselves?" She pulls a white mesh mask out of a back pocket. It looks exactly like the one Redmond pulled over his own head. Unhinged and wild-eyed, she shakes and dangles the mask in front of Andrew and Eric. "Come on. What's it going to be? You want me to put it on first?" She stuffs her right fist inside and holds it like a puppet that's going to say something obnoxious, scandalous, something only a puppet would be allowed to say. "There you go. You pick. One of you sacrifices yourself or all kinds of other people die." She makes crashing noises and pantomimes striking the mask-covered fist.

Andrew shakes his head and groans because he thinks he has waited too long to free his hands. So does he wait even longer? Wait them out like Adriane intimated? Are they really going to kill Adriane like they killed O'Bannon? Are they that committed to their obviously Revelations-inspired rituals? He still doesn't know why they are killing themselves. And at some point they would have to stop killing each other and turn on Eric or Andrew or Wen, wouldn't they?

Eric says, "Hold on! Wait, wait, wait!" He's loud enough that Adriane slows her cricket's bounce from her heels to her toes. She takes the mask off her hand and hides it behind her back, like no one was supposed to see it. He says, "Let's just keep talking, okay? Adriane, tell us about the restaurants you worked at. I want to hear about them."

Sabrina says, "Guys, this is it. You have to choose."

"There's time, there's time. Come on, let's talk a little while longer, okay?" Eric's deep, smooth voice has the faintest waver. He is obviously stalling with how he's trying to engage the others into talking about themselves and their old lives. They aren't answering him and they close in toward one another, clustering like molecules.

Andrew imagines everyone in the cabin is visualizing the same blow-by-blow transgression of violence to come, an act of collective foretelling, or summoning. The room feels like it did in the moments before the others killed O'Bannon. Andrew experiences an animal foreboding and an instinctual compulsion to flee from the inevitability, as well as an unsettling, vertiginous itch to become a willing participant. If the others swing their weapons again, even if only against Adriane, he will raise his hands and fight.

Andrew says, "Wen, you should come be with one of us now, I think." Wen is on the couch not looking at anyone or anything.

Leonard turns and says to her, "You can stay there, too. You can cover your eyes with your blanket. You'll be okay."

Andrew shouts, "Right, it'll all be fine! After a little bludgeoning, maybe you'll let her go outside and play with the grasshoppers."

Adriane says, "Our last chance, fellas. What'll it—"

Wen erupts into high-pitched screams of the kind she's only ever unleashed when suffering great, incomprehensible pain. "The grasshoppers! The grasshoppers! The grasshoppers!" She kicks away the blanket and spasms off the couch. She stands and trembles with her arms held out begging for someone to hold her, to take her. After the initial torrent, she is crying so hard no sound comes out; silent open mouth, wet cheeks, beseeching eyes. She remains soundless long enough for Andrew to worry she's stopped breathing, as he unconsciously holds his own breath. Then, finally a guttural, gasping inrush of air and she resumes screaming.

"They're in the jar! I left them! In the sun! They're gonna die! They're all gonna be dead! I'm sorry, I didn't mean to, I forgot. Daddy, I forgot! I forgot!" She runs unsteadily to Eric and scrambles into his lap.

Everyone says her name and there's a group murmur asking her to slow down and tell them what's wrong. The others form a semicircle around Wen and Eric, but none of them reach out for her, as though she's not safe to touch.

Wen grabs fistfuls of Eric's T-shirt and yells into his face. "I left it on the grass and ran inside because I was scared! The jar is still out there! You have to let me go get it! I have to check. Let them out if they're still alive. Maybe they're still alive! Let me go get them please, please, please!"

Leonard bends and leans forward, trying to get in her sight line. "Wen? Wen, honey? It's okay. I let them out. I did. After you ran inside, I let them out of the jar. They all hopped away. They're all happy."

"Daddy, he's lying. He's a liar. They're still there. There are seven in the jar. I wrote down their names. We have to let them out! I don't want them to die! I don't want them to be dead! Please! Let's go! Now! Please, Daddy!"

Wen dissolves in teary *pleases* and *Daddys*, and pounds on Eric's chest, her fists demanding why isn't he up and going outside with her already? Eric says, "Okay, okay," and wiggles and shifts his seated position, struggling to keep her balanced on his lap, and then his arms hesitantly appear from behind the chair, unfurling like great, unused wings. The skin of his hands and wrists is red, excoriated, and raw. He wraps his arms around her quivering form, and he kisses the top of her head and is crying now himself.

The others do a group double take at Eric's arms releasing from the ropes and releasing so casually. Sabrina and Leonard lay their weapons on the floor and share quizzical looks.

Adriane covers her face and whisper-yells, "We can't even tie a fucking knot right. Should've brought duct tape like Redmond said."

Sabrina places a hand on Eric's shoulder, like a friend might in a vulnerable moment. Leonard pokes and taps Eric's other shoulder and asks him, politely, to let his daughter go. Adriane bounces between the two suggesting Leonard pull his arms apart and Sabrina grab Wen.

Eric shouts at the others to leave them alone, to go away, to give them a minute, a minute more.

With the others frantic and occupied, the time for Andrew's escape has to be now. He doesn't hesitate. He calmly shrugs and lifts his right shoulder, a movement as innocuous and ordinary as a breath expanding within his chest. As his shoulder rises, he slides his right hand up. There's a pull, pinch, and burn on his palm and at the base of his thumb, and then his right hand is free. The rest of the binding sloughs off his left hand and wrist. The thud of rope hitting the floor is louder than he anticipated, but the others don't react to it. Andrew brings his arms around to his front, careful to not stretch them out wide, confining them to the width of the chair and his torso. He rests his hands and forearms on his thighs momentarily and flexes his swollen, chaffed fingers and knuckles. His hands are unable to fully close into fists. Andrew bends and reaches toward his feet and ankles, making no sudden movements, nothing to catch the corners of eyes, nothing to alert the others to his Houdini act. He is composed and considerate as he goes about the serious business of untying the leg ropes. The knots behind his calves are thick and obvious, and they give away their secrets to his battered fingers. Andrew does not look up and to his left until after the knots are solved.

The others are still struggling with Eric. His arms remain stubbornly locked around Wen. Not even Leonard is going to be able to simply pull his arms apart. Sabrina begs Eric to let go. Adriane has both hands on one of Eric's wrists and forearms, yanking and trying to peel an arm open. Leonard argues with Adriane, telling her to calm down and to let go of Eric's arm as he tries to snake his hands between Wen and Eric.

Wen yells, "Go away!" and windmills her arms, striking out at Leonard.

As Andrew gives in to haste and hurry while unwinding the never-ending loops of rope from his legs, he visualizes two potential paths to the SUV and the gun in the trunk compartment. The shortest path would be through the front door, but he'd have to wade through the others and take time to unlock the door, but if he could get outside, he'd be unimpeded to the SUV. The path of least resistance out of the cabin would be through the deck slider, but it's a much longer run down those wooden stairs, around the cabin, and to the driveway. One or more of the others would most certainly be out the front door and to the SUV before he could get there. Maybe if he is stealthy enough, he can sneak out onto the deck without the others seeing. Andrew stands on the creaky, rusty legs of the Tin Man and readies for a dash through the back slider.

Adriane points and yells, "Fuck you," at Leonard. She shuffles into the center of the room and stands directly in front of Andrew. They share a surprised, head-tilted look. Adriane yells, "Hey!" and lunges at him.

Andrew slide-steps and knocks his chair onto its side, then kicks it into Adriane's legs. She stumbles and plunges forward, her hands pressing on the inverted chair back to keep from falling to the floor.

Sabrina grabs Andrew's left arm and he spins to face her with his painful, crumpled-paper fists raised. She unexpectedly grunts, winces, and collapses onto her knees. Eric is behind her, still sitting and with one arm around Wen, and he gives Sabrina another backhanded kidney punch. She crawls away from Eric's reach, a hand pressed against her lower back.

Eric switches the arm with which he holds Wen and throws left jabs at Leonard's midsection. Leonard clumsily fends off the blows from Eric's pistoning arm with open hands. One punch catches him in the groin and he staggers back into one of the bedroom doorways.

Eric shouts, "Andrew, take Wen and go! Take her!"

Leonard recovers and approaches Eric from his left. Adriane has already discarded the chair-in-her-legs obstacle, but instead of going after Andrew she renews her grappling with Eric.

Eric alternates throwing quick punches at Adriane and Leonard while shielding Wen.

Adriane yells, "Hit him, Leonard! Hit him in the head!"

Leonard says, "We don't want to hurt you," and attempts to snare Eric's left arm when it lashes out.

Sabrina is upright now, too, has her weapon, and steps toward Andrew.

Andrew can't fight off all three at once. Not without his gun. He lunges for the front door, pulls the latch bolt to the right, turns the knob, and flings the door open wide all in one motion. With a rush of warm air and sunlight the door opens too wildly and the momentum of the pendulous swing almost sends him tumbling back into the cabin. He maintains his grip on the doorknob, leans all his weight forward, and stumbles outside, pulling the door shut behind him. His slow and heavy feet cannot catch up with his forward lean and he pitches down the small set of stairs, landing chest and face first on the grass.

His breaths are painful and short, air squeezing out of the pinched end of a balloon. He blinks away the shock and unsteadily restacks himself onto shaky legs. Once upright he starts the forward-moving engine again.

The cabin's front door opens behind him. Sabrina yells, "Andrew, stop! Come back!"

Andrew doesn't stop and he doesn't look to see if anyone else is with her. The SUV is ten to fifteen yards away. The driver's-side front and rear tires are flat and the side walls have been slashed. He assumes the other tires have been slashed as well. That car isn't going anywhere.

His right hand goes into his shorts pocket in search of the familiar lump of his car keys. They're not there. He remembers that he gave Eric the keys yesterday when the others were breaking into the cabin. If the car doors are locked, he won't be able to get to the gun and he doesn't know what he will do, what he can do.

Andrew races onto the gravel driveway, the loose stones part and grind under his feet, spewing clouds of dirt. The stomped-on-gravel crunch is too loud, all encompassing, like a mob is sprinting across the driveway, but he won't look back, can't look back. Maybe Sabrina has caught up to him. Maybe she isn't alone. He's almost to the passenger-side door that he'll open because it has to open, not opening is not an option, and then he'll jump inside the car and lock the doors, which will give him time to crawl into the backseat and to the trunk—

Something sharp and heavy crashes into the outside of his

right knee, which buckles and sings with jagged, white-hot agony. Andrew falls and bounces off the car door, absorbing most of the collision with his forearms and hands, before landing on his screaming knee. He flips over into a sitting position with his back against the car and faces Sabrina.

Sabrina stands over him and says, "You can't leave them. You can't leave us. We all need you. Come back inside. I'll help you," in an oddly detached, unearthly monotone. She lifts her weapon, raising the tapered edge of the curled-over and pointed shovel blade, appearing to reload for another swing despite her promise of help.

Andrew scoops up a fistful of gravel and dirt and he underhand throws it into her face. With her eyes closed and head turned to the side, he scrambles up onto his left knee and punches her in the stomach. An almost comical *oof* plumes out of Sabrina and she folds in half. He tries to snatch the weapon away but she falls backward, landing on her butt, one hand over her midsection, the other on the weapon, holding it so as to ward off more blows.

Andrew pivots and he flips up the car door handle. He grunts in triumph as it's not locked and the door clicks open. He slithers inside the SUV, coiling himself into the passenger seat, shutting and locking the door behind him. The pain in his right knee has dulled some but is now focused on the inner side, not where the weapon contacted him. Already swollen to twice its normal size, the knee is wobbly and as loose as a door hinge when he puts weight on it.

Sabrina rocks herself up into a standing position. She's hunched over, still holding her midsection, and gasping for air. She shambles to the SUV and, in a matter of moments, she will smash windows with that goddamn nightmare stick.

Andrew shimmies between the front bucket seats and worms

over the center console into the back, dragging his right leg behind instead of relying on it to propel him. His right foot snags between the console and passenger seat and while pulling it free doesn't exactly hurt, his stomach flips at how unstable and putty-like his knee is.

Sabrina's shovel blade clangs off the rear passenger window. The glass doesn't break but there's a gouge and crack dowsing a haphazard path to the window frame.

Hand over hand Andrew scrabbles over the middle of the backseat, where there is no headrest. It's still a tight, awkward squeeze to pull his torso over the seat back so that he can hang into the trunk area. The side panel storage is to his right. He paws at two black plastic knobs, turns them clockwise to six o'clock, and pulls away the plastic hatch.

The window to his left disintegrates, and jagged little glass cubes sting his bare lower legs and a handful ricochet off the rear windshield and roll around in the trunk. Andrew spasms, ducks his head between his shoulders and behind raised arms. With the window gone, Sabrina's rough and greedy gasps for air suffuse into the car. Andrew mule-kicks his left leg behind him. He yells and his body tenses up for another strike from Sabrina, anticipating the pain to come.

Within the opened side panel is his handgun safe. Less than a year old and not much bigger than an eight-hundred-page hardcover book, it's a the-future-is-now, aluminum alloy silver gadget with a sleek, edgeless design. Eric joked that it looked like a panini maker and asked if it could make him a tuna melt. The newest, lightest model he could find at the time of purchase, it's biometric, opening after the sensor on the top reads the owner's palm or thumb print.

Andrew extracts the gunbox out of the interior darkness of the side panel, dumps it onto the trunk floor, and waves his palm over the sensor. The cover opens on its minihydraulic arms. Inside, splayed on the black neoprene lining, are his snub-nosed .38 special, loose bullets, and a small cardboard ammunition box, the top flap tattered and open, which must've happened during transport or as the unit was roughly jostled from the storage panel.

Sabrina has the car door open. "Leave whatever it is you're going after. Get out of the car and come back inside. I don't want to hurt you."

Can she see the gunbox or the gun? Probably not from where she is standing and with his body likely blocking her view of the trunk. Andrew snatches the gun with his right hand. It's compact but solid, fitting purposefully into the folds of palm and fingers, which have lost some of their stiffness from the fight with O'Bannon and a day of disuse. With one hand he presses a thumb piece forward and pushes down on the cylinder until it swings open to the left. He shakily begins loading bullets into the five chambers.

Sabrina jabs him in the left side, the rusty tip of metal digging under his ribs. Andrew yelps, twitches, and tries to curl away from the repurposed spade, but he's bottled in by the adjacent rear headrest. He knocks the gunbox over, spilling the contents. The bullets scatter and roll to all corners madly eager for movement and to achieve their projectile apotheosis on their own. The jab from Sabrina hurts, but there isn't much oomph behind it, as maybe she doesn't have enough leverage given the constraints of the confined enclosing of the SUV interior or she's hesitant and isn't sure what to do to get him to come back inside the cabin and hasn't fully committed to stabbing him with a bizarre, customized weapon as the solution.

Andrew yells as though he's in more pain than he is and kicks out behind him, connecting only with the back of the front passenger seat. He plucks one last stray, teasing bullet from the trunk floor and fills the fifth and final chamber.

Sabrina says, "You have to come back inside, we don't have time for this," and jabs him again with the weapon and with more force, the tip prodding painfully between his ribs.

He closes the cylinder and pushes off the trunk floor with his left arm. With both arms outstretched over his head he sinks back onto his haunches, like a dive into water reversed, pulling his chest over the seat back. He twists and sags against the other rear passenger door. Sabrina is crouched within the opposite doorframe, her hands slid farther up the length of the wooden staff, a Little Leaguer choking up on a bat.

Andrew fires a wild, nominally aimed shot, the report ear-ringing loud. His aim is too high and the bullet chunks into the ceiling above the thicker metal of the SUV's doorframe.

Andrew and Sabrina look at each other for a beat, sharing in the surprise, lunacy, and possibility of the moment. Sabrina cowers and then looks over her head, as though the missed shot might bring the sky crashing down on top of her.

Andrew points the gun and says, "Drop that thing and back the fuck up."

She says, "Okay, I'm sorry. Okay . . ." She doesn't drop the weapon. She shuffles backward, and too quickly, so she's far enough away that his view of her is obscured by the SUV's interior and frame.

Andrew shouts at her to stop moving and slides across the backseat, his bare legs scratched by bits of shattered window. His left side stings where he was jabbed twice and his shirt is warmly damp with blood. His swollen knee throbs with a low but constant ache and is already turning an inky, storm cloud purple. The pain is bearable, but he's unsure if the leg will hold his weight.

By the time he's to the edge of the rear seat, his legs dangling over the gravel driveway, Sabrina is a blur, running away to the left.

He shouts, "Stop! Stop right now!" Using the open door, he pulls himself up so that he stands on his left leg. He lowers his right foot onto the ground and slowly adds weight. His knee holds.

Sabrina is twenty or so paces away, legs pumping, and her bulky weapon swaying side to side. She's close to being able to duck around a corner of the cabin and out of his sight. He yells at her to stop again, and when she doesn't, he steps to the right to avoid shooting over the car door or having to crouch to shoot through the smashed window. He takes a deep breath and aims low, for her legs, and as he unconsciously replants his right foot and fires a shot, his knee gives out, bowing outside his profile, insisting upon continuing in the lateral direction. The shot misses, the report echoing over the lake and within their little bowl of forest, and Andrew falls.

Sabrina is gone, disappearing around the side of the cabin. Is she going to run into the woods and hide or is she going all the way out back and to the deck or up through the basement and then back inside to warn and help the others? Will the others come outside now after hearing the gunfire?

"Fuck, fuck, fuck!" Andrew thrashes about on the ground as though he is drowning until he muscles onto his feet. He decides he doesn't have time to wait for the self-opening pneumatic rear gate to open or to crawl back inside the car and root around for more ammunition. He's already left Eric and Wen alone with the others for too long. Will the others be more inclined to hurt Eric and/or Wen because they heard one if not both gunshots?

He tests a forward step on his gimpy knee. It quivers, as loose as a Slinky, but he remains upright. He takes a second step, and then a third, and he makes a deal with his knee; it will continue to function as long as he walks only in a straight line and doesn't move brashly to either side.

Back on the front lawn and without the sound of gravel shifting under his feet, the abrupt silence is a new terror. The cabin, even with the benefit of the morning's wholesome sunlight, appears worn, tired, and bereft. The paint on the door and trim is dulled and sun bleached. The wooden shingles are blemished with dots of mildew and are loose and as asymmetrical as crooked teeth. The cabin is now a haunted house, baptized by yesterday's violence, and its passive accumulation of similarly vicious and desperate acts is as inevitable as dust gathering on the windowsills.

Even with the windows locked shut and front door closed, shouts, grunts, and the wooden thuds and knocks of physical struggle emanate from inside the cabin. His hybrid run/limp across the grass to the front stairs is as long and lonely as a doomed expedition. He passes Wen's grasshopper jar; sunlight flares off the glass and aluminum lid (screwed on tightly) as though saying *see me, see me*. Lying on its side and sunk into the taller grass, the earth is already absorbing it, consuming the evidence of its existence. He oddly hoped Leonard wasn't lying about setting the grasshoppers free. It's possible he let them go and resealed the lid, but unlikely. That Andrew finds the jar glinting sunlight and most certainly containing the dead bodies of Wen's seven named grasshoppers seems a cruelly mocking harbinger.

Andrew clambers up the cement front stairs, loading both feet on one step before moving on to the next. Lifting and bending his right knee is exponentially more painful than when walking straight and on flat ground. Once on the landing, he hears Eric yelling inside the cabin, "Stay away! Leave us alone!" and it sounds like he's on the left side of the common room.

Andrew leans, pressing his shoulder against the doorframe, allowing his right leg to rest a moment. He wraps his left hand around the doorknob, and before turning it, he quickly attempts to work out what he'll say or do or see after the door opens. He cannot open the door and start shooting indiscriminately. The rash first shot fired at/near Sabrina inside the SUV unnerved him as he doesn't remember actively deciding to shoot. It just happened.

Andrew closes his eyes and flattens his body against the door; he's as close to being inside the cabin as he can be without actually being in it. Adriane yells about not wanting to die. Leonard tells Eric to stop swinging and let's talk. He says, "Eric, let's talk," repeatedly. Leonard's voice is muffled, an echo across the canyon of the common room.

Andrew holds the gun up near his face so he can swing the arm down and instantly point it into the room. He takes a deep breath, turns the knob, and the door opens, the cabin greedy for his reentrance. Andrew lurches inside and he lowers the gun in front of him. No one seems to notice he's there.

Eric is to his left, stationed in front of Wen's bedroom doorway. His left leg is free, but his right leg is snared in twisted, stretched-out rope still attached to a fallen chair on the floor trailing behind him. He swings Adriane's flower-of-hand-shovel-and-trowel-blades-tipped staff in sweeping, menacing arcs. An inefficient machine, he sweats through his shirt and breathes in gulping hitches. His shoulders sagging and his spine curved, he grimaces before and after each swipe and whoosh of the weapon.

Leonard stands in front of the couch and the darkened TV on the wall. He says, "Everyone, let's calm down. Let's talk, this isn't good for anyone," in that insufferable I'm-just-trying-to-help tone. It's instantly clear to Andrew that Leonard—despite all the earlier talk about how they were running out of time—is perfectly content to let Eric work himself to total exhaustion. Leonard has his dual-tipped wooden staff, the one O'Bannon brought into the cabin, but he does not brandish it. It's hidden behind his back like the world's worst-kept secret.

If Eric is a cornered lion tamer, then Adriane is the lion, stalking, pacing, and darting forward at Eric and then skittering back when he swings what was once her staff. She has a steak knife in each hand, the blades thin but serrated. The knives appear comically small and ineffectual compared to the other weapons.

Andrew strays from the doorway, deeper into the room. Everyone else finally sees him. They stop moving and talking and they gape. Eric sways in place and he blinks like he doesn't believe what he's seeing or he's seeing something that isn't there. He lowers the bladed end of the weapon to the floor and holds his forehead with his right hand. Andrew can't tell if this is an expression of relief or anguish.

Andrew points the gun in the general shared direction of Leonard and Adriane. He wants to yell and scream and threaten and hurt; he yearns for both of them to hurt for this.

He says, "Drop the knives," to Adriane.

She screams with her mouth closed, a terrifying sound, one that makes Andrew fear that he is nowhere near in control despite the gun.

"Drop them now! Or I swear—"

She exaggeratedly opens her hands and the knives clatter against the hardwood floor.

"All right." Andrew takes a deep breath and alternates pointing the gun at Adriane and Leonard. "Where is Wen?"

Leonard says, "She's okay—"

"I'm not talking to you! Eric, where is she?"

Eric points behind him, and Wen appears in the bedroom doorway. Her eyes are puffy and red, her cheeks streaked with dirt and tears. Her thumbs have retreated inside the home of her fists. Her fists seek sanctuary next to her mouth.

A warm gust of wind at Andrew's back locomotives through the front entrance, across the common room, and rattles the deck's screen slider. Andrew is reminded that Sabrina is still out there and could be sneaking up behind him at any time. He tosses quick and uneasy looks to the front yard. He will not close the door, even though he probably should. Being reconfined to the cabin's space is not an option.

Leonard talks in an almost-whisper, the words too fragile, too strained with disappointment and melancholy to also burden with volume. "You're dooming us all, Andrew. You're dooming Eric and Wen, too."

"I'm done with you. I don't have to listen to another goddamn word you say." He imagines shooting Leonard in the thigh above the knee and the streamer of blood that would spurt out as he's cut to the floor.

"Andrew?"

"Shut your fucking mouth!" He stretches out his arm toward Leonard. The gun doesn't feel heavy, but his fingers twined around the grip and his pointer curled through the trigger guard are stiffening again, and there are twinges of threatening muscle cramps in his forearm.

Leonard doesn't react to the gun being shakily pointed at him. He's more resigned than calm; the one who believes he sees the end coming.

"Andrew?"

It's not Leonard speaking, but Eric. "Andrew? Let's go now.

We can go now. We'll leave them here and we can go." His voice
is hoarse, raspy. How is he going to be able to walk anywhere if
he looks and sounds as bad as that? They could try driving the
SUV on the slashed tires, but it wouldn't be long before the tires
disintegrated and the rims got hopelessly stuck in the dirt road.
It might not even make it out of the driveway and through the
quicksand gravel. They are going to have to walk a big chunk if
not all of the trip out of here, which if they were to walk all the
way to the main road would take upwards of five or six hours.
They could go in the opposite direction, deeper down the road
that snakes along the lakeshore, and search out another cabin
with people or a phone, but the nearest cabin is still miles—

"Andrew?"

"Yeah, all right. We're going to tie these two up first. Only fair,
right?"

Eric nods slowly and closes his eyes. He still has one hand
over his forehead like he's holding something in, keeping it from
escaping.

Adriane asks, "Did you kill Sabrina?" Her hands open, and
arms outstretched, frozen in their I-dropped-the-knives-like-
you-said position. "She wasn't gonna hurt you. We heard the
shots—"

"No. I didn't shoot her." Andrew regrets answering truth-
fully. Why let them think Sabrina might come to help them? He's
screwing this all up. "But that doesn't mean I won't shoot you."

Another breeze flutters into the cabin like a lost spirit and Andrew can't help but take another peek over his shoulder to look
for Sabrina. It's only a glance, one that lasts two seconds at the
most. When he looks back, Adriane is charging at him from a
semicrouched position, teeth bared in a silent snarl and a suddenly not-so-dropped knife raised above her head.

Wen

One Sunday afternoon in late winter Wen's dads asked her to come into their bedroom. They were superserious and had those half-amused, half-sad smiles they wore whenever she would tell them she didn't like Chinese school. They told her there was something important they wanted to show her and talk about. Wen thought she was in trouble because they found out she was sneaking into their bedroom to look through all her baby pictures. She worried if they were mad enough they might not let her watch TV for an hour after dinner or take away her phone; both were things they had threatened but never enacted. She knew going into their room without asking was why they were mad at her, but it was their fault for keeping the pictures in there. She didn't think it was fair those pictures were hidden away when they should be kept somewhere else for easier access, maybe even in her room. They were pictures of her after all. That was what she was going to say after telling them she was sorry for sneaking in and they were through being mad. But this meeting with her dads wasn't about the pictures, not really. This was about Daddy Andrew's gun and the gun safe hidden in the room (he wouldn't say where). He held up a chunky black container the size of a shoebox that had some buttons on a front panel, but he didn't let her look at it for long. They asked her if she'd ever found or seen it. They said she had to promise to tell the truth. She hadn't seen it before. And that was the truth. Daddy Andrew said he got a new gun safe and he showed it to her. It was silver, smaller than the other one, and it looked like a minispaceship. (In the weeks and months after this family meeting, Wen didn't say anything to her friends about having a gun at home, but she did tell Gita and Orvin that one of her dads had a special silver safe he kept in a secret place, and Wen and her friends spent a recess making a game out of guessing what he kept hidden in there.) Daddy Andrew turned around, holding the safe so she couldn't see it, and when he turned back, the top was flipped open like the rear hatch of their car. Inside was a gun. She wasn't sure what it would look like but she imagined it would be bigger, something she would have to hold with two hands. Daddy Andrew said it wasn't loaded but it still was a very, very dangerous thing. Daddy Eric kept saying it wasn't a toy and under no circumstances was she ever to touch the safe or the gun. He kept shaking his head when he talked like this whole thing was a terrible idea. They explained Daddy Andrew had a special license and had taken a lot of classes to learn how to keep and use the gun properly. They never told her why he had it and she didn't ask. They knew she was coming into their room and going under the bed to get her baby pictures. They weren't mad and her looking at the pictures was of course okay; they were going to move the pictures and put them in the hutch out in the living room so she could look at them whenever she wanted. Wen was embarrassed they knew about her sneaking in for the photos, but the embarrassment quickly faded. Daddy Andrew took the gun out of the safe and let it sit in his open hand and it looked bigger and smaller, more real and more fake. Daddy Andrew asked her if she wanted to hold it, but before she could answer yes, Daddy Eric said he changed his mind and he didn't want her touching the gun. Daddy Andrew didn't argue. As he put it back in the safe and shut the lid, they said so many kids got hurt and sometimes killed playing with guns, usually *found* guns that belonged to their parents. They said she wasn't allowed in their bedroom by herself anymore. Daddy Andrew said, "No more snooping around in here." They said, even though it had a special lock and it wouldn't open for her or anyone other than Daddy Andrew, she was never to move or touch the gun safe. They said these new rules were the most important rules ever.

Wen reviews those most important rules and stares at Daddy Andrew and his gun. She wonders where he hid the silver safe. She didn't realize the car had secret places in which to hide things.

Andrew says, "Yeah, all right. We're going to tie these two up first. Only fair, right?"

Adriane asks, "Did you kill Sabrina?" She stands still and with her arms out like a scarecrow, one mad it can't scare everyone away. It's Adriane who scares Wen the most now. Adriane would've clubbed her with the shovel-bladed weapon if Eric hadn't picked up Andrew's chair and knocked the thing out of her hands. Wen wants to tell Daddy Andrew to not listen to her, that she might find a way to hurt him with her words.

"She wasn't gonna hurt you. We heard the shots—"

Andrew says, "No. I didn't shoot her." He pauses and gimps forward half a step. "But that doesn't mean I won't shoot you."

Wen wants to dissolve back into the bedroom so she doesn't have to see anything. She doesn't want to see what Adriane will do when she drops her hands or when her dads tie her to one of the chairs. She doesn't want to see Daddy Andrew shoot the gun.

Wen tries to see outside the front door and to the lawn, but Andrew and the severe angle obscures her view. She again remembers the poor grasshoppers trapped in the jar and how horrible it must've been for them. Did they run out of air and die crawling and knocking into the lid? Did they wind down like little toys on juiceless batteries? Did they, like Daddy Eric said they would, get cooked by the sun, boiling to death inside their own exoskeletons? Maybe they're still alive but barely and they are suffering. It's all her fault and she quickly ticks off the grasshoppers' names in her head, and another crying fit begins to swell.

Andrew looks behind him, as though he hears Wen thinking about the jar left in the grass. As he turns, Wen sees the entire common room splayed before her and the adults animate, one movement begetting the next. She doesn't understand or even have time to react to all of it, but her brain catalogs everything to be parsed and dwelled upon later:

Andrew swivels at the waist, peering over his left shoulder. Adriane drops to one knee, snatches up a knife with her taloned right hand, and launches at Andrew. Leonard sprints away from the couch, triggered by Adriane's springing forward. Andrew spins back around to face the room and Adriane is only one or two steps from being on top of him. Her knife arm is raised triumphantly over her head. Leonard thunders across the room shouting Adriane's name. Andrew fires the gun. There's a pop, or a crack, sounding to Wen like two cars smashing together; its punchy loudness is as jarring as its brevity and the silence that fills the vacuum after. Wen covers her ears. Adriane is stood up, jerked upright, and lifted and pushed onto her heels like the gun spewed out a magic invisible wall. Her shirt is black and there is no visible, telltale red staining the cloth, but the bullet must've hit her somewhere in her now drooping left arm or shoulder. Eric lifts what was once Adriane's weapon and tries to run toward the others, but his foot is still snared in the rope attached to his chair and he trips. He falls hard and lands on top of the weapon. The wooden handle snaps near the base of the jury-rigged flower of blades with a weak, imposter gunshot crack. Leonard is almost to Adriane, and he stretches out a hand toward her. Adriane reraises the knife, but shakily, and her face is cleared of expression and emotion, rubbed out, erased. Andrew fires again. Underpinning the minidetonation of the gunshot, there's a soft, wet, sucking sound. Adriane's throat explodes into a geyser of blood. Leonard is close enough that blood sprays onto his face and the front of his shirt. Her arm drops and so does the knife. Then she falls, too, collapsing to the floor, landing on her back. Blood spurts and pumps from her neck in endless supply. Her gurgles become hisses fading in volume until there's no sound at all. Eric flips onto his back and tries to kick the tangle of rope from his leg. Andrew's mouth hangs open, his upper lip quakes, and his eyes are wide O's. The gun lowers, pointed at the floor or at the dying Adriane. Andrew doesn't initially react to Leonard's changing course, charging past Adriane and at him. Andrew raises his gun but he's too late. Leonard is right on top of him and with both of his hands grabs Andrew's hand and gun. Andrew's arms go above his head, pulled up by Leonard. The crown of Andrew's head is only at Leonard's chin because of the height difference. Andrew grunts and yells and rams his head into Leonard's neck and chest, and he lifts his knees, bouncing them into Leonard's midsection. Leonard doesn't flinch and doesn't let go.

Wen floats out of the doorway and into the common room, gravity sucking her into the orbits of the crashing bodies. She stares down at Adriane. Her eyes are half closed, and the skin of her face is a fancy doll's white, glowing above the gaping red hole of her throat. Her already dark hair is blackened by the expanding pool of blood.

To Wen's right, Eric frantically kicks his tied-up leg, and the attached chair skitters around like a dog happy to see its owner finally returned home. Wen dodges the chair and crouches next to Eric. She taps his leg just above the knee. He sees her and stops kicking. She says, "I can help." She tries sliding her fingers under the coils, but because of Eric's flailing about the rope is wound tight and haphazardly, and she can't find the original knot.

Eric sits up and his hands join Wen's. One of his hands is wet with Adriane's blood and he smears red onto the rope. He doesn't quite push Wen away, but he takes over tugging hard on the lines and pulling out knots and loops hidden within other loops. The rope begins to melt away, the tangled mass unwinding as though his leg is a spool. Wen leans back and sits perched on top of her feet. She folds her hands in her lap. Her fingers are pink with Adriane's blood.

Wen marvels at how much bigger Leonard is than Andrew. Despite the size difference, they continue to wrestle to a stalemate over the gun. Leonard lowers his right shoulder and drives it into Andrew's chest. Andrew twists enough to avoid the brunt of the force, which throws Leonard off-balance, and the two of them crash into the wall next to the doorframe with a cabin-shaking thud. Their arms fall from over their heads like a plummeting castle gate. Their hands swallow up the gun, but as they sweep their arms left and then back right, the black eye of the short, stunted barrel is visible, sunken into the entangled tree roots of their fingers. Leonard twists and slams his weight back into Andrew, pinning him against the wall.

Leonard yells, "Let go! Just let go!"

Wen yells, "You're hurting him! Stop!"

Eric is almost free from the rope and chair.

Andrew's face is red, and his body shrinks under the assault of Leonard's insistent size and strength. Andrew's breaths are coarse and irregular. His feet slide and stab out from behind Leonard, desperate for purchase and a path to freedom, but he isn't going anywhere. Andrew drops suddenly—perhaps purposefully—to his knees as though his ankles and shins are made of thin cardboard and crumple under his weight. Leonard stumbles, loses balance, and bashes the side of his head against the wall's wooden panels. He pops back upright and vigorously attempts to shake the gun free, yanking Andrew's arms up and down, and side to side, and then Wen doesn't see or hear or feel anything anymore.

BLOODY LIKE THE DAY YOU WERE BORN

FIVE

Leonard

Andrew and Eric are with Wen's body. They are huddled on the floor to his left. They hold her. They surround her. They shield her from Leonard. They wail and scream her name, and then they are just screaming.

Moments ago, the gun and Andrew's hands were nested dolls inside Leonard's hands. Andrew was fatigued, weakening, and ready to yield. Leonard felt the waning resistance in Andrew's quivering, failing attempts to push him away. Leonard was going to graciously accept surrender without judgment, without threat of reprisal, and gently guide the gun out of Andrew's hands, and salvage salvation from ruin, but then Andrew wrecking-balled himself to the floor and pulled Leonard off-balance, bouncing his head painfully off the wall. Anger flashed like a bright and hissing road flare. He was not cold, blank, removed. Leonard was not *not-him* as when Redmond was killed. Leonard was as angry as he's ever been and he wrenched and torqued Andrew's arms like he wanted to rip them off, discard them, and tear the rest of the cabin and then the world into irretrievable pieces. Andrew's hands were a fistful of hornets inside Leonard's hands, and he squeezed, trying to crush them all. And when Leonard squeezed, he felt the subtle vibration and click of the trigger under his palms. (Leonard's hands are currently pressed flat against the floor, yet he is still feeling that trigger click, which is now a physical time stamp delineating his brief history into *before* and *after*.) There was the gunshot and the jolt that reverberated up his arms. It was only after Wen fell that he noticed the heat of the passing bullet glowing on his fingers still wrapped around the gun.

Leonard wasn't looking directly at Wen, but in the instant after the gunshot, there was a blooming flower of red, a sunspot in the blur of her face. He wasn't looking directly at Wen, but he saw her fold backward.

He is on all fours and he is crying. His head is down. He will not look at Wen now. He cannot look at what happened to her. He won't. He is a coward and a failure, and he doesn't deserve to see her ever again.

Leonard whispers, "I'm sorry," over and over. He says it out loud and he says it in his head, hoping someone will believe him.

He is still going to do what must be done, what he was asked and then commanded to do. He crawls and Adriane's legs pass below his carriage like the yellow lines of a lonely mountain road. He makes sure to witness and remember every detail of this small journey over the length of her body. This is the first penance of many to come for breaking a promise to a child, for the hubris of issuing the promise in the first place.

Adriane's death, he knew, was a possibility, a probability even. Leonard says, "Sorry," again, and this one, the quietest one, is for Adriane. He is sorry because when she was shot, he felt relief and a spark of joy that the burden of her death was taken away from him; he wouldn't have to kill her like he killed Redmond. That Redmond might have had another name and assaulted Andrew (right now, he believes Andrew) shakes his faith in what he is doing here more than he has let on. But what choice does he really have at this point other than to continue? Continuing is neither brave nor cowardly, and it is both. Having seen what he has seen and felt what he has felt, Leonard puts his faith in the soothing power of having no choice. He reminds himself that he is only a vessel, and an imperfect one, but he fears all that has gone wrong—so terribly, horribly wrong—is his fault and his alone.

Leonard continues to crawl over Adriane's body and his hands sluice through her still-warm blood. His hands have always been bloody and are finally being honest about it. He was born in blood like we all were.

He slides his right hand under Adriane's waist and backside. He retrieves her mesh mask from a back pocket. It is soft and as fragile as a baby bird. He tries to not get blood on the mask, to keep it white for as long as he can. He has the same mask in his pocket, too. He imagines what he will see when it slides over his face. Will he see the world through it or only outlines and dark shapes? Will he no longer see the blood? He wonders if he'll be afforded the opportunity to put the mask on himself or if there will be anyone left alive to fit it over his face after he is dead.

Mask in hand and knees wading deeper into her blood, Leonard crawls until his face is directly above Adriane's. Her throat is a mess of ruined anatomy, still leaking blood and fizzing air bubbles and a coppery odor tinged with the acidity of bile. He does not want to linger on the ragged skin and exposed tissue of the wound, but seeing her turned-to-stone face is worse. Her lips are parted, a door thoughtlessly left open. Her squinty brown eyes are obscured by sagging upper eyelids, one hanging lower than the other. This malfunction of her smallest muscles and the resulting asymmetry is a final indignity, and he already has difficulty recalling what she looked like when she was alive.

Leonard does not want to disturb her head or body. He fears

the mask erases who you were, but he must put it on her. The mask is part of the mysterious, seemingly random ritual he doesn't understand, that was never fully explained beyond vague, dire consequences of incompletion; the ritual must be followed bureaucratically; otherwise, Wen's and Adriane's deaths would be wasted. If they die for naught, what would be the point? At this thought he remembers the cabin's TV hanging on the back wall, that eerie portal to the wider world, and he feels its black screen, that single unwavering eye leering at him. He is afraid to turn on the TV and witness its judgment, but he will have to soon.

He stretches the mask open and slides it over the crown of Adriane's head. There is no maybe about it; he is erasing her with this mask, and it is a blessing, one he hopes he is worthy to receive. Leonard only wants this to be done and then to be taken away from this cabin and never be made to remember the promise he broke. He is careful to not jostle or displace Adriane's head, but his hands were not made for this task and he is rough and clumsy. It takes two attempts to get the mesh over the back of her skull and all that blood-soaked hair. When he finally coaxes it onto her, the mask hugs her face and features, a new simplified skin. Given how much blood is on his hands, the mesh is remarkably white. He has the defiant urge to protest what has happened and all the shitty things he's been made to do and smear a red slash over her mouth and dots over her eyes.

Andrew is now standing next to Leonard and pointing the gun. He shouts, "Fucking get up!" His eyes are glowing coals. His teeth are bared and his cheeks are blotchy red; the blood underneath is eager to come out and be free.

Leonard does not fear the gun. He does not fear for his own safety. That will never again be his concern. Whatever happens to him, he deserves. He says, "I promised Wen she would be okay and I wouldn't let anything happen to her. I'm sorry. I'm so sorry—" This is not the right thing to say and he knows this confession will only torment both Andrew and Eric, but he has to say it; he selfishly has to have it on record. For all the blood already spilled and for all the blood to come, he still meant to keep that promise to Wen for as long as he was standing, until the end of everything.

Andrew pistol-whips the side of Leonard's face, just below the temple. A bright light goes supernova, washing out his view of the room. A stabbing pain quickly morphs into the simmering sting of an open cut and the dull ache of swollen tissue. Leonard falls off his knees and returns to all fours, a reversal of the evolutionary ascent-of-humans pictograph. His hands are again baptized in Adriane's blood. There's a high-pitched tuning fork ring in one ear, and he is gazing into Adriane's masked face when Andrew kicks him in the ribs. Leonard remains prostrate, penitent, and ready to accept more. He deserves this.

Andrew shouts at Leonard to stand up. His shouts degrade into incoherent, larynx-shredding growls. He presses the gun's barrel against Leonard's face in the same spot where he hit him.

Leonard stands up slowly, an electric current of agony splintering through his head. Over Andrew's shoulder he sees Wen's body on the floor and the red on her face and he looks away. He says, "I'm sorry. I'm so sorry . . ."

Tears, spit, and snot stream from Andrew's face. His arm shakes; his whole body is shaking. He hits Leonard with the gun again, smashing his jaw, spinning his head, and redlining the volume of the whine in his ear.

Leonard looks at Wen's body again because he can't help it. He prays for her to get up, yet another prayer of his that won't be answered.

Eric lumbers up from his crouched position by his daughter's side. After two foal-like steps, he stumbles and falls to the floor, blocking Leonard's view of Wen. Eric throws up and he sways and swoons into a sitting position, a line of vomit hanging from his open mouth.

Leonard says, "I'm sorry, I'm sorry, I'm sorry..."

Andrew limps backward, never taking the gun off Leonard, and grabs the chair Eric was tied to. He drags it across the short distance and it tumbles into Adriane's legs. "Sit in that chair. And don't fucking move." He asks Eric, "Are you all right?"

Eric rocks back and forth. His eyes are closed and his head is lost in his hands. He says, "No." His voice is a sigh, as heavy and lonely as a name whispered into an empty room.

Leonard says sorry again and again. He'll be doomed to say sorry for eternity and no one will listen and no one will believe him. He picks up the chair and takes two small steps toward the kitchen so he is not sitting in Adriane's blood. Before placing the chair upright on the floor, he kicks aside a coil of rope with which he tied up Andrew. The rope careens into the end table and wobbles its little yellow-shaded lamp, which spins in two slow, drunken circles, waiting until he places the chair on the floor before going still. He sits, ending the concatenation. He will follow Andrew's instructions. He will not move. He will sit there and he will wait for Andrew to do whatever it is he's going to do.

Andrew goes to Eric and coaxes him onto his feet. Eric says, "We have to leave. We have to take her with us," and they both look behind them at Wen, and they rest their foreheads together, and they break down into more tears, the kind that bow, bend, and mesh the men's bodies into the shapes and symbols of grief.

Andrew breaks from their embrace, is the first to stand upright, and he props up Eric. He whispers in a flash flood of words, "I need your help. We need to tie him down. We'll tie him down so he can't follow us and then we can go. The three of us will go away."

Eric says, "Okay, okay," but he doesn't appear able to focus and he sinks to his knees. Eric is not well. Because of the physical strain and exertion of the fight, he must be experiencing renewed symptoms of his concussion.

Andrew speaks in a conspiratorial lower register. "You hold the gun, and hold it on him. I'll tie him to the chair. All right? I'll tie him, you watch him, make sure he doesn't get up. You can do that, right? I know you can do it."

Eric says, "No." He shakes his head as deliberately as a shadow creeping across a sundial. "I can't do that."

"You have to, please. I'll tie him down and you hold this." Andrew looks at the gun in his hand and his eyes widen as though utterly horrified by what he sees, or horrified by what he saw.

"I'll tie him. I can do that." Eric staggers and careens away.

Andrew continues talking as though Eric is still next to him, leaning on him, listening to him. "And you shoot him if he—" He can't get it all out and he breaks down and the gun rattles in his hand.

Eric wobbles like he's navigating a high wire. He veers around Adriane's legs instead of passing over her and plops himself onto his butt in front of Leonard. Eric's eyes are all whites and pupils. He looks at Leonard once, or through him. He reels in coils of rope; one end is still tied to the leg of the chair in which Leonard sits. Eric then winds the nylon around Leonard's legs, making no mind of knots, snares, and tangles. He isn't doing a good job; there's no pattern or reason to the loops and he isn't pulling tightly on the rope to ensure there's no slack.

Leonard initially thinks he will be able to wiggle free if he wants to, but there is a lot of rope and Eric uses it all on Leonard's now mummified legs. Eric then belly-crawls behind the chair and gathers the other rope Leonard kicked away moments ago.

Leonard puts his hands behind the chair before Eric asks him to do so. He tells Leonard to do it, anyway, and his voice floats up like he's speaking from the bottom of a hole. He winds a couple of lines around Leonard's chest, under his arms, the back of the chair, and then spindles the rest of the rope around his hands and wrists.

A blast of wind crashes the open front door into the wall and drags into the cabin its tail of dirt, dried grass, leaves, and pine needles. Eric cries out, startled and terrified, and he collapses to Leonard's left. Eric cries and talks to himself, and he crawls to the front door that indecisively hovers on whorls of air, pushed and pulled by unseen hands.

Andrew limps over Adriane's body and stands in front of Leonard, well within arm's reach if Leonard had a free one. The gun is lowered. He isn't looking at Leonard and he isn't looking at Eric. He looks at his red swollen hands and the gun.

Leonard knows what he is thinking. How can he not think it? Saying it will not help, but he says it anyway. "It's not your fault, Andrew. It was an accident. You can't blame yourself. I know you didn't—we were wrestling and the gun was in both our hands and . . . and . . ." and Leonard can't bring himself to say that he squeezed his hands and the gun went off. He is not going to say that out loud. He is not going to say that he knows, ultimately, Wen is dead because he and the others heedlessly went along with what they were told to do and he couldn't say no because it was too hard, maybe even impossible, but he still should've tried to say no anyway. He is not going to say that despite the horror of what's already taken place, he will still try to save the world, even as he fears it is no longer worth saving.

During Leonard's stammering pause, Eric makes it to the door, which winnows in and out of his grasp.

Andrew's face is stippled with overnight growth of black beard stubble and his hair hangs in front of one eye, and the other doesn't blink. He presses the end of the gun barrel, that black dot rimmed in steel, against Leonard's forehead.

Leonard hopes he shoots. He wants this to be over. He is sorry he couldn't save everyone. He couldn't even save one child.

The front door slams shut and Leonard jumps in his chair and exhales the breath he didn't know he was holding. He grieves that the slamming door was not a gunshot. He wants to cry that he is still here with Andrew looking at him the way he's looking at him.

Leonard finishes off his long pause because he's selfish. "The gun just went off, Andrew. It's no one's—it just went off. And I'm—"

Andrew pulls the trigger. Leonard hears the empty click. He hears it even though Andrew is screaming in his face. Andrew pulls the trigger again and again and again. He presses the gun harder into Leonard's forehead, forcing his head back until Leonard is looking up at the ceiling. The dusty old wagon wheel hangs above. Leonard's eyes water and the wheel is blurry and it sways slightly, acknowledging the struggle below it, but the wheel is not turning and it will never turn again.

SIX

Eric

"You don't have to worry about me doing anything. I'm not leaving this chair until it's all over. Andrew—hey, you should check on Eric. Eric, are you okay? Listen, Andrew, we need to talk. I—I don't know if this is over yet. We have to check. Andrew? Andrew?"

Leonard prattles on. His voice is a burring rumble, looping inside Eric's skull while there's certainly no room for Leonard in there at all. Eric feels worse than he did yesterday in the initial agonizing hours after he bounced his head off the floor. This second round of concussion symptoms is more intense. While breathing and seeing are bearable acts now, the pressure and pain before this most recent blackout was near blinding. His throat stings and his mouth tastes like puke. He doesn't remember vomiting. He doesn't remember sitting against the front door.

He remembers his hands holding and manipulating rope but not feeling it. He remembers walking and then crawling through a miasmic haze. He remembers the open doorway and the light as an amorphous, malicious entity, so bright it was impossible they all weren't burned to cinders. He remembers being afraid it was coming to take Wen away if he didn't shut the door. He remembers Wen sitting on her knees next to him as he untied his legs. He remembers a bang, and Wen falling away from him.

He remembers seeing her face and knowing she was gone. He remembers praying in his head *please, God, no* over and over, and maybe he was screaming it, too.

Leonard is still talking, as fuzzy as an old recording. "Eric? You should take it slow, Eric."

Outside the sky has turned cloudy, overcast, as gray as November rain. Eric sits with his back against the front door, barricading the cabin, preventing the terror of the light from reentry.

A few steps away Leonard is tied to a chair. A thin trickle of blood leaks down the left side of his face. There is more blood on the cabin floor, dark swollen ponds of it. One tributary leads away from the middle of the floor to Adriane's body, which lies perpendicular to the screen slider. A gaggle of flies, as black as crows, flitter on and off her body; some flies linger on her neck and others spiral over her white mask and bounce madly off the screen door and kitchen windows. To Eric's left and on the floor in front of Wen's bedroom is a spread-out comforter. Thick and puffy, its light green has gone darker in the spots where it absorbs Wen's blood. Andrew is sitting on the couch, his head is down, and his hair hangs in front of his face like the leaves and branches of a weeping willow. His arms vine underneath Wen's body draped across his lap. She is swathed tightly in their flannel bedsheet. Queen-sized, there is enough material to transform her body into an oblong, formless cocoon, a chrysalis from which she will not emerge. The sheet is white and decorated with clusters of small blue flowers; they brought the flannel set from home in case it got cold in the cabin.

Eric says, "Andrew. Andrew?" He flashes to another time, lost but not forgotten, when Andrew was sitting like this and he smiled, held a finger to lips, and mouthed *shh, she's asleep.*

Eric says, "Let's get in the SUV and go."

"They slashed the tires."

"Drive on the flat tires then. It doesn't matter."

"It's not going to make it."

"We can try."

Andrew speaks in sentences made of broken glass. "The SUV won't get far. We can try, but it won't make it all the way out to the main road. Might not even make it out of the driveway. Maybe we can find their car, which has to be parked somewhere on the road, right? Leonard doesn't have keys on him, neither does Adriane. I checked. Even if we find keys, we're still going to have to walk the dirt road. Some. All of it."

"Then we'll walk." When Eric talks, the volume of the flies' buzzing increases, a dangerous, collective thrumming, a warning so loud he wonders if a bee's nest isn't stirred up somewhere. Two flies, as plump as thumb heads, land on Leonard's face. Leonard doesn't so much as twitch as the flies explore his skin.

"Eric?"

"Huh? Okay. Yeah. I'm here." Eric sits up straighter, catching himself from slouching and sliding away into the black-hole center of the cabin.

Andrew says, "We'll go when you are ready."

"I'm ready now."

"Sabrina is still out there somewhere, and she has her weapon. I'm out of bullets. There're more in the trunk. One of us has to carry Wen."

"We're not leaving her here."

"Never. She's coming with us. Wherever we go."

Eric says, "Okay, come on, I'm ready." Eric presses his body against the door and grinds himself into an upright position.

Leonard says, "Wait, please, wait! Before you go, you have to turn on the TV. Listen: Adriane's dead so we have to turn on the

TV and see what's happening. See if there's anything happening. Like we did yesterday, after Redmond. He died and we turned on the TV and we saw the cities drowning like I said we would. So we have to turn on the TV now. We have to see if—" Leonard pauses with his mouth open, like he cannot believe what came out of his mouth. Then repeats, "We have to see if—" and stops again.

Neither Andrew nor Eric asks for further explanation. Andrew's head is down again, making a hermit's cave out of himself.

Leonard continues. "We have to see if what happened here in the cabin stopped what is supposed to happen out there next. We have to see if Wen's death is enough to stop the end of the world."

Andrew rocks back and forth on the couch. He says, "I'm going to kill you if you say one more goddamn word."

Leonard says, "If you do, you'll still need to watch and find out if her death is accepted as the . . . the required sacrifice. A willing sacrifice. It has to be a willing sacrifice. That's why we kept asking and begging you both to choose. We couldn't sacrifice one of you. That wasn't allowed. We told you; it was *you* who had to choose. It had to be a choice. I'm afraid she might not, um, might not count."

Andrew shouts, "She doesn't count? She doesn't fucking count?"

"No, no, no, that's not what I mean. Of course she counts, she counts more than anything in the world. I'm saying you were supposed to choose. The sacrifice was supposed to be a willing one. And it wasn't. It was an accident, a terrible accident. No one chose this. Maybe it's enough but I don't know. It—it doesn't feel like it's over. Turn on the TV and we'll know. Just turn it on . . ."

Leonard rambles on about the television and how sorry he is

for everything. Eric closes his eyes and sends out a general *please, God in the name of your son Jesus Christ, help us* prayer. He feels an oddly focused heat radiating through the front door along with the chainsaw sound of a mass of gathering insects. No, this— whatever this is—doesn't feel like it's over.

Andrew stands up, turns around, bends, and gently places Wen's body on the couch. His right hand lingers, resting on her covered head.

Eric wanders away from the door and into the cabin. He says, "I'll take her, you can give her to me. I won't drop her," and he holds out his arms. He isn't sure Andrew hears him over the flies and Leonard's continued, voluminous pleas.

Andrew hovers over Wen for a moment, and then he leans sharply to his left and grabs the dual-tipped weapon propped against the far end of the couch and wall. He spins and limps to Leonard, brandishing the sledgehammer end.

Leonard says sorry once more and goes quiet. He doesn't beg or plead or ask for mercy. He doesn't flex or strain against the ropes. He doesn't close his eyes. He lifts his chin, neither defiant nor proud. He breathes audibly through his nose, and his body tremors and quakes.

Eric says, "Andrew? What are you doing?" and slides in front of him. His arms are still held out for Andrew to give him Wen's body. "No, you can't."

The sledgehammer wavers as though caught in an irresistible magnetic field and itches to dart forward, and then Andrew drops that end of the weapon to the floor. Leonard jolts in his chair at the thud of metal and wood. Andrew says, "I already killed one of them," and he motions at Adriane's body. Then he looks over his shoulder at Wen on the couch. Tears glisten in his glassy eyes and he lifts the weapon again. "So I'm going to kill him, too."

"You're not a killer. Adriane attacked you with a knife and you defended yourself. He's tied up and helpless."

"He's not fucking helpless."

"This is different. You can't."

"Wen is dead because of him! Eric, he fucking squeezed my hand and when he did . . . and when he did . . ."

Leonard sobs and says he didn't mean to even though he promised nothing would happen to her. More flies leave Adriane's body and orbit around Leonard like they are pets called to their owner.

Andrew says, "He made me shoot. The bullet came from the gun in my hand, my finger on the trigger. I shot her—"

"It's not your fault." Eric pushes the weapon down.

Andrew doesn't resist and lets Eric guide the weapon until the rake-claw end is on the floor. He says, "It is my fault. I'm so sorry . . ."

"No, it isn't." Eric hugs Andrew. "It's not your fault. I will never allow you to say it is."

Andrew doesn't drop the weapon to return the embrace, but he leans into Eric and rests his head on his shoulder. "Eric, what the fuck are we going to do?"

"We're going to leave like you said." Eric holds on for another moment and listens to Andrew breathe in and out. He releases Andrew and steps back, noticing they are standing in Adriane's blood. He says, "Take the weapon in case Sabrina is out there waiting for us. I'll get Wen." For an irrational moment, Eric fears their feet will be forever stuck to the floor, the blood as amber. They'll be fossilized, frozen in time, and not be found for millions of years.

Eric lurches to the couch, not so much dizzy as lacking any sense of equilibrium. Every step must be thought about and planned or the whole cabin will tilt like an unbalanced seesaw. Each correction he makes teeters into an uncoordinated over-correction that threatens to topple him. He anchors himself by standing with the tops of both feet under the couch's low frame. Now that he's not concentrating on walking, he closes his eyes and prays, hoping God can parse the loose and stretched-out thoughts in his head. He asks for the strength to be able to carry his daughter away from this place. *Away from this place away from this place away from this place* becomes an interior mantra, and with its harried, manic repetition, the syllables and beats transform into unrecognizable noises not of language.

Eric opens his eyes, and the sheet covering Wen's body is blackened with flies. They hover and they crawl over and weave between one another. Eric cries out and waves his arms frantically over her body. The flies ignore him. They are fat and drunk. They are greedy. They are cruel and fearless. They are the darkening knots and threads of her shroud.

Andrew says, "Eric! Eric? What are you doing?"

"I'm getting them off her. I want them off her."

"Getting what off her?"

"The flies. They're all over our baby." The enginelike roar of their collective wings is deep and guttural, a growl that turns into derisive laughter. He would be willing to spend an eternity crushing the flies' bodies, one by one, between his fingers, if it'll keep them away from Wen.

"I don't see any . . . hey, if you can't lift her—"

"There's just so many."

"Are you sure you're okay? How about you hold this thing and I'll carry—"

"I'm fine. I can do this."

Another voice worms into the cracks between the buzzing

and Andrew and Eric's conversation. Leonard says, "Eric, turn on the TV." He says it twice. He says it like it's nothing more than a hey-try-this friendly suggestion.

The television. It's there on the wall in front of him. The black screen is not quite a mirror, but it reflects his face and the cabin behind him, filtering the images in dark, muted tones. There's color in the reflection, but at the same time there's not. The rope around Leonard is white, Andrew's long hair is black, and the pooled blood is a black red, so opaque the floor appears to be full of holes.

"Eric, turn on the TV." Leonard's patient request sounds like his own thought verbalized. Yes, he could turn the TV on. It would take very little effort and would not prevent them from leaving. He could turn it on and see whatever it is they might see. Maybe it would be an answer. Maybe it would be nothing. He remembers yesterday's tsunamis and the filmed drownings and devastation. He can't remember what promised calamity is supposed to be next. What could he see that's worse than what he's already seen in the cabin? He remembers his shame and guilt while watching the rising ocean swallowing the Oregonian coastline and its denizens and fleetingly believing the four strangers were who they said they were. Does he believe them now? Does he believe it enough to turn on the television? What if the screen stays blank and dark? Would that mean it's all over, that everything and everyone is gone? Would he be relieved? What if the screen flashes on and bathes the cabin in light? What if the void isn't darkness, but is instead a sea of burning, unrelenting, unforgiving light?

Andrew shouts at Leonard, only inches from his face. He tells him to shut up and he doesn't give a fuck about the TV.

Leonard says, "Just turn it on, please. We have to know if we stopped it, or if we didn't," and he says it as though there's only him and Eric in the room, using the minimum amount of volume to be heard, to be understood.

Eric says, "We're leaving now," but he doesn't move to pick up Wen.

Andrew says, "Eric? You're not listening to him, are you? Hey, are you all right? Maybe you should sit down for a minute."

One fly lands on the TV screen's lower right corner and crawls in looping, sideways eights. Eric says, "We're going to leave right now," or maybe he doesn't and only thinks it. He reaches out and the fly guides his hand to the power button on the inside edge of the almost invisible plastic frame. The button is hidden and half the size of his finger pad. He presses it.

After a second or two delay, a confusing, bracing collage of colors and images fills the screen to its borders, accompanied by the sound of an authority, a narrator talking offscreen. Eric squints and is initially unable to focus on what's happening: the scrolling text banners with blurry words and numbers, images changing from overhead shots of an airport to a hospital with doctors wearing hazmat-esque shields and gowns, crowded side-walks, bustling markets, and packed-beyond-capacity subways, many of the people wearing surgical masks over their noses and mouths, and quick cuts to iconic images of a metropolitan city Eric would normally recognize instantly. He succumbs to the withering onslaught of sight and sound and slinks away from the TV and the couch, and he bumps into Andrew.

Andrew puts a hand on Eric's shoulder and turns him so they face each other. He asks, "Why'd you do that?" and he gives Eric a confused look of betrayal.

Eric doesn't recall deciding or deliberating whether to turn the television on or not. He says, "There was a fly . . ."

"A what?"

"We're going. I'll get Wen," Eric says. His voice is a decayed echo.

Leonard cries out. "We didn't stop it! We didn't stop anything! We're another step closer to the end."

Andrew says, "Shut up," but there isn't much oomph behind it. His head is turned slightly to the television, giving it the same distrustful side glance he gave Eric.

Leonard sniffles and coughs and shouts between deep, shuddering breaths. "Remember, I told you yesterday. Oceans would rise and drown cities—which happened, you can't deny that, you saw it—and I said then a plague would descend—"

Eric interrupts and says, "Then you said the skies will fall and crash to earth like pieces of glass and then a final everlasting darkness." He didn't plan on reciting that doomed litany, just like he did not plan to turn on the television.

Leonard appears nonplussed at having his words repeated back to him. "Yeah. Right. Um, yes, I said that—yeah, a plague, a plague would descend, and it's here, it's happening."

On the screen is a slideshow of images from Hong Kong. Among them: the Blue House in Wan Chai. Andrew's favorite building from their trip, it features a museum on the ground floor called the Hong Kong House of Stories, which was where they spent their last morning in the city before heading north to Hubei Province. Back home, hanging on the wall above their computer desk are two framed photos: one with the two of them standing in front of the Blue House, their chests puffed out in Superman poses, their smiles equally heroic; the other is of the Jardine House, a beanstalk-tall skyscraper with windows shaped like giant portals, or holes (this is Eric's favorite building and Andrew playfully teases him that he only likes it because it's full of bankers). The collage of this-is-the-city images ends with a field reporter in the middle of the bustling Kowloon City Wet Market, her surgical mask pulled away from her mouth so it hangs limply around her neck.

In the lower left corner of the screen, stacked above the omnipresent news scroll, is a red, rectangular box. The text inside the box is the name of the program: *City Zero: Hong Kong and the Fight Against Bird Flu*. The reporter talks about the surging number of human cases of H7N9 in Hong Kong since January with a mortality rate at almost 40 percent. The government has ordered millions of chickens and ducks culled throughout the region in recent months, and within Hong Kong there is the growing probability of quarantines for the hardest-hit neighborhoods and would include the closing of open-air markets. In recent weeks, dead birds with the avian flu strain have turned up in Suffolk, England, Germany, and at a Grayson chicken farm in Tennessee, increasing fears of a possible pandemic.

"Why did you turn it on?" Andrew asks again.

Eric shakes his head even though it's not a yes or no question. He wipes his eyes with the backs of his sweaty, bloody hands. He repeats his *away from this place* prayer in his head.

Andrew leans in and whispers, "Are you starting to believe him, Eric?"

Eric wants to say no. He yearns to. But he is in so much pain and grief, and he is confused and fatigued and he wants to lie on the couch next to Wen and close his eyes, and he's afraid if he says no to Andrew's question, they'll never be allowed to go away from this place. He says, "I'm sorry."

Andrew stutters through saying, "Eric—what are you, what are you saying? You can't. You're not, you're not thinking clearly."

Leonard says, "Guys, look. You didn't choose to make a sacrifice. Wen's death was an accident so that won't stop the apocalypse from happening. I said a plague would come next and here it is. Don't you see it? Everything that's happened—you have to see it now. The only way to prevent the end of everything is for you to willingly sacrifice one or the other."

Andrew dives at Leonard, throws both hands forward, and hits him in the face with the wooden handle, connecting at the bridge of his nose. Leonard's head snaps back with a grunt and blood gushes from his nose and down his already stained shirt.

Eric grabs Andrew's arm and pulls him away from hitting Leonard again. He points at the TV and says, "He said there would be a plague."

Andrew's voice goes high pitched, filled with the helium of incredulity. "This? I've been reading about these bird flu cases for months already. This isn't a fucking plague—it's, what, a news report. It isn't even being broadcast live." He stalks to the TV and points at the red title-box on the screen. "It's preprogramming. It's a TV show. It has a fucking title for Chrissakes. Breaking news doesn't have a title. Leonard, Sabrina, all of them knew this bird flu show was going to be on and knew what time."

Leonard says, "Come on, Andrew. How can you—"

"Shut your fucking mouth or I'll bash it in." Andrew swivels his head, looking around the room. "Where's the remote? Find it, and hit the guide button. You'll see the title show up in the menu. It's a fucking preprogrammed show. They knew about it before they came out here and made it part of their narrative."

Eric has both arms around one of Andrew's. What Andrew is saying is rational, but it sounds desperately rational.

Andrew says, "So God drops a couple of earthquakes but then had to wait for us to eat dinner and get a good night's sleep before dialing up the slow-moving-already-been-in-the-news-all-summer plague? Eric, they were all checking their watches this morning; all of them were, just like Leonard was yesterday. Do you remember them doing that? It was so obvious. They weren't even trying to hide it."

Leonard says, "I check my watch when I get nervous." He sounds sheepish, like he's apologizing. "I don't even realize I'm doing it most of the time."

Eric says, "The others were checking their watches, too." He doesn't remember them doing so, but assumes that Andrew isn't lying or misremembering. Eric says this because he wants to still be on Andrew's side.

Leonard says, "I'm sure they were nervous, too. And the thing is, we all felt it, felt the time coming, you know. And we were made to know that your choice had to come soon. So, like anybody would, we checked our watches."

Eric is beginning to believe Leonard, yet even to his ears that explanation is awkward and clunky.

Andrew says, "Who even wears a watch anymore? You all just check your phones. Especially people your age. You're telling us you four all show up and just happen to be wearing watches? No. You knew you were coming out to this cabin and there'd be no cell reception and you had to be able to tell time."

"That's not it at all, I swear . . ."

"Listen to him, Eric. Can't you tell he's lying? They knew this bird flu show was on today at this time just like they knew the Alaskan earthquake and the tsunami warnings had already happened before they showed up to the cabin . . ."

"I know. You're right." The buzzing is all around Eric. He thinks he knows what Leonard meant when he said he *felt the time coming*, like it was a physical thing made of presence and purpose. He remembers the figure made of light and maybe what he was saw was time made manifest, and that's not right but it feels closer to the truth, and he wants to tell Andrew about it. Instead, he says, "But there was another quake after the Alaskan one. That was the one that killed all those people. Leonard and the others didn't hear about that one before they showed up. That one happened live, while we watched." Eric silently prays that he's wrong and that they will be allowed to leave.

"And?"

"That was the one they predicted, and Adriane said she saw it happening at the beach with the giant rock."

"She didn't see anything but *The Goonies*. That quake was triggered by the first one, the one they knew about, and they got lucky—why are we even talking about this, Eric?"

"Now this bird flu outbreak. And in Hong Kong, our special place, our city, Andrew. Remember when we were there and we called it *our* city?" The trip to China was Eric's first time out of North America. Eric was so anxious and excited on the plane he couldn't sleep and watched five in-flight movies in a row. During the four days spent in Hong Kong, they crammed in as much as they could see and do, a rapturous final fling of their old lives before the adventure of their new one with Wen began. "It means something that it's there, that it's happening there."

"It doesn't mean anything. I already told you; China has been dealing with this outbreak for months. I'm not going to argue about this with you. It's what he wants. So let's go. You and me and—and Wen." His voice breaks and his indignation and anger evaporate. His eyes tear up. "If you're ready, then let's go. I can't—we can't stay here."

Sabrina's voice billows into the cabin from below. "Hey, it's me, Sabrina. I'm coming up the basement stairs, now, okay? I'm not going to hurt anyone, so please don't hurt me."

No one answers her. Her footfalls echo on the wooden stairs, a slow, uneven dirge that changes in pitch and tone the closer she gets to the main cabin floor. She has her curled shovel blade–tipped weapon with her, but she does not hold it threateningly. She carries it more like a scarlet letter, a final judgment she cannot escape.

She says, "I've been down there for a while. Listening to you and the TV. So I know—so I know we didn't stop it." She looks at Andrew and Eric and sidesteps away from the basement stairs. Her face is streaked with dirt, her hair dark with sweat. Her off-white shirt is a crusted map of yesterday's blood. "I don't know what—I don't know how it happened, but I'm truly sorry about Wen. I don't know what to say."

Andrew says, "Then fucking don't say anything. And don't come near us."

"Yeah, okay." Sabrina leans against the wall separating the bedroom doors and cranes her head toward the screen slider. "I'm sorry about Adriane, too. But she shouldn't have been threatening you. That wasn't supposed to happen."

"Turn out your pockets," Andrew says to Sabrina, and motions at her with the sledgehammer.

"Why?"

"Keys. Keys to your car that has to be parked somewhere near here."

Sabrina pulls out her empty pockets. The white cloth sticks out from her hips like mocking tongues. She rotates and runs hands over her smooth back pockets.

The news report rattles on in the background with a narrated video of dead birds bulldozed into piles and incinerated.

Andrew says, "Eric, can you shut that off, please?"

Eric goes to the TV and with the vivid, flashing images close to his throbbing head he squints and looks away. He fumbles about the side control panel pressing buttons until he hears the commentator cut out while discussing the most recent administration's ill-advised and crippling funding cuts to the Centers for Disease Control's pandemic preparedness programs. Eric only mutes the audio, however, and the video continues to broadcast.

A spinning bout of vertigo strikes and Eric sinks into the couch, sitting next to Wen and with the flies. Eric knows they are eager to crawl on him, too. He lifts Wen's body and slides her across his lap. She is rolled up like an ancient map to a lost place.

Andrew says, "Eric? Are you okay? We should go now, don't you think?"

"I can't—not yet."

"Are you sure? I think we really should go."

Eric says, "I don't feel right—I need a few minutes. Just a few minutes. Then we'll go. Together, I promise." He prays he will be able to keep that promise.

The flies leave Wen's body and disperse like released spores. Eric is relieved they are leaving Wen, but their forming an indoor storm cloud is an awful sight. They swirl and they land and they creep over the walls, tables, chairs, and they crawl on Sabrina and Leonard, on their hands and their mouths and over their eyes. Their unremitting buzzing sounds like it's crackling through the muted television speakers, and theirs is an ancient message of immutable decay, rot, and of ultimate defeat.

Sabrina and Leonard

"I don't feel right—I need a few minutes. Just a few minutes. Then we'll go. Together, I promise."

"That's okay, take some time, but we have to go as soon as you can. We can't stay here." Andrew puts a hand on Eric's shoulder and rubs his back. Eric mumbles something they cannot hear and he leans into Andrew's hip.

Leonard is battered, a diminished and broken King Kong after the swan dive off the Empire State Building. Sabrina is pressed against the wall as though standing on the crumbling ledge of a cliff face. They share a look. They wonder what the other is thinking, what the other believes, and what the other is going to do. They wonder if they've truly shared the same visions, the same commands. They wonder if the other is who they say they are. They wonder if the other is what they would consider to be a good person before they were called here. They share a protracted, probing look. They realize they do not know each other, not in the slightest. They realize in this darkest hour of the darkest day they are alone, fundamentally alone.

Sabrina says, "This should be over, Leonard."

"But it isn't."

"I know, I know. But what happened should be enough. Why isn't it enough?"

"She wasn't a willing—"

"I don't care. It's not right. They've already lost too much. It's so not right I can't even say how not right it is."

"I agree but it's not up to us."

Andrew halfheartedly tells them to be quiet.

Sabrina says, "I don't care what you do, but I'm going to fight it. I fought it before—I did, I swear I did. But now—no more of this. I'm done. We should've—I don't know—done something more to resist this. To reject it. There's no way—"

"There will come a point when you won't be able to. You know that." He isn't mocking or threatening. He's being commiserative.

"Why us? Why are we being made to do this, Leonard? Why

is this even happening at all? This is barbaric and vile and evil shit. And we're a part of it, all of it."

"I don't know, Sabrina. I really don't. I don't understand and we're not supposed to understand."

"That's such bullshit."

"We're trying to save billions of lives. The suffering of a few for—"

"It's still not right. It's all capricious and cruel. What kind of god or universe or whatever wants this, demands this?"

Leonard sighs and doesn't answer. He stares at Sabrina and blinks.

"No, no. You have to answer. I know what my answer is. I need to know yours. I want to hear what Leonard—" She pauses and laughs. "I was gonna say your last name but I don't know what it is. Isn't that fucked?"

He says, "It's—"

"I don't care about your last name! I want your answer. Tell me. What kind of god is making all this happen?"

"The one we have."

They share another look. Leonard is misshapen, grotesque, an unfinished monster. Sabrina stands at the disintegrating edge of a lava flow and the air she breathes is poisonous. They wonder if one or both or neither of them is crazy and they wonder if it even matters. They wonder if the other has always been as weak as they are now. They share another long look. This one is reserved for ill-fated observers in the moments before impending, inescapable calamity, whether it be natural disaster or the violent failure of humanity; a look of resigned melancholy and awe, unblinking in the face of a revealed, horrific, sacred truth. And they realize again, in this darkest hour of the darkest day, they remain alone, fundamentally alone.

Sabrina nods and she drops her staff and it lies on the floor like a borderline. "I never believed in it. But this is fucking hell."

Andrew

It's clear Eric's concussion has left him more compromised than Andrew originally thought. He can't possibly give Eric the rest needed to recover enough for him to be able to walk any sort of distance, even if it's only to the others' car parked presumably somewhere nearby. Does he leave Eric here and go for help on his own? No, that is not an option. He will never leave Eric or Wen alone again.

Andrew looks at Wen's sheet-covered body and he can still feel Leonard squeezing his hands, his finger folding in, collapsing on the trigger, and the hitch and the click, and the gun kicking back. He didn't know where the bullet went and then Eric screamed and scrambled on all fours to Wen. She was lying on her back with her knees and legs bent under her. Andrew saw her shattered face and he dropped to the floor next to Eric. His eyes flooded with tears he did not wipe or blink away so his view would remain distorted, refracted as though looking up from the bottom of a well. A blur of seconds later Eric was passed out against the door and Andrew stood alone in front of a tied-up Leonard, his gun empty of bullets but his finger pulling the trigger. Eventually he stuffed the gun in his back pocket and then checked Leonard's empty ones for keys. He checked Adriane's pockets, too. He dragged her body to the deck because he didn't know what else to do. He was going to check O'Bannon's pockets, too, but he didn't want to leave Eric alone inside the cabin while he was unconscious and he didn't want to leave Wen lying on the floor. He went into their bedroom and gathered the flannel sheets. As he carefully wrapped her body, everything was under water again, and he said her name. He lifted her off the floor and sat with her on the couch, and he said her name. He didn't know what else he could possibly say. He rested his forehead against hers, gently kissed the tip of her nose through the sheet, and he whispered he was sorry. He wanted to tell her the gun going off was an accident, wasn't his fault, but he couldn't. Instead, he said her name again and again. He said her name like he was afraid she would never hear anyone say it again. He said her name like it was a solemn oath to take her away from this place and bring her home.

Sabrina drops her staff. The twisted shovel blade clangs at contact with the floor, knocking Andrew out of his paralyzing fugue. She says, "I never believed in it. But this is fucking hell."

Leonard says, "There's still a chance. They still have a choice. They can choose to save everyone."

Sabrina says, "Everyone else, you mean."

Andrew imagines hitting Leonard with the sledgehammer until his head is the lumpy, spent wax of a used candle. The gaping pit of grief and rage demands to be filled with this act. Sabrina is now unarmed and if she attempts to intervene on Leonard's behalf, he can chop her down, too.

Leonard says, "Sabrina?"

"What?"

"Will you put the white mask on me, after? I don't think I'm getting out of this chair alive."

Andrew imagines bludgeoning both Leonard and Sabrina and then sitting on the couch with Eric and Wen. He and Eric will cradle her on their laps and they will wait in peace for as long as Eric needs, until he is ready to go.

Sabrina ignores Leonard's question, slowly walks across the room, and stops in front of Andrew. She says, "You never asked why we killed Redmond."

Andrew takes his hand off Eric's back and regrips the weapon.

Eric says, "Don't, Andrew."

Andrew says to Sabrina, "You mean your pal O'Bannon? That the guy you mean?"

"He was never my pal. I never trusted him but—but I still came here with him, I know. I'll never be able to explain it, or even believe it myself . . ."

Andrew says, "I'm pretty sure I can."

Sabrina nods. "We didn't come out and tell you about what our part in this is. I mean, besides presenting you with the choice. Have you figured that out yet?"

"Back away now or I start swinging. And find yourself a chair to sit in, too." Andrew has taught apocalyptic literature for years, calling his course *This Is How the World Ends*. The course has occasionally included a literary analysis of the Bible's Book of Revelation and the Four Horsemen of the Apocalypse riding their red, black, white, and pale horses. Over the years the course syllabus has evolved, but one of the main arguments/discussions he has with his students remains a constant. No matter how bleak or dire, end-of-the-world scenarios appeal to us because we take meaning from the end. Aside from the obvious and well-discussed idea that our narcissism is served when imagining we, out of all the billions who perish, might survive, Andrew has argued there's also undeniable allure to witnessing the beginning of the end and perishing along with everyone and everything else. He has impishly said to a classroom, to the scowl of more than a few students, "Within the kernel of end-times awe and ecstasy is the seed of all organized religions." Of course Andrew has figured out the four strangers' quasi-Christian endgame, but he doesn't want Sabrina explaining it and making biblical connections in front of Eric—his Catholic faith is as confounding and mysterious to Andrew as it is endearing—while he's in this addled, vulnerable mental state.

Sabrina doesn't move. "I will sit and do whatever you ask, just let me explain, let me tell you this first."

"Back the fuck up now."

Eric interjects, "If Andrew and I didn't choose to make a sacrifice, then you four had to make one."

"Don't talk like that." Andrew crouches so he can look Eric in the eye. His right knee gives out on the way down. The looseness, the detachment of his swollen knee from the rest of his leg makes his head go dizzy and hot. He wonders if he'll be able to complete any sort of hike on this knee. What if they can't get car keys from Sabrina or Leonard? Do he and Eric risk walking down the road, finding their car, and hoping they hid a key somewhere? Andrew's dad used to hide a spare to his truck in the driver's-side wheel well. Maybe they go up the road in the opposite direction, deeper into the woods, and to the closest cabin that's a few miles away, break in, and hope the cabin has a phone.

Everything in Andrew screams to get out of this place of death and madness and figure it all out after. He leans on the staff and says, "Eric," until Eric looks at him. "Listen to me. I love you, and we have to go now. All right? I know you can do it."

"I love you, too. But I don't—"

"We can take breaks and rests when we're on the road, as many as we need. We'll make it." Andrew stands, slides an arm under Eric's, and tugs him up.

Eric doesn't stand and stays sitting with Wen. "Not yet. One more minute, please."

Sabrina says, "He's right, Andrew. When you didn't choose, we were forced to kill Redmond."

"I don't want to fucking hear any of this!" Andrew shouts.

Sabrina holds up four fingers. "After he died, the earthquake and tsunami hit." She folds down her pinky, making the number three. "Adriane dies, then the bird flu spreads." She curls another finger into her palm. Two fingers held up, a mocking peace sign. "There's only two of us left. If you don't choose to make a sacrifice, then Leonard and I will be the sacrifices. Each time one of us dies"—she folds down another finger—"another calamity—"

"The skies will fall and crash to pieces like glass," Eric says, like he's participating in a call-and-response prayer.

Sabrina continues, "—and the apocalypse is another step closer. And if you don't choose and the last of our four dies—" Her fist swallows up the last finger.

Eric says, "The final darkness. That's what Leonard said."

"—then it'll be the end of everything. When the last of us are dead, there are no more chances for you to stop the apocalypse."

Andrew wobbles across the room toward Sabrina. "I said stop talking."

"Before we got here, Leonard and I wanted to spell it all out for you, tell you everything we knew as soon as we walked into the cabin. Redmond and Adriane talked us out of it. We knew we had an impossible sell and, look, we're not stupid or crazy—I wish we were crazy . . ."

Leonard says, "You're not crazy."

"I think it's both now," she says without explaining what she means. "Andrew, you weren't going to believe us, believe why we were here, believe in the choice and the consequences, especially when we first presented it to you, and maybe not ever. So we couldn't risk telling you we would kill each other off one

by one if you chose to never make a sacrifice. We were afraid
you'd wait us out, watch us kill each other, and then the world
would end."

"Get a chair, put it against the front wall, and sit down," Andrew says.

"Maybe the world should end if any small part of it was made
to be like this." Sabrina nods as though she's made a decision or
a pact. She faces Leonard and points at the television. "Did you
know this bird flu show was going to be on?"

Leonard is surprised by her sudden pivot. "Huh? Y-yeah.
Well, no. I mean, I didn't know there would be a show like this,
or what kind of, um, plague, there'd be, or even where, but I knew
there'd be some kind of deadly illness."

"How'd you know?"

"Sabrina, why are you—?"

"Before we came up here, you told us the plague would happen around nine o'clock if they didn't make a choice in the early
morning of the second day. Adriane and I had a vague sense of
a plaguelike calamity happening after the tsunami but not the
precise time. You gave us a time."

"I don't know what to tell you. I just knew the time it would
happen, like it was always there in my head, waiting for me to
find it."

"You didn't check the television programming schedule before we met up with you?"

"No, of course not."

Andrew doesn't know what Sabrina is doing, why she's now
grilling Leonard about the show and the timing, why she has
seemingly flipped to arguing Andrew's side.

She says, "Redmond said he knew the time, too. Did he tell
you first?"

"No, I knew the time before he and I—or any of us—talked about it."

"Are you sure?"

Leonard sighs. "Yes. I'm sure."

"So he only knew the time because you told him?"

"I have no idea what he knew or was shown. Why all these questions now? You can't doubt what's happening—"

Andrew says, "I really don't care anymore. You guys will have plenty of time to figure it out once we're out of here. Take that chair and sit, Sabrina, or I'm going to have to hurt you both. Know that I won't hesitate to hurt you."

Sabrina says, "I'm going to help you and Eric leave here if you'll let me."

Sabrina

I tell you, Andrew and Eric, the four of us hid the keys to Redmond's truck, buried them a few paces away from the dirt road. Or maybe I should say O'Bannon instead of Redmond because even if Andrew is mistaken, I believe that's who he is now. Redmond was awful even when I first encountered him on the online message board. He made jokes about posting dick pics and asked what Adriane and I were wearing while we shared the dreams, nightmares, messages, and visions we were all experiencing, and what it was doing to our lives. Despite Redmond, I was relieved there were others living through the same thing. Yes, obviously our shared visions were terrifying, but as frightened as I was, finding the others meant I wasn't alone, and it meant I wasn't having some sort of psychotic break and I could stop the obsessive self-analysis and self-diagnosis. The first night on the message board together, we didn't know yet what the visions meant or that we had any part to play. I hoped we were going to be like prophets, or something. Warn people, you know? Warn them about what might happen if we didn't stop doing all the shitty things we're all doing to one another and to the environment. I told the others how it started with me hearing whispers a few nights before while I was in line at In-N-Out Burger. The burger was my reward for a long day of entrance exam prep; I was planning to apply to nurse practitioner master's programs in the California State University system. So at first I thought some creep behind me was whispering in my ear. And it wasn't just hearing the whisper; I felt breathed-out air pushing through my hair and brushing the rim of my ear. I turned but there was no one in line behind me. I must've looked like a lunatic spinning around like I did. I tried to pass it off as my own yammering brain unable to come down from study mode and I pawed at my ears like there was a fly or mosquito dive-bombing me. I nearly shouted my order at the confused kid behind the counter. The whispering continued and I thought maybe it was the clunky air-conditioning operating at some weird frequency, so instead of eating at the restaurant like I'd planned, I scooped everything off the tray and ran out to my car. I was exhausted and now totally freaked out and the voice was still there with me. It wasn't in my head. It sounded like someone talking through the tiny speakers of a cell phone but when the phone wasn't against my ear and was instead crammed inside my jeans pocket, or lost inside my bag, or it had fallen down underneath the driver's seat. Believe me, I've thought long and hard about this and I know it's what a crazy person who doesn't know she's going crazy would say, but it wasn't in my head. That small voice existed independent of me and it was coming from somewhere inside the car. I drove home with the radio tuned to KRock and blasting at full volume. I shouted and I sang along with songs I didn't know the words to. I parked and ran up to my little second-floor studio apartment, fumbling with the keys at the front door like some slasher movie victim moments before the knife blade flashes, and then I was inside and I dropped my food on the kitchen table, which was covered in papers and the exam practice booklet. The apartment was quiet but for the ticking of the central air and muffled steps coming from the floor above. No voice or whispers, but my apartment seemed off, like it had been staged to look like the way I would've left it, but there were imperceptible inauthenticities. Something was wrong, or would be wrong, and all I could do was wait for the wrong to happen. The more I listened, percolating up from below those everyday background noises I usually ignored, there was a high-pitched ringing, the kind you get in your ears after a really loud concert, but it wasn't coming from inside my head or my ears. A spanned distance was communicated in how it sounded. A great, impossible distance. The ringing pitched lower, like the hum of slowing fan blades, and focused into words that were in my own voice but not a voice I've ever used. I sat and I listened. I never ate that stupid burger and I fell asleep at the table and I dreamed. Those dreams from that first night are a deck of used playing cards, the colors faded, corners bent and peeling, and some of the cards are missing and I don't know which ones are gone but they are the important ones, the most important. I do remember everything the voice said to me, though. And I remember the physical part of listening. I remember what those words felt like.

I tell you, Andrew and Eric, the morning after finding the message board (I'd stayed up into the early morning hours typing, reading, and rereading everyone's posts), I woke with a compulsion to drive to Valencia, a town twenty miles north of Los Angeles. I hadn't been there since I was a kid and I had no idea why I was supposed to go or what I would find. I was still buzzing after connecting with the others online so I indulged this compulsion instead of denying it. This might sound strange, but the idea of dropping everything to drive to who-knows-where was both terrifying and thrilling, and it was a relief, too. It was relief to give in, even knowing this act of belief would irreparably change my life. I didn't want or crave that change, at least not consciously. Until the night at In-N-Out, I was 100 percent focused on my job and getting into a master's program, to the detriment of my already meager social life, but that didn't really matter to me. I was happy, or if I wasn't happy, I was all right, and that was plenty good enough. But that morning I called in sick to the hospital, although I knew the written recommendation I needed from my supervisor for my school applications was becoming less glowing with each passing sick day, now the third in a week. She was royally pissed but I had no choice. Or I convinced myself I had no choice. Either way, for this once proud and life-long agnostic, the possibilities and implications of the fucked-up adventure were intoxicating. For some reason I'd been chosen. I was being given proof there was something out there greater than me or greater than us, something beyond our everyday, and it was communicating with me, and telling me what to do. Do you have any idea how delicious it is to give yourself over to something else so completely? So I did.

I say to you, Andrew and Eric, trust the process, right? Dad's favorite saying, applied to everything from sports to career to politics to relationships to dealing with grief after Mom died a few years ago. God, I hated that saying and how often he'd say it. It made this big strong guy seem so mealymouthed, passive, weak, resigned to failure. *Trust the process* and a shrug. Might as well wear a shirt that reads FINE, I GIVE UP. I yelled at him in front of the oncologist, after hearing the details of proposed and (I knew) desperate treatment, he said, "Trust the process," like it was a goddamned hallelujah. I should tell him I'm sorry, now, because I can't count how many times I've said *trust the process* to myself over the last seven days. My holy mantra. I said it when I was home and ignoring the pleading *where are you?* texts and voice messages from work, friends, and Dad, too. I said it when I took mesh from orthopedics and made our four white masks as a vision instructed me to, no reason yet to be given for their existence and usage. Never a reason. I said it when I bought the plane ticket. I said it when I met Leonard, Adriane, and Redmond for the first time at a Burger King rest stop on the highway, and I said it when I saw they were all wearing jeans and button-down shirts like me and Redmond joked that we looked like a lame indie rock band, and I said it when the shirts' different colors made sense and told me all I needed to know about who each of us was or was supposed to be. I said it when we first verbalized what it was we were actually going to do out here at the cabin, and I said it when I looked into Redmond's pickup truck bed and saw he made the staffs for us with their spiked metal tops and the one with the bonus hammerblock tacked on, each of them right out of a dream I had on the plane ride out here, like he'd plucked them out of my head and dropped them in the truck, and I said it when he told us about how he'd made them without remembering or knowing exactly how he'd made them, and I said it when I climbed into Redmond's truck cab, and I said it as those awful things rattled around the truck bed with each bump and turn, and I said it when we parked on the dirt road and I said it when I picked up the weapon built for me to use and I said it when we knew we could use the rope but not the rolls of duct tape, and I said it when I tried to text Dad, "Trust the process. I love you," and then we left our phones in the truck and we started walking here, and I said it before we forced our way into the cabin. And I keep saying it. I even fucking said it before I walked up the basement stairs like ten minutes ago. *Trust the process.* Dumbly believe things are how they're supposed to be and that they will work out simply because of that belief, even if you know better.

I tell you, Andrew and Eric, about my impromptu trip to Valencia, how I drove north on the I-5 without any maps or GPS and I got off at a random exit. I didn't know what I was looking for and I navigated through suburban sprawl and then to San Francisquito Canyon Road, which goes rural in an eyeblink and carves through rolling hills and forest like a winding river. At a severe bend in the road, I pulled over and parked in a small gravel lot buffeted by a cement divider. Beyond the divider was the former San Francisquito Road. It'd been closed and rerouted after numerous washouts. The closed road follows alongside the ruins of the St. Francis Dam, which collapsed in the middle of one night in March 1928, sending giant chunks of cement and billions of gallons of water rushing through the valley, wiping out houses and ranches, killing more than four hundred people, washing bodies all the way to the Pacific Ocean. I didn't know anything about the dam until after I got home and looked it up online. While I was there walking the path of the ruins, I walked alone, dutifully following the closed road, which was being overrun and swallowed up by the surrounding vegetation and clay and dirt. I walked through the valley, dry and bleached and as empty of people as the surface of the moon. There was a cloudless blue sky above the craggy, shadowed faces of the surrounding hills and the only sounds came from bugs and it felt like I was walking through a postapocalyptic landscape. My earlier excitement quickly faded. Whatever I was going to be shown, I was sure I wouldn't be able to stop it and my only purpose was to be a witness.

I tell you, Andrew and Eric, I now wish my only role was to be a passive witness of the end. I took my time and I was careful not to walk too fast so I could see and mark everything, and maybe thirty minutes in, there was a fifteen-foot-tall, cube-shaped boulder of dam just off the road and squatting in the brush like a sunning tortoise. Its sand-colored, crumbly concrete was striated, and from the road it looked like a section of a staircase for a giant. Like I said, I didn't know it was a piece of the St. Francis Dam until I got home, so I didn't know what it was other than a man-made ruin, a leftover, a gravestone for a doomed past. I kept walking and following the road, and maybe another thirty minutes later I stopped. I was made to stop. I now think I was in the spot where the dam had been built and spanned across the valley. I left the road and hiked over to an area covered with rubble, a mix of stones and small bits of porous cement. I stood in the lowest point of the valley and it was as quiet as the bottom of the sea. I expected, I don't know, to see someone or something (I still can't bring myself to say God, or a god) come over the hilltops and—this sounds crazy, I know—grab me, pick me up because I felt doll-sized, and I didn't think I was alone anymore, and it wasn't a good feeling. Then everything went black.

I tell you, Andrew and Eric, I know Adriane said she saw *The Goonies* rock and the tsunami before we saw it all on TV. I never saw that. I won't lie to you. That's a promise I can keep. I'd marched the path of a great flood without knowing it and I didn't see anything other than darkness. It wasn't like I'd lost time or something and it had become night in the valley. It wasn't night-dark; I couldn't see anything. There was nothing. I was nothing. But then I heard groans and high-pitched sounds of stress and I could only imagine one of the hills was going to burst or break above me. There was a thunderous crack and a low vibrato whoosh sounding like the earth itself giving a defeated sigh, and then an ocean of water cascading and rushing over me, past me, and into the landscape I could no longer see. There was the per-cussive snapping of trees and crunch of collapsing houses and buildings. There were people, so many people, screaming and screaming, and the worst part was the screams went unfinished; the screams cut out and left me to fill in how they were supposed to continue. In the valley I listened to an apocalypse that already happened and I was listening to the end of everything else, and that end would never cease. The callous rush of water didn't stop and continued long past the final echoes of destruction and death. It went on forever. I went along with it, neither cold nor warm, or anything really, another piece of detritus floating away. Part of me is still there now. At some point I was extracted out of that endless time, and I wasn't in the dark, and I was back at my car and it was almost noon. I don't remember walking back to the car. Trust the process, right?

I tell you, Andrew and Eric, there are other gaps in my mem-ory. Gaps I don't care to fill in. I already told you how I tried not to come to New Hampshire and how I just sort of came back to myself, from wherever I was, and I was sitting in a cab on the way to LAX.

Just let me tell you this, Andrew and Eric: I wasn't me, or I wasn't all there when the three of us killed Redmond. It was like a trance, I guess, though I've never been in a trance so how would I know? I think a part of me, the best part, the important part, got sent back to the nothingness, floating along in the never-ending end in the valley, but enough of me was left behind here to see Redmond grinning through his masked face and to feel the wooden handle vibrate in my hands as I smashed his head and to hear the sound it made. I wasn't there for all of it. I can't tell you how many times I swung and hit him. I can't tell you which one of us landed the final, killing blow. I tell you, Andrew, I already cannot recall specifics about our struggle at your SUV. It's like trying to remember something from early childhood. There's only the barest and broadest traces of *this happened and I was there*.

Eric asks me if I've seen anyone else here or there (he doesn't specify where *there* is) and he mumbles something about a figure and light. Andrew talks over him, nearly shouting, telling Eric to stop talking to me and he asks Eric if he's ready to go yet. Eric doesn't look at Andrew. He only looks at me. I try not to stare at his daughter, wrapped in a sheet and on his lap. It only occurs to me now that I'm being a terrible nurse for not insisting I look under the sheet at Wen, to make sure she's beyond saving.

I tell you, Eric, I've never seen a figure like you described, but that doesn't mean there wasn't one here.

Eric says that right before Redmond was killed, he sensed a presence in the room with us. It was sort of like when you drop an egg into a pot of water and the water rises, is displaced. He says it was like that.

I don't like what he is saying and I like how he looks even less. He has a lights-are-on-but-no-one's-home glaze. I wonder if I looked like that when I was talking about my experiences and I already can't remember how much or how little I actually said out loud to them or just thought.

Eric says he could feel the space in the room being displaced.

He says he saw something appear, join the circle around Redmond before we started pummeling him. He says he tried to pass it off as a flash of light from the deck or a concussion- and stress-induced hallucination or migraine, one that looked at him, one that regarded him. Eric enunciates "regarded." He says he hasn't seen the figure again, but he's felt it hanging around. It was here somewhere after Adriane and Wen died, and Eric says he shut the cabin's front door to keep it outside.

I ask you, Eric, is it here now?

He tells me no, but he thinks it will be soon.

Andrew charges across the room at me. He is crying and yelling, telling me to stop talking to Eric, to stop filling his head with nonsense and lies. To Eric he says you're hurt and whatever you saw was a hallucination and you're not thinking clearly.

I tell you, Andrew, I'm sorry and I'm not trying to convince Eric of anything and I want to help you both leave the cabin. That's all I want to do now. That's my only mission left in life, to help you both leave here and leave here alive.

Leonard says they have to choose again, and soon. His voice is a reveille, and the new part of me that isn't an actual part of me stirs and I say yes without being able to stop the affirmation.

Andrew ignores Leonard and he tells me to sit in a chair and if I say another word he'll kill me.

I hold my ground. If Andrew is going to swing that block hammer at my head, so be it. I tell you, Andrew, listen, Redmond's truck is exactly three miles away from the cabin. On the side of the dirt road, about halfway between here and the truck, we hid the keys under a flat rock the size of a Frisbee. It's slate colored, and half of it has a light-green beard of lichen and it's maybe four steps off the road and into the brush. The rock is in front of a tree with a goiter-sized knot on its trunk. I don't know what kind of tree, and I tell you, Andrew and Eric, I'm sorry. You can go now and try to find it yourselves, but it'll be difficult to pick out the tree if you haven't seen it before. So I am going to go with you.

Andrew says fuck you.

I say to you, Andrew and Eric, the four of us left our phones and wallets in the truck. Leaving the phones and the keys behind was our safety net. We'd decided we couldn't risk having you over-power us, take the keys to the truck and simply drive away, leaving the world to die. Now that's exactly what I'm going to help you do. I believe in what's happening here, but I also don't believe.

Leonard says my name like he's a disapproving, disappointed parent, a self-appointed expert, an authority who has none. He tells me to stop talking about the truck and convince them to make the selfless choice. He says time is running out more quickly now.

I tell you, Andrew and Eric and Leonard, I don't believe in this kind of god. I pause and laugh at myself. Instead of saying *someone* or *something* I've finally deigned to say the g-word, haven't I?

I tell you, Andrew and Eric and Leonard, I don't believe in this kind of devil, either, or in this kind of universe. I'm sure all of them will be disappointed to hear it. I laugh again, and I'm sorry, this is not funny. Not in the least.

I tell you, Andrew and Eric and Leonard, I don't believe any of this is right anymore. I mean, I never believed it was right or moral, but I thought it had to happen to save the world, no matter what. Now I don't. I am done trusting the process.

Eric tells Andrew that he should listen to me. That they should take me with them.

I am going to say that after we find the truck, I'll go with them to the police and tell them everything about our four and the kidnapping and admit to all the crimes perpetrated here, even though I know I will not live long enough to speak to anyone who isn't already in this cabin. I am going to tell them this and more, but Eric and Andrew fall into a shockingly ferocious argument and they ignore me.

I pick up the staff at my feet, the one Redmond custom made for me, the one with a function that was never explained but was wordlessly obvious, and it feels right in my hands and it feels so wrong I'd be happy if someone cut my traitorous hands off so I could never hold it again. I return to the darkness in the valley, and I'm alone and flowing away in the nothingness, and I'm alone in the cabin and the presence in light or whatever you, Eric, tried to explain to me is nowhere to be found. There's no light. There never was. There's only emptiness and lack and void and it all explains why the world is the way it is and I would scream if I could. Andrew, you're pleading with Eric to stop listening to me, to consider that I might be lying about the keys so I can ambush you, that it should be so obvious I can't be trusted. And, Eric, you're telling Andrew to let me help, that you believe me and you need me to find the keys, you need me to get out. I run across the room on feet that do not feel the floor. The curlicued blade is raised over my head like a banner, a flag, an emblem of death, sorrow, and never-ending violence. Andrew, you tell Eric that you're leaving now and you're not taking me with you. Eric, you see me sprinting across the room, but you don't warn Andrew.

I swing the staff down like I'm aiming to split a log. My torso bends and my legs squat autonomically so the full force and weight of my body is behind the strike. The edge of the blade smashes into Leonard at the top of his head with a wet smack and a chunky thud. I'm brought back from the nothing so I can feel the impact reverberate through my hands and arms. Leonard screams, high pitched and algorithmic, his damaged brain stuck on a wailing siren setting. The shovel blade has sunk into his skull and I anchor a foot on his lap for leverage to help pull it out. Leonard convulses and thrashes about and his screams are now a dying prey animal's desperate and betrayed squealing. I finally work the shovel free and then I swing it horizontally and I swing it madly, sending the warped blade into his face and his neck, again and again. And at the end of it, I'm all me. I am swinging the weapon and I hit him as hard as I can until he isn't screaming or moving.

I pitch the staff behind Leonard. It bounces once and plows into the end table with the yellow-shaded lamp, which tumbles and crashes to the floor. I tell you, Andrew and Eric, I'm sorry.

I will never pick up that weapon again. This, at least, has been promised to me. Leonard's face is unrecognizable as having once been a face. His white shirt is only white in spots. I am dizzy but not dizzy enough to be on the floor, but that's where I am now, on my hands and knees. I pull out his mesh mask from his back pocket and stuff it in mine. Going for the mask is as inexplicable as it is instinctual. Then I root around under Leonard's chair. I find a tooth and I twitch and flick it away as though I'd accidentally picked up a poisonous spider. Drops of warm blood drip from Leonard onto my head, neck, and arms. I cough and wretch and keep searching the floor until I find the remote control for the television.

I stand up behind Leonard. My limbs are tremulous from overexertion, like I'd just finished a hard workout. Leonard's hair is matted and dark with blood and mashed scalp. I tear up, but the tears aren't for him, not really. Andrew and Eric gawk at Leonard and then at me. I am sorry for your blank, blood-sweat-and-tears-stained faces. I am sorry for everything. Eric looks at me like I'm about to give an answer. Andrew lifts and lowers the sledgehammer weapon indecisively, moving it like a clock's pendulum.

I wipe each hand on my jeans, careful to swap hands with the remote and not drop it. As my arm raises on its own, a mechanical arm full of wires and gears that function and perform their duties in secret, I tell you, Andrew and Eric, I have to turn the volume on but you don't have to listen and you don't have to look at the screen, either. My thumb unmutes the TV without having to search the bloodied remote for the correct button.

On the terrible screen, the one always filled with apocalypses big and small, breaking news has already interrupted the bird flu program. On the terrible, awful screen is the smoking wreckage of an airplane. The smoke is thick and the deepest black, a writhing toxic column that billows and expands into a cloud, a mass, a tumor in the sky. Quick cut to an aerial shot of the crash site and debris is scattered in the grassy field like confetti. Quick cut to another wrecked plane cratered in the middle of another field. There is more black smoke, and within its hypnotic undulations I know there is a message. Then a cutaway to another downed plane, its pieces floating in an ocean only a few hundred feet offshore. The plane's tail section is intact and breaches the surface like the fin of a leviathan. Silver panels from the fuselage bob serenely in the blue waves. If left alone they will sink, and I imagine them becoming part of a reef, a habitat, a new ecosystem, but of course that won't happen. Life isn't the promise.

Eric stands and backs away from the couch so he can better see the television. He still has Wen in his arms. The paper-towel pad taped to the back of his head hangs loosely and is about to fall off. He says what Leonard said yesterday: the skies will fall and crash to the earth like pieces of glass, and then the final, everlasting darkness will descend over humanity.

I want to tell you, Eric, to stop saying the words Leonard said. They are not Leonard's words to begin with. The four of us were given them and you cannot trust who gave them to us. I want to tell you, Eric, to ignore the words and the planes and the blood. I want to lie to you, Eric, and say that you and Andrew can leave the cabin and everything will be all right.

I tell you, Andrew and Eric, we should leave now. We shouldn't spend one more second in this place. I don't tell you I am the last of the four and I am next and it will be a relief when it happens. Maybe the truth is the end has already been happening long before we arrived at the cabin and what we're seeing, what we've been seeing, is not the fireworks of the world's denouement but the final flickering sparks of our afterword.

The commentator says they have confirmation of as many as seven airplanes having crashed without warning, without issuing distress calls, amid fears and increasing speculation there may have been a coordinated cyberattack on the planes' flight management systems. TSA has yet to issue a statement. Airports around the globe are canceling flights—

Andrew swings the sledgehammer, punching a hole in the middle of the television screen. The hole is as black as the smoke spewing from the planes.

THIS IS THE END

Andrew and Eric

We can't go on. We stare at the television. The hole in the screen is a porthole in a sunken boat. It's an open mouth ringed in rows of small, asymmetrical, jagged teeth and it once spoke of unimaginable places and things. It's a wound, one from which the blackest ichor will begin flowing. It's a telescopic view of the universe before stars, or after.

In the new silence of the cabin, Andrew only hears his own breathing and the quickened metronome of his heartbeat. He imagines bashing the television and frame with the gore-stained hammer until there's nothing left to bash and until he's beaten back the icy tendrils of doubt.

Eric stares at the screen as though he is afraid to look else-where; the very act of staring is a talisman that already failed to protect us. He has Wen in his arms and he sways in rhythm with the frenzied buzz of flies echoing from inside the hole. Only one of us ever hears and sees these flies just as only one of us saw a figure in light.

Eric silently tells Wen he will not put her down or ask Andrew to hold her until after we leave the cabin, even though his arms are tiring. Then he says, "We should go right now." Is he only saying this because Sabrina suggests we should leave? He closes his eyes and he sees planes falling like drops of rain from a darkening sky.

Andrew says, "All right. Let's go. Maybe I should carry Wen." Andrew hates the defeat and need in his voice.

"No, I have her. I can do it. I can make it." In his head, Eric prays for the strength to carry Wen until his strength is no longer needed. For a few weeks after her third birthday, Wen went through a phase insisting we carry her on endless jaunts around our condo so she could count the number of laps as a measure of how strong we were. We would both purposefully complete the same number of laps, which frustrated Wen greatly, and she reacted like we were keeping a secret from her. We would jokingly tell her that our arms were always at the same strength level and we only got tired because she was growing, getting bigger by the second as we held her in our faux-shaky arms.

Andrew says, "I know you can. Just—let me know." Wen's body is all but made shapeless by the sheet he wrapped around her. He wants to hold her again, right now, and he wonders if her arms, which he'd carefully positioned at her sides, have shifted or bent, and he wonders what her hands are doing, and her feet, and maybe he should unwrap her and make sure she's okay underneath, and then kiss her forehead and not look at the lower half of her face.

Eric says, "I will."

Andrew is weeping. "All right. I'm sorry." For as long as he lives, Andrew will wonder if Eric partly blames him for Wen's death because of his unwitting part in the hellish Rube Goldberg device that took over our lives, because he snuck the gun up to the cabin, because the gun was in his hand, because his finger was on the trigger, because he couldn't stop the trigger from being pulled. The lump of the handgun, the cold machine, is in his back pocket. Andrew's hands are currently filled with the wooden handle of the cursed weapon O'Bannon made. He wishes to hold Wen instead.

"Why are you sorry?" Eric doesn't know what to say to him. He wants to tell Andrew that he loves him but is afraid that it would sound final.

Andrew doesn't explain and says, "I'm sorry," again. He doesn't like how Eric stands, wavers, leaning one way and then the other, or how he talks with no inflection. He doesn't like how inscrutable Eric's eyes are. It's more than the concussion and dilated pupils and the shock of everything. Does he look this way because he has given up?

Eric says, "I said we can go now."

"I know. We're going."

We say the right words again, but we don't move. We stand there. Now that Sabrina is the only one of them left and unarmed, we're more afraid of what we are thinking and of what the other one of us is thinking. We're afraid for each other and we're afraid of ourselves. How can we go on? At this shared thought, we turn away from the television screen and away from each other.

Sabrina is behind Leonard with a mask stretched between her hands. She pulls it down over the pulpified, eroded mass of his head. The mesh conforms to his new, unrecognizable physiognomy, and the white immediately reddens. His concealed and misshapen head is grotesquely small, a bump atop the mountain range of his broad shoulders and prairie-wide chest, which strains to be contained within the looped ropes. His grisly, trussed corpse is a garish cartoon, a ludicrous exaggeration of the human form.

Andrew motions at Sabrina. "You and I are going out onto the deck first."

Sabrina asks, "Why?"

"To check O'Bannon's pockets for the truck keys."

"They're not there. I told you we hid them under a flat rock, and I promise I'll help you find them." She looks at Eric and her half smile turns into a wince as though she's ashamed, guilty to be appealing to him for support.

Andrew says, "There's no way a wannabe redneck like that would leave behind his truck keys."

Sabrina doesn't argue or protest. She walks the line between the kitchen and the common room to the deck and straddles Adriane's supine body as she fumbles with the screen slider, which stubbornly continues to reject its track.

"Just take it off and chuck it outside."

Sabrina carries the screen door onto the deck and stashes it between the picnic table and cabin wall. Andrew instructs her to stand next to O'Bannon and with her back against the wooden railing. Once she follows his directions, Andrew joins her on the deck. The air is warm and humid, ready to burst. Wind rattles through the trees and small waves lap at the lakeshore below. The gray sky is a smear, a *Neuromancer* sky, dead and anachronistic.

Eric walks behind Leonard and in full view of the doorway so he can see what's happening on the deck. The sun is muzzled, but the sky's grayness is too bright for him. He doesn't hear any birds chirping or whistling, only flies gathering on Leonard's corpse. He tries to drown out the buzzing with silent prayers and entreaties and *what do we do*s. Planes are falling in his head; one dives into the lake and sinks to the bottom, the water is nothing more than a curtain to be brushed aside.

Andrew says, "Lift the blanket and check his pockets." He hopes against hope that the keys are with O'Bannon. If they are, then he will have caught Sabrina in a lie and it will be easier to convince Eric she and the others have been lying all along and all this end-of-the-world bargaining insanity is in fact insanity.

Sabrina peels the blanket up from O'Bannon's lower half. She coughs and recoils from the release of a rancid, cloying, fecal smell that brutally imperializes the deck. Andrew reels backward. He holds a forearm over his nose and mouth, a gesture as feckless as building a wall of sand to hold back high tide.

Regathering herself, Sabrina is careful to fold the blanket so that O'Bannon's torso and head remain veiled. The bloodstains on his jeans have dried into a hardened crust. On her knees, she searches inside each front pocket, grimacing and grunting, and then turning them inside out.

Andrew asks, "Nothing in your hands? Did you palm a key?"

Sabrina holds up her empty hands.

"Check his back pockets." He's so desperate for the keys to be there he repeats himself. "Check his back pockets!"

"There's nothing there—"

"Check them! Now!"

Sabrina lifts O'Bannon onto his side and the smell impossibly becomes more intense, more physical, a thing clawing through membrane and matter. Sabrina's eyes water and her heavy breaths hiss through clenched teeth. She turns her head away from O'Bannon, gasping for clean air. "There's nothing in them. I can't pull these pockets out. You're going to have to have a look yourself." She balances the body on one hip.

O'Bannon's blue jeans have turned inky from an unholy mix of blood and shit. The back pockets appear to be bulgeless and fitting flush against the body, but Andrew can't know for sure if there isn't a single key in them. Sabrina drops O'Bannon's body before Andrew can make up his mind as to whether he was going to stick his hand in either pocket. She twists away from the body and drops to all fours, coughing and dry heaving.

Andrew says, "Maybe he tucked a key inside his socks. Check those, too."

"The keys aren't here."

"Just do it."

She rolls O'Bannon's pant cuffs over his thick, mottled calves. She sighs and says, "Look. He has those no-show ankle socks on. They don't even cover his—"

"Take his shoes off. He could've stuffed one key in his shoe. It has to be on him somewhere."

Sabrina shrugs and says, "Seriously?" She's losing her calm and I-just-want-to-help composure, which is fine by Andrew. She'll be more likely to slip up in a lie if she's frazzled and on edge.

Sabrina unties O'Bannon's shoes and she works them off his club-thick feet. "Andrew, we hid the keys in the woods. I promise. I'm not lying." She tumbles the clunky black shoes to Andrew. They clatter and flip and come to rest on their sides. No key comes clinking out. "Go ahead, check them. I haven't lied to you since I've been here. Not once." She stands up and re-covers the body's lower half.

Eric calls out from inside the cabin, "I don't think she's lying, Andrew. I really don't."

Sabrina says, "I'll show you where the keys are. It's possible you can find them without me, but I really don't think you will. I'm not saying that to taunt you. It's just the truth. But I'll find them and then you can leave me there on the side of the road, tied to a tree, or put me in the trunk and take me with you to the police, turn me in. Your choice. Whatever it is you want. I swear."

What Andrew wants is to have Wen back and to have Eric be his Eric and not this brain-bashed proto-zombie. And if he can't have that, then he wants to sit down and cry and never move again. He wants to cover himself with the blanket, the one that used to belong to us, used to be ours. He wants to tie Sabrina to the deck railing and leave her behind forever. He wants to know what exactly is going on in Eric's concussed head. He wants to yell and lash out at Eric for defending anything Sabrina says. He wants to take Wen away from Eric; rip her out of his hands.

Andrew says to Sabrina, "All right. Back in the cabin. Be quick."

Eric asks, "Aren't we going? Is she coming with us? I think we need—"

"We're all going!" Andrew yells.

That barking roar spikes through Eric's head, and he winces and closes his eyes. When he opens them, he looks past Andrew and to the lake, and a thought scurries: Eric could walk into the water with Wen in his arms, and he could walk until the water is over his head. He could walk until his feet sink into the muck and then weave binding chains from the weeds so he would never surface, never be exposed to the light. Then everything would be over; he would've made the required sacrifice and the world would be saved. Aren't those the rules? The rules some growing, metastasizing part of himself believes to be true? There is still doubt, but it has become easier to believe than not. Has it always been easier to believe? Either way, the lake solution doesn't feel right, and it wouldn't be fair of him to take Wen with him, take her away from Andrew. Eric drifts over to the couch and sits down. He spreads his legs wide, balances Wen's body on his thighs, and pulls his arms out from under her to give them a break. He needs the rest if he is going to carry her for the duration of the walk, however long or short it might be. Flies land on his arms and not Wen's body this time. He doesn't shoo them away.

Sabrina steps over Adriane and back into the cabin. Andrew follows. He sidesteps into the kitchen and grabs an eight-inch chef's knife from the cutting block. He tosses the sledgehammer weapon out the slider doors and it lands on O'Bannon. Andrew

says, "Good." With that nightmare stick back with its dead pro-
genitor, the cherry on the top of that refuse pile, Andrew is invig-
orated and more able to concentrate on what needs to be done to
survive the next minute and hopefully more minutes after that.

Andrew stalks back to the center of the cabin's common area
but slows down when there's a hiccupping click in his right knee,
a warning from his shifting bones to slow down. He navigates
more carefully over the blood-slicked floor. Sabrina stands with
her back against the front wall, and Eric is on the couch with Wen's
body across his lap. It's as though the trip to the deck didn't happen and no one has moved and nothing has changed. And just
like that Andrew's energy dissipates and a near-incapacitating
sadness and despair swells at the realization that even after we
walk out the front door, part of us will be trapped in the cabin
and in these positions forever.

Andrew says to Sabrina with his best impersonation of his
own stern, professorial voice, "Turn around, drop to your knees,
and put your hands behind your back."

Sabrina does as is instructed. Facing the wall, she says, "You
don't have to hurt me. I'm going to help you as much as I can."

Eric asks, "What are you doing?"

"I'm going to tie her hands together and then we'll all walk to
the keys."

Andrew saws lengths of rope away from Leonard's bound
legs. The size of the chef's knife makes it unwieldy for the job.
He accidentally pokes and jabs Leonard's body twice. Red beads
leak sluggishly from the puncture wounds like sap from a tree.
He manages to cut four arm-length pieces of rope loose. He carries them over to Sabrina, who is still on her knees, waiting. He
considers threatening her with consequences if she doesn't com-
ply but instead simply tells her not to move. He squats behind

her. His swollen right knee is a bowling ball. Sabrina's fingers and hands are pink with memories of blood. The back of her shirt is as white as a single puffy cloud in summer.

Andrew doesn't say anything to her and she doesn't say anything to him. He does a quick and rough job of tying her hands and wrists together with the first rope length. It will keep her bound long enough for him to take more care with the reinforcement lengths. If any of this process is uncomfortable or painful, Sabrina doesn't react to it. When he finishes, her hands and wrists are all but swallowed up by a thick dual spindle. He tries to pull her forearms apart and there's no movement, no give in the rope.

Eric is off the couch and standing behind Andrew. He looks at the door and is as afraid of what's outside as he is afraid of what's inside. He says, "We're doing the right thing."

Andrew does a double take because he thinks he hears *We're going to do the right thing.* He says to Sabrina, "Okay, you can stand up. Do you need help?"

"No, I don't." She lifts her right knee until her foot is flush against the floor and she stands smoothly and without much effort. She turns and flashes a friendly, I'm-on-your-side smile that slides into pity, an ugly transformation familiar to us both.

She says, "I'm ready."

Andrew walks to the front door and swings it open on creaking hinges.

Eric holds his breath and prays, asking for the light and whatever entity might be housed within to not be outside waiting for us. That there hasn't been another sighting of the shimmery figure only convinces him it will return. The cabin interior brightens by a few shades, enough to wash out color and add more shadow. This light is from a nowhere time, neither before nor after the golden hours of dawn and dusk. Nothing in the cabin moves; even Eric's flies are stilled.

Andrew stands in the open doorway and glances back inside the cabin. With bent metal pieces of the television frame and wires hanging limply from a splintered, jagged hole in the far wall and the blood on the floor congealing into colossal scabs. The room was thrashed and scored from within by parasites so greedy as to have killed the host.

Andrew waves his knife and says, "Come on." Sabrina is the first to walk outside, and she does so silently. Eric and Wen are next with Eric walking dutifully and with his head down. Andrew thinks about reaching out to touch his husband's shoulder as he passes, but he fails to lift his free hand in time. Eric is already down the stairs and to the grass. Andrew is the last to leave and he closes the door behind him, keeping whatever is left inside the cabin from following.

It's darker outside now than it was only minutes ago, and windier. The cloud cover is charcoal tinted. The cabin and surrounding trees block any attempt at distance viewing. At least from the deck, we could see across the lake to the forest and mountains and more easily imagine the wider world beyond us, beyond what we saw on the television. Without the elevated perspective, the front yard is the bottom of a grasshopper jar.

We walk across the lawn and to the gravel driveway. Our footsteps are loud and grinding. We don't feel safe. We're exposed and vulnerable, and we suppress the urge to run back inside the cabin and hide from this world.

Andrew says, "Hold up," and stops at our SUV. The passenger-side rear door is open, shark-tooth-shaped chunks of glass clinging stubbornly to the frame. The slashed tires have melted into pools of rubber. The vehicle is lopsided, a sunken derelict ship.

"We can't drive it. It's not going anywhere," he says as though having to explain or excuse leaving behind anything that belongs to us. He opens the rear hatch, which hisses as it lifts over his head.

The hissing is a shriek in Eric's ears and it echoes through the woods, stirring up a susurrus similar to but not the same as the mocking chorus of flies in the cabin; it's a deeper sound, the humming of power lines. Maybe it's a mistake to be outside, attempting to leave, acting like we can simply go on.

Eric asks, "What are you doing?"

"This will be quick." Bullets, those shiny brass threats, are seeds spilled and spread over the black-as-potting-soil trunk interior. Andrew ghosts over the evidence of his earlier struggle with Sabrina and those leavings now read like tea leaves, a forecasting of the events in the cabin that followed.

Andrew pulls the handgun from his back pocket. He studies the snub-nosed barrel from which exploded a bullet that looked no different from the ones lying dormant in the trunk, a bullet that passed through his daughter's—

"Stop it," Andrew whispers. He's going to reload this gun and bring it with him just in case Sabrina or anyone else has another surprise for us. Andrew says into the vehicle's interior but loud enough for Eric to hear, "When this is over and when we are safe, I am going to throw this gun into the woods or the lake or preferably a bottomless pit."

"I'll help you find one and we'll throw it in there together," Eric says. It comes out too eager and sentimental, so it feels like such a damned and obvious lie. Andrew reloading that gun, *the* gun, and then Eric's awkward attempt at commiseration is yet another microevent within the greater, grander days of horror and evil that will mark us whether we live another sixty seconds or sixty years, together or apart.

Andrew gathers the loose bullets quickly, before he can change his mind. They are small chilled things in his fingers and he loads the five chambers of the handgun. He returns the gun to his back pocket. He places the knife in the trunk next to the gun safe, leaving an offering for a bloodthirsty, violent god, were there any other kind.

Andrew faces Eric and is desperate to say something, anything besides *the gun is loaded so we can go.*

Eric adjusts Wen's body in his arms and walks down the driveway, toward Sabrina, who is as still as a photographic image.

Andrew leaves the SUV trunk open, hurrying to catch up to Eric. His right knee audibly grinds and clicks, and he catches himself as the knee buckles and gives out, leg quivering like a loose spring. "Shit!"

From the mouth of the driveway and standing next to Sabrina, Eric asks, "What's wrong?"

She sneaks glances at Eric as though she wants to tell him something that's meant only for him. Maybe she wants to tell Eric this is his last opportunity to save the world: leave Andrew behind while he and Sabrina continue down the road and along the way Eric can make the sacrifice, a self-sacrifice, without Andrew having to suffer through witnessing his suicide, without Andrew being there to stop him, and once it's done then Andrew will live. It will be hard but Andrew will live. And everyone else will live.

Eric says, "Maybe you should—" He pauses long enough, and purposefully, to let Andrew interrupt and to keep Eric from finishing his statement. *Maybe you should stay here.*

"Don't worry about me. I'm, um, rebooting the leg." Andrew regrets not taking one of the weapons with him as he could've used one as a cane. He walks more cautiously and with a pronounced, sputtering limp, only putting as much weight on his right leg as is absolutely necessary before skipping back onto his left. He scans the woods along the edge of the driveway for a walking stick and finds one that's long enough but might be too skinny to hold his full weight. It's a gnarled, arthritic finger and the bark is black, knotty, and dotted with green and white blossoms of lichen. It'll have to do. He says, "All set," and hobbles forward.

Sabrina calls out to Andrew in an overly cheery, high-pitched voice. "It's not that far. You can do it." And did he see a flash of a smartass smirk, the we're-on-to-you kind his better students give him when he's playfully obtuse in a group discussion? Sabrina holds Andrew with a look that pins him, and he now reads it as *I can sprint away at any time and you can't catch me and you won't shoot me.* Andrew quickens his pace, putting all his weight on his inadequate and warbly stick, desperate to prove he can achieve a brisk, healthy-legged walking speed. He should've gathered more rope and tethered a line between himself and Sabrina. What was he thinking? But it's too late now. There's no going back inside the cabin for more rope. There's no going back for anything.

We make a right turn at the end of the driveway. It's darker on the dirt road, which is narrower than we remember, only wide enough for one lane, and it might be our imaginations, but the road appears to be thinning, winnowing as we progress. The trees crowd our procession, wanting to be closer, to hold us, to stop us. They are our jurors and their whispered deliberations occur above in the canopy. The treetops sway and peer down for a better look, or a final one before they hold their thumbs down. Above the conspiratorial trees, the clouds have lost their individuality, pressed tightly into thick layers of ash. It's darker ahead, the road leading to a point beyond where we can see, to a point we may never reach.

After a few hundred paces of silent walking, the little red cabin is no longer visible. Sabrina is a few steps ahead of us. She walks evenly and with a confidence neither of us feels. We stagger behind, side by side, glancing nervously at each other.

Eric looks down at Wen and another panicked thought slithers in: later (however long or brief his *later* might be), when he remembers what it felt like to hold Wen in his arms, will he only and forever remember this death march? It doesn't feel like it's her that he's carrying. This isn't what he wants to remember, and her body is suddenly as heavy as a wooden cross. Eric recalls his Sunday school teacher, Mrs. Amstutz, a middle-aged woman who always wore blue print dresses, black patent shoes with silver buckles, and tan pantyhose that made her legs look wooden. She didn't smile and a tight-lipped pucker of disapproval was permanently etched onto her ruddy face. Eric's mother didn't like her very much. Mom never said so outright, but he could tell by how she referred to Mrs. Amstutz as "your teacher" and never by name. Mrs. Amstutz once spent an entire class harping on how heavy the cross was that Jesus was made to carry. She wasn't speaking metaphorically, either. She asked each of the children in the class to give a weight comparison. The other children enthusiastically compared its weight to cars, boulders, elephants, an offensive lineman for the Pittsburgh Steelers, Jabba the Hutt, and someone's overweight uncle; the kids did not take the question anywhere near as seriously as she intended. When it was Eric's turn, he was near tears and his heartbeat was a drumroll. In a regular classroom setting, Eric was composed, confident, and according to all his teachers, mature beyond his years. Sunday school was different. It wasn't the teacher that had him rattled and afraid. This was God's class. God was watching, listening, keeping track of what Eric said and did, and what he thought.

Mrs. Amstutz asked Eric three times how much he thought the cross weighed. He thinks of the question every time he goes to church and sees the cross hanging over the altar, and every time, he remembers his answer: the ten-year-old Eric squeaked out that he couldn't imagine anything being that heavy.

Andrew says, "Talk to me. How are you doing, Eric? Need me to carry her for a bit?"

Eric shakes his head not as an answer but at the uncanny timing of Andrew's inquiries. He needs to tell Andrew what he believes might need to be done. The *might* is still there within him, like a crumb of conscience in an unrepentantly guilty person, but it is shrinking. He says, "I know I'm injured. Concussed. Not thinking straight. But—"

"But what?"

We continue to walk together. Our feet grind into the road at different rhythms, leaving two separate paths of footprints in the dirt.

Eric says, "This might be real. I think it's happening."

"*It.* Tell me what it is that's happening." Andrew wants Eric to quit obliquely referring to the others' proposal of choice and apocalyptic consequence. If Eric can be made to spell it out in detail and stop with the midwestern, polite vagueness—like how people discuss but not-discuss a serious illness in the family— then Eric might understand how irrational it all is. Andrew, too, would benefit from having the illogic of what the others are proffering reinforced. In these dimming, implausible hours, he is not immune to doubt.

Eric feels like he's being made to answer his Sunday school teacher's *how heavy* question all over again. He cannot explain how heavy this is. Andrew should know; he's supposed to know.

Eric has too much he wants to say at once and is unable to

organize it all. What's happening to us is this big unwieldy thing in his head, changing form and shape with each passing second. There's no beginning at the beginning, so he says, "Those planes all crashing and crashing when they did, at the same time. Leonard said they would fall from the sky."

"No. He didn't say that."

"Yes, he did."

"He never said anything about planes. Did he ever say the word *planes*?"

"No, but—"

"Leonard said the sky would fall into pieces. He didn't say planes. Like a scam psychic, he made a general statement, one culturally associated with end-of-the-world stories, essentially saying the sky is falling, and he let you fill in the details. What if we'd turned on the news and saw a skyscraper collapsing? That means the sky is falling into pieces, right? Or how about a monsoon or a nasty hailstorm; one could argue either of those would be closer to a literal interpretation of *the sky is falling*. Or it could've been a mass die-off of birds, or chunks of falling satellite or, I don't know, space stations, goddamn Skylab 2.0 plummeting to Earth . . . whatever. Metaphorically, you can retrofit almost anything to—"

"Come on, Andrew, it's not much of a metaphorical leap from sky to planes. The planes literally fell out of the sky and in pieces. He said 'pieces.'"

"Frankly, so what?" Andrew pauses and flashes on the images of the wrecked planes, and he remembers the fear coursing through his nerves like a rabies virus, and then his giving in to the impulse to destroy the television so he wouldn't see them anymore. With as much of the voice of reason as he can muster, he adds, "Planes crash all the time."

"All the time? Yes, they just drop like leaves in the fall. We're always having to look up and take cover and—"

"All right, an exaggeration, but only a slight one. Crashes do happen frequently. It's a numbers game: there are thousands and thousands of planes all over the world in the air at any given time. The day before we drove up here that little pond hopper crashed into a house in Duxbury."

"Yes, fine, but this is different than a little two-seater going down. These were commercial airplanes all crashing at the same time. You smashed the TV, but it sounded like there were more planes, maybe even all the ones in the air, and crashing right after Leonard was killed."

"You know, it's only occurring to me now that that's not true, either."

"What's not true?"

"The planes crashing *after* Leonard was killed. Think about the timeline here: the planes had to have crashed before Leonard died, probably at least twenty minutes or so before."

"What are you talking about?"

"If the planes had crashed at the exact moment Leonard died, the news wouldn't have had enough time to gather and air the footage we saw."

"Video is practically instant now. Everyone has a camera."

"They weren't broadcasting phone videos, certainly not the fly-over footage of wreckage, that plane in the ocean especially. Those crashes had to have happened before Sabrina killed Leonard."

"I guess so, maybe, but that's not the point. I mean, are you quibbling over the timing?"

"The timing is pretty important, don't you think?"

"Yes, of course, because everything Leonard said would happen did happen, and it happened each time after one of them was killed. You really think everything we've seen, everything we've been through has been a coincidence?"

Andrew says, "I do," as more of an affirmation to himself. "They knew about the Alaskan earthquake before they came to the cabin and then, yes, that second quake and tsunami hit was coincidental. But then they knew the preprogrammed, scheduled bird flu show would be on the next morning and had it timed to the minute with their watches, and then—"

"And then all those planes just happened to crash when Leonard died."

"They didn't crash when—"

"Andrew!"

"Yes, fine, a coincidence, but not an outlandish one. Maybe the planes were a preplanned part of their narrative, too. It's possible the others were aware of reports, government warnings about terrorists or—what did they say?—cyberattacks on planes and we didn't hear anything because we were up here and hadn't watched TV or been on the internet for days. Even if that isn't the case, all they had to do was make us watch cable news where it's bad news all the time. Turn it on and within minutes you're bombarded with breaking news of wars, suicide bombings, mass shootings, trains-planes-and-automobiles crashes . . ."

"It doesn't work that way. They can't get that lucky with guesses and maybes and turn on the TV and hope for something random to fit. Not like this."

"Think about the psychological stress and state they put us in. They break in, terrorize us, tie us up, and you seriously injure your head. Then they tell us pseudo-Christian-biblical-end-of-times vagaries knowing that at any moment they can turn on the news and in our fried and frazzled brains something will very likely stick."

"So I believe them because I'm Catholic, right? That's so unfair and—"

"No, Eric, no, I'm not saying that, not trying to make you feel bad, I'm trying—"

"And they aren't vagaries—drowned cities, plague, sky falling into pieces. Those things happened. I know you want me to hear how preposterous it all sounds, but you should listen to yourself. You're bending yourself into a pretzel rationalizing the impossibilities."

"That's just it. I'm telling you it's not—" Andrew cuts himself off and starts over. "Eric, I'm going to ask you straight out: Do you think one of us has to be killed by the other to keep the world from ending?"

"Why would those four make it all up and make us go through this?"

"You didn't answer my—"

"Answer mine."

"Jesus, Eric, the fucking guy who hate-crimed me broke into our cabin. O'Bannon and the others came here with a plan to terrorize the queers. There's your why."

"If it was him."

"Eric—"

"I know, I'm sorry, but I'm not as sure as you are that it's the same guy. He—he looks different to me, but even if it is him, is that enough of a why? I mean, why go through everything else? If it was only about us, they wouldn't have been killing each other, would they?"

"They're cultists. That's what they are. Homophobic, doomsday cultists. They take meaning, identity, and purpose from believing they know the end is coming. Not only that, these pious soldiers of their god believe they have the power to stop the apocalypse if they can manipulate the gays into hurting each other. If that fails, then they get to start the end of the world themselves. They're broken and delusional and everything they've done and everything they do serves to keep their delusion intact, to keep it alive. Think about it, it's a no-lose for them, as far as their delusion goes. If one of us kills the other and then the world doesn't end—because it's not ending, not right now, anyway—then they were right, yeah? And if they all kill themselves instead, it doesn't matter that the apocalypse won't then happen, because they won't be around to see the world going on without them."

"I know but—that makes sense, and it sounds right. But it isn't. Maybe all the stuff we saw and if Redmond is really O'Bannon, it's all proof God is really testing—"

"Are you going to answer my question?"

"What question?"

"The one you haven't answered. Do you think one of us has to kill the other in order to—?"

"Not yet."

Andrew isn't sure what Eric means by that two-word answer. Does the "not yet" mean he's not ready to answer the question, or does it mean we do have to make the sacrifice, just not now, *not yet*?

We are finally on pause. Our manic, rapid-fire quid pro quo leaves us breathing heavily and as skittish as rabbits in an open field. Our minds replay everything we said and didn't say. We don't look at each other. Sabrina remains silent, a few paces ahead of us, plodding along with her head down. We keep our eyes on the road veined with ruts, pitted with sunken holes and loose stones, and flanked by a forest that will one day reclaim it. We can no longer imagine the road's end. Our eyes float upward trying to escape.

Andrew sees darker, threatening storm clouds. He tastes and smells rain in the air. His ears pop with the decreasing atmospheric pressure and temperature. The low rumble of thunder announces itself in the distance.

Eric sees an alien sky gone more purple than black, like a bruise. Its color changes the longer he watches; the sky becomes more gray than purple, and then more black than gray, and another change to more purple than both colors, then a color he's never seen before and could only describe as being more purple than purple. The sky is so low and looks like a painted ceiling. The thunder rolling into the valley isn't thunder; it's the sound of the avalanching sky. Eric's head throbs, sending hot stinging waves to the backs of his believing eyes.

We walk and we watch and we wait for Sabrina to tell us we are where they hid the truck keys. Rain falls tentatively. We hear the light patter of raindrops on the leaves before we feel it on our skin.

Andrew clears his throat and says, "Eric." He clears his throat again, more loudly and protracted. "What about Wen?" His voice cracks and spills open on the rocks of her name.

"What do you mean?"

"On top of everything else, they expect us to believe Wen's death isn't—"

Sabrina shouts, "No! No!" and dashes into a graceless sprint, her twisting torso a poor substitute for free-swinging arms.

Andrew yells at her to stop where she is. He pulls out the handgun from his back pocket with his left hand and holds it out in front of him, as far away from his body as he can reach. She doesn't stop or slow down. He doesn't shoot, and he limps after her.

Sabrina's and Andrew's shouts, grunts, and their grinding, leaden footfalls are an overture to the end, their spastic move-

ments an asymmetric ballet to the chaotic, atonal fuss. Eric
doesn't run or walk faster to keep up with them. He feels like a
fool, a hopeless, helpless fool for ever believing we could survive
this.

The rope tied around Sabrina's hands and wrists does not un-
wind or unspool or turn slack and spaghettify and become an
elongating white tail. Seemingly without effort on her part, as
though the act of her running simply triggers release, the ball of
rope slides off completely intact, keeping its shape and splatting
onto the road like a wad of putty.

Sabrina alternates pumping her arms and covering her ears
with her freed hands, yelling what might be, "I'm helping them!"

Andrew considers a warning shot in the air to keep her from
growing the distance between them. Before he swaps hands with
the gun and walking stick—he has never shot with his left—
Sabrina veers into the woods. Only three or four steps away from
the road, she drops to her knees in front of the broad knotted
trunk of a pine tree. Grunting, she flips up a sizable flat stone and
rotates it away to her left. She then roots around in the under-
growth with her hands.

Andrew staggers to the road's edge. Eric is not far behind
and quickly catches up. With Andrew on his left, Eric steps off
the road and into the greenery. Sabrina, in profile, is crying and
talking to herself. Eric is close enough to see her dirt-and-mud-
smeared hands appearing and disappearing.

Andrew tucks the walking stick under his armpit and points
the gun at Sabrina's back. "What the fuck was that? You should've
told us we're here. You didn't need"—he glances back at the plop
of rope in the road—"you could've just shown us where the keys
are. What are you doing? Are you digging? You didn't say any-

thing about digging. I want you to stand up and show me your hands."

Sabrina stands and turns to face us. In her right hand she dangles car keys on a red keychain. She underhand-tosses them. The keys fly a brief arcing trajectory, passing between us, and they land with a muted jingle in the middle of the road. Her left arm up to the elbow has disappeared inside a dark blue vinyl drawstring bag.

Andrew shouts, "What's that?" He raises the gun, but he hasn't been able to bring himself to slide his finger over the trigger. He doesn't want to feel it, doesn't want to remember how it felt when it was last pulled. His finger is instead curled over the front of the guard. "Drop it, Sabrina. Hey, you said you were going to help us. Remember? This isn't helping . . ."

She says, "The truck is only another mile or so down the road. Take the keys. You can make it." Her rhythm and inflection is off, like she's reading a statement presented to her without punctuation or proper form.

Eric wishes Sabrina would look at him instead of Andrew, though she's not really looking at Andrew, either; her eyes are unfocused, somewhere beyond us. Eric needs to see the terrible light's reflection in her eyes, and then he'll be sure of what he has to do.

Sabrina pulls the bag away and drops it to the ground, revealing a handgun bigger than Andrew's. The black brick of polymer filling her left hand appears to be a semiautomatic Glock. She says, "I didn't know Redmond left this here. I swear to you both. It had to have been Redmond. Oh my God . . ."

"Come on, Sabrina. Open your hand and let it fall," Andrew says.

"How did I not see him leave this here? I watched him hide

the keys under the rock and that's where they were and now this bag is here, too, buried underneath. I never saw the bag and I never saw the gun—"

"Put the gun down, now, Sabrina."

"I would've seen Redmond carrying the bag here. I walked next to him the whole time down the road. Unless it was Leonard. Maybe Leonard buried it here first, before we got here. When we parked the truck, Leonard took off, running ahead of us so he could be the first one at the cabin. Like he was supposed to, right? Like he was supposed to. . ."

The gun being here makes perfect sense to Andrew. If everything went wrong at the cabin, the others would still have this hidden weapon, their trump card. Andrew slides his finger through the guard and over the trigger of his gun. He doesn't know if he can do this. Any of this.

Sabrina finding the gun makes perfect sense to Eric, too. As she is the last of the four, this gun is her chance to make the final sacrifice if we don't choose.

Sabrina's gun is down by her hip, pointed at the ground. She reaches into her back pocket and pulls out a white mesh mask. She roughly pulls it over the top of her head with one hand. It goes on askew, tilted, and it only covers the top half of her head and face. An unfinished concession to ritual, her mouth and the tip of her nose remain uncovered.

The rain is falling heavier now, turning the red clay of the road to dark brown. The blood on Sabrina's shirt runs, becoming pink.

She says, "You have the keys. You should go, please. Just go. Drive, away from here, and then you'll—" She pauses to allow herself to cry, openmouthed and silent. She presses the back of her hand over her mouth and then says, "I'm so sorry. I wanted to help you. I tried to help you, help you more than this."

Andrew says, "Put down the gun and you can still help by coming with us to the police and telling them everything that happened. We need you to do that for us."

Sabrina shakes her half-obscured head. "I want to, believe me. But I can't. I won't be allowed to."

Eric bends and reverently lays Wen's body on a bed of fern-like plants. He kneels next to her, and fat raindrops darken her shroud. The bandage on the back of his head finally gives way and slides off.

Sabrina swings the gun up in a smooth and precise motion. Her left arm is animatronic. The arm moves like it is not of her. She presses the muzzle against her temple. Her right arm waves and flutters, a confused mash-up of *go away* and *please help me* gestures. She is still crying with her mouth open, now wide enough to fit a scream.

Andrew points the gun at her left shoulder and cocks the hammer back. "Put it down, Sabrina! Don't do this!"

Eric stands up too rapidly, and his vision fills with stars that turn into oozing inkblots of light. He closes his eyes and takes three deep breaths. When he opens them again, Sabrina is turned toward him and whispering, in an almost comically open manner. "You still have time to save everyone. Eric. You still have a chance. Even after. But you have to do it quick." Sabrina shakes her head no, disagreeing with what she just said. Then she says, "You are—" and her gun goes off. The bullet plows through her head and exits with a ribbon of blood. Her body collapses against the fir tree and lands with her torso partially propped up. Her head lolls to her right, conveniently allowing its contents to empty through the exit wound.

Andrew shouts, "Fuck!" and spins away. He screams the curse repeatedly and bends over, his hands on his knees. Rain beats down on his head and back. He delicately uncocks the hammer of his gun.

Eric walks through the brush to Sabrina's body, and he takes the gun from her hand, which is open. The gun is lighter than he anticipated. The forest darkens; there's no end to how dark it can get. Flies swarm Sabrina's body, crawling over her mask and in and out of her uncovered and open mouth. Their buzzing adds an undercurrent to the thunder, which he realizes isn't thunder, not anymore. He's hearing ancient gears grinding and clicking into place, and perhaps irrevocably turning.

Andrew remains bent over and facing away from Eric. Should Eric do it before Andrew turns around? It would be easier that way. He prays silently, fills his broad chest with air, and says, "She said I could still save everyone."

Andrew straightens and finds Eric in the woods and standing in front of Sabrina's body. He has her gun in his right hand and his arm is angled across his chest.

"Eric . . ."

"She said I have to do it quick."

Andrew asks, "Where is Wen?"

"She's right there. Close by. I wouldn't leave her. I didn't want to put her down, but I had to."

Seeing her on the ground alone is like seeing her on the cabin floor all over again. "Maybe I should carry her now."

"I think you might have to. Sabrina said the truck isn't far."

Andrew doesn't move. He's afraid to move. "Hey, I didn't get to finish what I was going to say about Wen because Sabrina took off running and then—" He stops talking and points at Sabrina's body.

"What were you going to say about Wen?" Eric understands what the others were experiencing when they kept telling us that time was running out. It's a physical sensation; he can feel it splashing in his blood.

Andrew says, "Forget O'Bannon, Redmond, and all the co-incidences and the rules and everything else. Focus on this: they expect us to believe that Wen's death isn't a good-enough sacrifice for their god. So you know what? Fuck them and their god. Fuck them all." He says it all in one breath and then gives in to full-on sobbing. Tears and rain mix and wash down his face, blurring Eric and the forest.

Before today, Eric has only seen Andrew cry once. It was when Andrew returned to their apartment after the two-day hospital stay, post–bar attack. Eric sat next to Andrew on the edge of the bed and wrapped his arms around him. No one spoke. Andrew cried and he cried, and when it was over he said, "That's enough of that."

Eric says, "You're right. You are. And I know you can give a reason for everything that happened, that's happening, but—" He waits and gives Andrew a chance to say the right thing, the impossible right thing that would make this all go away and take us and Wen back home safe.

Andrew doesn't know what it is Eric needs him to say, so he'll just keep talking until he lands on it. "I'm really sorry about the Christian crack earlier." He sputters a half cry, half laugh and Eric only blinks at him. "But you—"

"I saw something in the cabin you didn't see, Andrew. I think I was supposed to see it. And I felt it, too. I experienced it. It was real and it was made of light and it was there when they killed Redmond, when they were pushed to kill him. And then it was—it was all light the next time and I closed the door to keep it out."

"I have no doubt you saw and felt something, just as I have no doubt they were concussion induced—"

"Stop saying that."

"I won't, because I love you and I won't let you do this."

"I—I know. I love you, too, more than you know. But I'm sorry; one of us must."

"Is the light thing here now?"

"No." Eric wishes it was here. He hopes it will show up and take him over like the others were taken over and lead him by the hand. But it's not here. He feels its lack of presence. There's only woods, darkness, rain, thunder, and us.

Andrew drops his gun to the wet road. He limps into the woods without his walking stick and stops within arm's reach of Eric. "So which one of us is it going to be, then?"

We stare at each other's beat-up, red-eyed, blood-streaked, beard-stubbled, still-beautiful faces waiting for an answer, waiting for the answer.

"Please don't try to take the gun away from me." Eric pivots and lifts his forearm so that the gun is pointed under his chin.

"I won't touch the gun. I promise I won't." Andrew inches closer. "Look at me, okay? Maybe you won't see anything you don't want to see if you look at me."

"Stay away, please." Eric steps back and his heels bump into Sabrina's legs.

"That I can't do. It's all right. I'm not taking the gun. I'm taking your other hand. That's all. That's okay, right?" Andrew reaches out and his fingertips make tentative first contact. The back of Eric's hand is cool and damp. Eric's fingers clench into a fist as Andrew's touch springs them shut. "Are you're going to leave me all alone then?"

Eric unclenches his fist. Andrew closes his hand around Eric's.

"You're too close. You should back up. I don't want you to get hurt," Eric says.

"Would you shoot me instead? I'd rather not be here alone, without you. Not for one second."

Eric gazes into Andrew's face, an ever-evolving landscape more familiar than his own. He doesn't pray, not to the light or to God. He whispers, "I don't want you to be alone," and then he gasps as Andrew gently places a hand on his wrist just below the gun.

"It's all right. I'm not taking the gun from you. I said I wouldn't." Andrew pulls the gun out from under Eric's chin. He leads Eric's arm until the gun is turned on Andrew, the muzzle pinned against his chest. "Shooting me would be your ultimate sacrifice, wouldn't it? Because then you'd be the one stuck here alone."

"Unless I shoot you and then myself. I don't think that's against the rules."

Andrew doesn't say anything. He drops his hand away from Eric's wrist. The gun remains pointed, adhered to his sternum.

Eric says, "I don't know what to do."

"Yes, you do. You'll throw the gun away, Eric. It'll be hard, but we'll pick up the truck keys and we'll walk down the road."

Our faces are only inches apart. We breathe each other's breaths, blink each other's blinks. We squeeze our hands together. The rain traces the lines of our expressions, those characters of the most complex language.

Eric asks, "What if it's all real?"

"But it's not, I—"

"Andrew!" Eric yells and Andrew jerks his head in surprise. Eric wants to pull the gun away from Andrew's chest and nestle it back under his own chin. But the gun stays where it is, and Eric implores, repeating his question. "What if it's all real?"

Andrew inhales, and his defiant answer is in the exhale. "If it is. Then it is. We're still not going to hurt each other."

"What will we do? We can't go on."

"We'll go on."

We stare, and we watch the rain and we watch our faces, and we don't say anything, and we say everything.

Eric pulls the gun off Andrew's chest, lowers his arm, and drops the gun to the forest floor. He leans into Andrew. Andrew leans into Eric.

We lean into each other and our heads are side by side, cheek to cheek. Our arms hang at our sides like lowered flags, but our fingers find each other's fingers, and we hold on.

The sky is a depthless black, impossible to not attribute malignancy and malice to it as strobing flashes of lightning split it open. Wind and thunder rattle through the forest, sounding like the earth dying screaming. The storm swirls directly over us. But we've been through countless other storms. Maybe this one is different. Maybe it isn't.

We will pick the truck keys out of the mud. We will lift Wen into our arms and we will carry her and we will remember her and we will love her as we will love ourselves. We will walk down the road even if it is flooded by raging waters or blocked by fallen trees or if greedy fissures open beneath our feet. And we will walk the perilous roads after that one.

We will go on.

ACKNOWLEDGMENTS

First and foremost, thank you to my family and extended family who support, love, and put up with me.

Thank you to my beta readers: my cousin Michael Coulombe, who was among a small group of family to read the first short story I ever wrote more than twenty years ago and I brought him back to beta read for this one; one of my favorite writers and a great friend, Stephen Graham Jones; and my friend and go-to beta reader, John Harvey, who has been reading and critiquing my stuff for more than a decade now. Their input was invaluable.

Thank you to my editor and friend, Jennifer Brehl. In early discussions about this book, she saved me from making a disastrous choice, and after I wrote the book, she was there to clean it all up and pick me up when I stumbled. I can't imagine writing a novel without her in my corner.

Thanks to everyone at William Morrow for their hard work and getting the book-word out.

Thank you to my agent, Stephen Barbara, for his friendship, enthusiasm, advice, and general awesomeness. I can't imagine a literary life without him. Thank you to my film rights agent, Steve Fisher, for his tireless work, support, our excellent lunches, and his enthusiasm for this novel in particular.

Thank you to all my friends and colleagues for their inspiration and for indulging my blathering and fretting, with special thanks to: John Langan for our weekly phone calls and his oddly threatening cacti; Laird Barron for being the devil on my shoulder who makes me do right; the band Future of the Left and Andrew Falkous for his friendship, our monthly late and later-night chats, and for another epigraph; the band Clutch and Neil Fallon for two great shows and conversations during the summer of 2017 and for the epigraph; Nadia Bulkin for her inspiring writing, taste in film, and her epigraph; the band Whores, who get extra bonus thanks for loaning their song title "Bloody Like the Day You Were Born" to the third section of this book; Stephen King for turning me into a reader, for his kind support of my books, and for his all-around awesomeness; Sarah Langan, Brett Cox, and JoAnn Cox for being my generous and always-positive friends and Shirley Jackson Awards coconspirators; Jack Haringa for his friendship, his whiskey expertise, his book release interviewer prowess, and being the president we all deserve; Anthony Breznican for being unfailingly kind and taking Sarah Langan and I on a hike through the St. Francis Dam ruins in Valencia; Jennifer Levesque (my slightly older sister-cousin) and Dave Stengel for their love and generosity in always letting me stay at their place whenever I visit NYC, though I suspect I might not be able to with that older crack; Brian Keene for being a superhero and my gun consultant—any mistakes in that area are mine and not his; Kris Meyer for never giving up; Stewart O'Nan for helping me get started and stay started; Dave Zeltserman for fighting the good fight; and you for reading this book.

About the author

About the book

Read on

Insights,
Interviews
& More ...

Meet Paul Tremblay

Michael Lajoie/Crimson Imagery

PAUL TREMBLAY has won the Bram
Stoker, British Fantasy, and Massachusetts
Book Awards and is the author of *Growing
Things, Disappearance at Devil's Rock,
A Head Full of Ghosts,* and the crime
novels *The Little Sleep* and *No Sleep
Till Wonderland.* He is currently a
member of the board of directors of
the Shirley Jackson Awards, and his
essays and short fiction have appeared
in the *Los Angeles Times, Entertainment
Weekly* online, and numerous year's-best
anthologies. He has a master's degree in
mathematics and lives outside Boston
with his family. ༶

The Cabin at the End of the World: Extended Liner Notes

That was fun, right?

(I assume you read the book before turning to the back to read this here thing. You really should read the book before wandering back here. No good will come from the following otherwise.)

Below is a collection of somewhat disjointed thoughts on the writing of the book.

Origin

The novel started with a sketch in my notebook. I was flying back to the East Coast from Los Angeles and doodling in one of my writing notebooks. Tucked underneath a random joke from *Young Frankenstein*, I unconsciously or subconsciously drew a little cabin. The cabin made me think of the home-invasion subgenre. Oddly enough it's probably my least favorite kind of horror subgenre. Home-invasion stories are so personally frightening, but it seems so many of the movies focus on the violence/torture over character. So I thought, Okay, big mouth, how would *you* write a home-invasion story then? When I got home I moved the cabin ▶

sketch/idea into a more serious notebook (I have issues . . .) and fleshed out who the characters would become.

(The watching-a-film thing is something I wrote about in my short story "The Teacher," and here it evolved into the family being shown news clips on the satellite television. I still don't know what "fancy pen horror" is.)

Chapter 1

• The only book that I reread before I started to write *Cabin* was the classic *Lord of the Flies* by William Golding. It's not a home-invasion story, clearly, but I wanted the mind-set of that novel. I wanted my book to (hopefully) make the reader feel the way that book makes me feel. The opening lines of *Cabin* are a riff on the opening lines of *Flies*. • Being a math person by day (um, no math at night; them's the rules), I couldn't help but play some numbers games with the book. Its original, working title was *The Four*, in reference to that special number of invaders who show up. The book is broken up into four sections and I was going to include a fourth epigraph (more on that in the last chapter). Anyway, yes, it was purposeful that Wen and Leonard catch seven grasshoppers (the same number of main characters in the novel) and then have a discussion about that number. Seven seals (not the cute aquatic mammals; different seals), perhaps? • The sizable Leonard was named after *Of Mice and Men*'s Lenny. • Leonard and Wen sitting across from each other on the grass is meant to recall an iconic scene in James Whale's *Frankenstein* (1931).

Chapter 2

• A yellow canoe glides by the cabin. For years I've been borderline obsessed with using the color yellow in many of my stories without ever really being able to explain why. In an older novella called "The Harlequin and the Train," reprinted by Concord Free Press as one half of a free book called *Another Way to Fall* (Yes, I said *free*; all you have to do is write them and ask for a copy.), the color yellow was used to mirror the yellow letters crawling across the news ticker on a television screen. In one of my earlier novels, *A Head Full of Ghosts*, yellow was a reference to the classic short story "The Yellow Wallpaper." In *Cabin* (or at least in my mind), yellow represents death. • Eric's nondescript thriller about a child going missing—yeah, he's reading (and not really into) my novel *Disappearance at Devil's Rock*. Everyone's a critic. • I mention Andrew reading aloud passages about Gabriel García Márquez's novel *One Hundred Years of Solitude*. There are many academics who think yellow represents death in that novel. So that was a tiny, yellow clue, I suppose, not one I would expect anyone to pick up when reading my book. Sometimes I play little games with myself to keep the novel-writing process fresh and interesting (interesting to me, anyway). And playing with yellow here was a fun way to keep my gears spinning instead of ▶

grinding during the writing process. Let's keep track of the end table and its little yellow lamp going forward, okay? • Leonard, Sabrina, Adriane, and Redmond. Their names all have seven letters. Their names have origins/meanings that correspond to the color of their shirts. The colors correspond, mostly, to the color of the Four Horsemen. • Redmond knocks over the little yellow lamp and that means he's going to be the first to die. You'll see.

Chapter 3

• One of the tropes of crime fiction is the hero getting knocked in the head and passing out at the end of one chapter and then waking up in the next chapter, confused and in trouble, but physically none the worse for wear. That's not how concussions work, particularly if it's a serious one. If you black out, it's a serious concussion. I coach a couple of sports as a part of my teaching day job and part of that responsibility includes my having to take and pass an online concussion course at the start of every school year. Glad I could finally make use of all those classes when I wrote Eric's concussion. I mean, of course, besides keeping my players safe and all that. • I have to admit I'm partial to *Adventure Time* but *Steven Universe* is a nice show. • If a novel is to have a thesis statement then this one has two. The last line of the novel is one and the following line is the other: "As though *everyday people* have nothing but love in their hearts and are always reasonable and have never committed atrocities in the name of their self-proclaimed *everydayness*." • Masks of all sorts have been worn by slashers and would-be killers in many a horror movie. Those masks tend to lend the killer personality or character. I thought the featureless white masks that rubbed out the wearer's identity would be creepy. • I spent a long time writing the different POVs of the sacrifice of Redmond. That was hard to write. • In January 2018—about a month after advance reader/review copies of *Cabin* had already been printed and sent out into the cold, cruel world—there was an earthquake off the coast of the Aleutians. I know, right? And parts of the Pacific Northwest were then put on a tsunami watch. I KNOW, RIGHT? Well, thankfully, no tsunami and everyone was okay. Later that afternoon I got an email from a more-than-kind-of-famous horror writer who'd already read the book. The email referenced the earthquake and ended with "Quick, sacrifice someone!" Cooler heads prevailed. • Adriane tries turning on the yellow lamp so that means she'll be next to die.

Chapter 4

• The POV here is an odd (odd to me, anyway) third-person plural using both Andrew's and Eric's perspectives; a warm-up for the odder POV in the final chapter. • Maybe this is weird but I was really excited to write this nothing-really-happens part of the book. I thought that the remaining intruders cleaning up and then making dinner and sitting around chatting like everything was fine and okay could be a quietly disturbing scene. Not to bring you down, but I wanted to reflect our own day-to-day and the awful stuff we have to ignore (or at least forget about for a few hours) to be able to go about the business of living without going totally mad. Also, this might be the first time I've written characters having to use the bathroom. Felt like gritty realism to me! • Wen wakes up in the middle of the night, and yeah, I'm sorry, but she tries to turn on the yellow lamp, so that means . . . • The name "Jeff O'Bannon" is a splicing of two politicians' names together. • The Penalty Box is a real bar/place. • The story Andrew told Wen about how he got his scar is from my childhood. I was eight years old and playing in a neighborhood baseball game (unsupervised by adults, which is how it should be, despite what ▶

happened next). We were using only a tennis ball so I thought
it would be okay to play catcher without a mask. Oops. One batter
flung his bat back right into my head. I saw literal stars and then
passed out briefly. There was lots of blood. And then there were
eight stitches on the right side of my forehead. I will not age
myself by telling you the year this occurred, but it was long ago
enough that *concussion* was not part of any diagnosis or concern.
My bell got rung, as they used to say. And hard. • "Targeted
Individuals'," or TIs', eschewing treatment and congregating
online is a real, sad, and frightening thing. • Andrew's escape
from the cabin and the run to the SUV for a gun was the section
of the book that took me the longest to write. My hope was to
realistically stage the action (and set up the big and terrible end
to the chapter) without losing the tone of what came before.
• Poor Wen . . .

Chapter 5

• One of my biggest concerns about the book's construction
relates to the transition here. I didn't want Wen's death to be
the emotional climax of the book with another eighty or so pages
still to go (and maybe it is, I don't know . . . but at the very least
I was fully aware of that potential issue). I thought switching to
Leonard's POV, even briefly, was important to keep the reader on
unsteady footing while adjusting to Wen's death. In my first draft
this Leonard chapter was written in second person. I thought
it might be a way to implicate the reader in the action and further
prep the reader for the jarring POV in the final chapter. But
I switched the voice from second to third person because I
didn't want readers thinking I wanted them to sympathize
with Leonard. • Leonard throws rope that knocks into the
yellow lamp, so you know he's next.

Chapter 6

• Maybe the lesson learned here is to never trust young people wearing watches? • More odd POV switches here. I thought it was especially important to dip into Sabrina's POV. I do not want readers sympathizing with the invaders. But I did think their experience was a horror worth exploring: the horror of feeling like you have no freedom and no choice. That's a horror partly because abdicating personal responsibility is kind of attractive. Living without conscience, maintaining that you have no choice because of a set of beliefs, I imagine, could be quite intoxicating. That break with the social compact is terrifying to me. • I wanted to use a reference to some kind of drowned city event. Friend and writer Anthony Breznican told me about the collapse of the St. Francis Dam in Valencia, California. Then he did one better and in April 2017 he took me on a tour of the ruins, which are as described (to the best of my ability) in the novel. I tried to capture how eerie that walk through a past disaster felt. • After Sabrina kills Leonard, she tosses her staff away, and it knocks over the yellow lamp. She's next.

Chapter 7

• Andrew's and Eric's POV, presented as first-person plural. We. Would it be too cheesy of me to say that *we* are Andrew and Eric by the end? • I originally intended to have a fourth epigraph at the start of the novel, quoting Samuel Beckett's novel *The Unnamable*, but then I thought it would give away the end of my book. • When I conceived of *Cabin* and during the first quarter of its life in my head, I had a much bleaker ending in mind. But for a variety of reasons, I couldn't do it and didn't want to do it. I needed to go out on a note of defiant ▶

hope. The movie *The Terminator*, of all things, helped me reshape the end of the book. That movie ends with Sarah Connor (played by Linda Hamilton) in the desert, fleeing south, and a boy takes the Polaroid picture the nice man from the future (the father of her son) would then carry around with him in the future and bring back with him to the past. She's sad because he's dead and sad because Skynet is going to blow up the world, but. . . . But. She's still a badass. And she's still going to fight. That's defiant hope. I could be petulant and say if you must admit you failed the book's empathy test, feel free to add a line of your choosing to the end: "Then the world ended" or "Then the world didn't end." But I won't be petulant! My defiant hope for you is that this book ultimately becomes about the choice Eric and Andrew make and not whether or not the world is actually ending. I mean, shit, their world has already been definitively shattered, don't you think? It's about the choice: do they and do *we* choose fear or that most defiant of all hopes, love? ∿

Have You Read?
More by Paul Tremblay

DISAPPEARANCE AT DEVIL'S ROCK

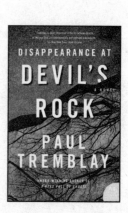

Late one summer night, Elizabeth Sanderson receives the devastating news that every mother fears: her thirteen-year-old son, Tommy, has vanished without a trace in the woods of a local park.

The search isn't yielding any answers, and Elizabeth and her young daughter, Kate, struggle to comprehend Tommy's disappearance. Riddled with worry, pain, and guilt, Elizabeth is wholly unprepared for the strange series of events that follow. She believes a ghostly shadow of Tommy materializes in her bedroom, while Kate and other local residents claim to see a shadow peering through their windows in the dead of night. Then, random pages torn from Tommy's journal begin to mysteriously appear—entries that reveal an introverted teenager obsessed with the phantasmagoric; the loss of his father, killed in a drunk-driving accident a decade earlier; a folktale involving the devil and the woods of Borderland; and a horrific incident that Tommy believed connects them. ▸

As the search grows more desperate, and the implications of what happened become more haunting and sinister, no one is prepared for the shocking truth about that night and Tommy's disappearance at Devil's Rock.

WINNER OF THE 2015 BRAM
STOKER AWARD FOR SUPERIOR
ACHIEVEMENT IN A NOVEL

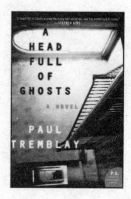

"*A Head Full of Ghosts* scared the living
hell out of me, and I'm pretty hard to
scare."
　　　　　　　　　—Stephen King

The lives of the Barretts, a normal
suburban New England family, are
torn apart when fourteen-year-old
Marjorie begins to display signs of
acute schizophrenia.

　　As their stable home devolves into a
house of horrors, they reluctantly turn
to a local Catholic priest for help. Father
Wanderly suggests an exorcism; he
believes the vulnerable teenager is the
victim of demonic possession. He also
contacts a production company that is
eager to document the Barretts' plight.
With John, Marjorie's father, out of
work for more than a year and the
medical bills looming, the family
agrees to be filmed. When events in
the Barrett household explode in
tragedy, the show and the shocking
incidents it captures become the stuff
of urban legend. ▸

Fifteen years later, a bestselling writer interviews Marjorie's younger sister, Merry. As she recalls those long-ago events, long-buried secrets and painful memories that clash with what was broadcast on television begin to surface—and a mind-bending tale of psychological horror is unleashed. ∾

Discover great authors, exclusive offers, and more at hc.com.